Borrowed Bride

NOAH HARDY

IS THIS LOVE?
PUBLISHING

Is This Love? Publishing

ISBN: 978-1-9995591-2-0 (paperback)

NoahHardy.com

Cover Illustration by Liza Rusalskaya

To Nathalie,
You're my happily ever after.

CHAPTER One

This is the wedding of the year and I'm marooned in the parking lot.

I couldn't be happier.

It's been months of intense preparation. I've been working so hard that I fell asleep in the bathroom last night. I woke up hugging the toilet.

This day must go *perfectly*. I've been desperately trying to get catering contracts from Washington D.C.'s rich, fancy-party-throwing politicians since I started Catering By Zoe eight years ago and today is my opportunity to shine. It's my opportunity to impress, to dazzle, to put my name on the catering map.

Senator Whitfield's son is getting married and I'm an official caterer for the wedding. Appetizers, cocktail snacks, four-course meals—you name it, I'm shoving it into the guests' mouths.

My team isn't as dedicated as I am, but I'm hoping they're going to step up in a big way today. Everything must be flawless.

"Aya!" I screech. "What are you doing?!"

She looks up at me as she plops an ice cream scooper into the duck liver pâté like a toddler playing with a bucket of mud. "Preparing the appies, what does it look like?"

A shiver racks up my spine as I watch her *shlop* the spoonful onto a cracker, splattering the twenty-three dollar an ounce pâté all over the recently polished silver tray.

My back tightens. "This is the—"

"Wedding of the year," Aya and four other employees say at the same time.

It almost sounds like they're mocking me.

I suck in a tight breath and try not to frown as I look around our large white tent at all of my team members who are trying not to snicker. "These hors d'oeuvres aren't supposed to be prepared until *minutes* before serving. The wedding is in two hours! Aren't you following the chart?"

My jaw clenches when I see the manilla envelope still sealed on the table beside Aya. We both lunge for it, but I snatch it first.

"Seriously?!" I ask as I tear it open. "You didn't even open it?"

She shrugs.

"You didn't read any of it!" I say in disbelief as I rifle through the four dozen crisp pages of pertinent information I spent a week preparing. "The bathroom schedule, the uniform checklist, it's all untouched!"

I whip my head around and frown when I see more manilla envelopes disappearing.

"That's it! Meeting. Right now. Gather around."

I hear a cacophony of sighs and groans as I flip over a milk carton and stand on it like a General about to address her troops. These people wouldn't last a day in the army. I, on the other hand, would thrive. I'd have the crispest uniform in military history.

"How many of you have read the manual I provided?"

No hands. No freaking hands. I don't believe this.

All of my thirteen workers stare at me with blank faces.

My gut tightens as I force out a breath. "We're catering the wedding of the—"

"We got it," Aya interrupts with her hand in the air. "But we're not *really* catering the wedding of the year. Are we?"

I stare at her in shock.

"We're in the parking lot," she continues as she points to the white painted line on the concrete ground at her feet. "We're only serving the limo drivers and secret service. We're not even allowed in the hotel!"

"We got hired for a job catering an exclusive wedding," I say, trying to keep my voice from cracking.

"*Parking lot* of an exclusive wedding," my cook Jason says in a long cough.

My eyes shoot laser beams at him. "Do you need a cough drop or something?"

He shakes his head as his cheeks turn red.

"We got hired for a job," I continue, "and parking lot or not, we're going to do the job as perfectly as humanly possible. When you hire Catering by Zoe, you get the best experience possible whether you're a US Senator or the Queen of England."

"Or Gary the Queen's driver," Aya mutters.

My eyes narrow on her. "Exactly."

She shakes her head, clearly disagreeing with me. "We could serve these guys macaroni and cheese with sliced hot dog wieners in it and they'd be happy."

Right on cue, two drivers with round bellies and bushy moustaches, looking like Mario and Luigi after a career change walk in.

"Is this the catering tent?" Luigi asks as his eyes drift over to the food.

"Yes!" I say as I step off the milk carton and spring to attention.

My crew disappears back to their stations even though I didn't dismiss them. My jaw clenches. I walk up to our guests while forcing my lips from a tight line into a wide smile.

"What can I do for you gentlemen? Are you hungry? Thirsty? Perhaps a hot moist towelette?"

"What's that?" Mario asks as he points to Aya's station with a scrunched-up nose.

"That is our mouthwatering duck liver pâté served on homemade crispy fig and olive crackers. It's delightful, delectable, and more than a little bit daring. Would you like to try some?"

My pulse is racing with excitement for my first guests of the day to try my new dish. Although, they're not looking like they're sharing my enthusiasm.

"Do you have any hot dogs or pizza?" Luigi asks, desperately looking around.

Aya snickers.

I'm about to offer them something a little less adventurous like our fried artichoke hearts with a creamy kale dip when the rumbling of a motorcycle fills the air. It's obnoxiously loud.

The roaring of the motorcycle gets so ear-piercing I can't think, let alone talk. I step out of the tent, gleefully excited to watch the secret service kick this guy out.

My catering tent is located on the side of the huge Royal Inn on the Bay, a gorgeous eighty-four-room hotel on the water in Maryland. The Inn has been featured on the cover of every wedding magazine in the country and is first class all the way. The spectacular views are dramatic and stunning. A sunset from the balcony will turn the most cynical cynic into a teary-eyed dreamer.

The inn is about an hour from D.C. so the summer weddings booked here are the who's who of America's blue-blooded families.

That's why they're being so strict about who they let in. I don't mind. It's not like I'm insulted or anything. I understand why they kicked me out earlier. I was being a "security threat."

And it's not like the view from the parking lot isn't just as spectacular. There's a nice maple tree over there, and past the dumpsters, you can see a bit of the water if you stand on your toes.

My eyes narrow on the red motorcycle as the male driver obnoxiously lets the whole area know he's arrived with a metallic rumbling theme song. He curves through the mostly empty parking lot and heads right for my tent.

Hell no!

I step in front of him and frantically wave my arms, but he just rolls around me and disappears into *my* tent.

My muscles quiver and my heart pounds as I charge in after him. The dinnerware on the tables are violently clattering from the vibrations.

"Excuse me!" I shout as he turns off the bike and swings his leg off. It's the fast kind of motorcycle—you know the kind that flings their drivers into orbit if they hit a pothole. The guy is wearing ripped-up jeans, a loose blue shirt, and a red helmet that covers his entire head.

I glare at him as he peels it off. "You can't just—"

The sight of him stuns me for a second and I jerk my head back when I look into his bright blue eyes, my words disappearing in my throat. He looks just like a hairy version of the groom. It's uncanny.

"Carter?" I ask as confusion sets in, muddling my brain up.

That can't be the groom. I saw the groom this morning. He was clean-shaven with a nice slicked-to-the-side hairstyle. Carter Whitfield is a magazine cover-worthy groom. He's charming and smooth and gives you tingles when he smiles at you. This guy is not that. He's obnoxious and scruffy and gives you tingles, but it's the nails on chalkboard kind.

"I'm his twin," the man says in the same smooth voice as the groom. "Luke Whitfield."

"Yeah. Great. Get this motorcycle out of here please."

Aya pops up beside me. She's staring at the bike with wide eyes. "I'll park it!"

"No!" both Luke and I say at the same time.

Our eyes meet for a long moment and I turn away, flustered.

"We're caterers, not valet," I say to Aya. "Will you please get those two gentlemen something to eat?"

"They went to the dive bar down the street to see if they serve food," she says with an I-told-you-so grin.

"What?!" I spin around as Mario and Luigi walk away. "Wait! We have food!"

"That's not food, lady," Luigi says before they disappear through the flap in the tent.

Damn it! I have a one hundred percent walk out rate, an unruly staff who's this close to mutiny, and a freaking motorcycle parked in my tent between my tables. I'm about to blow.

This is supposed to be the event that turns things around for me and my company. A shot at better parties and events with a higher class of clientele who don't scrunch their noses up at duck liver pâté (and who don't think twice about cutting a fat check). I was hoping to expand, hire more capable staff, and maybe start to make enough money that I can get an apartment without roommates and buy a car that doesn't hate me.

I'll be damned if I'm going to let all that slide without a fight.

My nostrils flare as I turn to my staff who's gathered around watching. "Get back to work!" I snap. They scatter like gazelle fleeing from a roaring lion.

Luke is watching me with an amused grin on his infuriating face. "And *you,*" I hiss. "Get that abhorrent ER-visit-waiting-to-happen out of my tent. *Now.*"

He just shrugs his big shoulders as he looks at me. "Where do you want me to put it?"

"In the parking lot!" I snap. "Or, I'll be happy to roll it into the bay for you."

"I thought I was in the parking lot," he says as he looks down at the concrete. "You're standing on an oil stain."

I suck in a sharp breath and step to the side as I glare at him. "This is a service tent. *My* service tent."

"Located in the parking lot."

My body tenses. Geez, what is with this guy? It's like he knows how to push every button I have.

"Regardless of where the tent is located," I say, trying to keep my voice nice and calm, "I am the captain of the tent and I have the final say of what—"

"The captain of the tent?" he repeats with a laugh.

"Yes," I say with my chin in the air. "The captain."

He gives me a lazy salute and drops his helmet onto the seat. "Well, Captain, this has been fun, but I have to get inside and get ready."

"Nope," I say as he turns his back on me. "We're not done here."

The mother of the groom, Kathleen Whitfield, prowls into the tent and I step back with my heart pounding. She's terrifying. She'll give you a nice warm smile while simultaneously murdering you with her words.

With a mother like her, I can understand why biker boy is such a delight.

"Luke," she says in a tone that can only be described as the opposite of motherly. "I thought I heard that obnoxiously loud yokel cycle."

At least we're on the same page with that one.

Luke rolls his eyes to me and then turns around to face his mom. "Hello, mother. I thought I smelled that obnoxiously strong perfume of yours. What's it called again? Eau de corpse?"

She struts up to him with her designer purse dangling from her arm and kisses the air beside his cheeks.

Her pink dress and huge sunhat look like they cost more than my car. This family is insanely rich. Walter Whitfield inherited the largest insurance company in the US before he started his very successful career in politics. The Whitfields are practically American royalty at this point. I saw a picture of Walter dining with Angela Merkel and Justin Trudeau.

I don't normally follow politics but a good caterer always does her research.

Kathleen makes a lizard face as her eyes roam over Luke's shaggy beard. "How nice of you to grow your hair like a prepubescent Sasquatch to make your brother look more handsome on his wedding day."

"Thank you," he says with a playful grin. "And how nice of you to wait until noon to get blackout drunk."

"Who said anything about waiting until noon?"

I gulp as she turns to me. "Cocktail. Strong."

"We don't have any alcohol here," I say with a quiver in my voice.

"This is a wedding tent, isn't it? We're not Mormons."

"We're serving the drivers and the secret service," I explain with a nervous laugh. "We don't want them to get drunk, do we?"

She just stares at me.

I shift from foot to foot. "It could get dangerous."

"You clearly have never seen my mother without a drink," Luke says with a grin. "Now, that's dangerous."

To my surprise, Kathleen laughs and hugs her son. "I've missed you. How come you never visit?"

"Mom," he says as he tilts his head.

She slaps his shoulder. "I know, I know. But maybe you can come visit when he's gone on one of his sailing trips."

"Maybe."

I walk behind the folding table and start arranging the tiny strawberry shortcakes on a tray as I eavesdrop on them. A good caterer always listens in to better anticipate a guest's needs.

"Oh, right!" Kathleen says, remembering something. "We're looking for the Turk. Have you seen her?"

"Mom, you have to stop calling her the Turk. She's going to be your daughter-in-law in a few hours."

"Not unless we get lucky and she gets deported."

Luke shakes his head. "That's not going to happen."

"You're right. ICE won't take my anonymous tips seriously anymore. Damn it. I wasted them all on my maid."

"Seriously, you can't find Taliah?" Luke asks as he runs a hand through his messy brown hair. My eyes dart to his hard tricep as his shirt sleeve slides down. *Stop it,* I scold myself before dropping my eyes back down to the sweets.

"A runaway bride," Kathleen says with a laugh. "Who would of thought it would have been your brother and not you?"

"Not me *yet,*" Luke answers. "I'm sure my future bride will lace up her shoes as soon as she meets my loving family."

"Sounds about right," she says as she starts to walk away. "Keep your eyes out for her, will you? And if you see any cocktails around, send them my way."

"I haven't even met Taliah yet," Luke calls out to her. "What does she look like?"

"Like a Turk," Kathleen says in a sharp tone before disappearing out of the tent.

I'm starting to understand why the bride is getting cold feet. This family is a lot to take.

It's times like this that I'm glad I'm running solo. I mean, I have parents, but I only see my mom about once a year and I've only seen my dad three times in the past five years. We talk on the phone every couple of weeks, but it's always short and always about superficial things like his hot water tank or the new pair of shoes he bought. My mom just complains about my dad even though they haven't seen each other in over ten years.

I cover the strawberry shortcakes and duck out of the tent to bring them to the large fridges plugged into the side of the building.

When I'm sliding them in, I spot the gorgeous bride Taliah sitting on the freezer smoking a cigarette. There are tears in her beautiful brown eyes.

Darn it.

I've never been good at this kind of stuff. I'm not a people person. I'm usually the one who causes the tears, not wipes them away.

But I have to try.

If this wedding gets canceled, all of my potential new contacts are going to get canceled along with it.

I suck in a breath and walk over with my pulse racing.

"Taliah?" I ask. "Is everything okay?"

CHAPTER
Two

Taliah sucks in a deep drag of her cigarette as she looks at me with red puffy eyes. She's so beautiful it's almost diabolical. I mean how is it possible to look even more beautiful when you cry? Asking as a legit ugly crier.

She's one of those natural dark-haired beauties who was made to wear a wedding dress. It's not just looks with her either. She's as smart as she is gorgeous. She's a very successful real estate developer with projects spanning the globe.

"This is all wrong," she says as she stares ahead blankly. "I hate this wedding."

"It looks pretty perfect to me," I say as I look around at the gorgeous hotel on the water. The sun is shining with a nice cool breeze. It's the perfect day for a wedding, although I would have gone with a pink and grey theme to match the building's—

"It's perfect for a magazine," she says before taking another aggressive drag of her cigarette. "But not for me. This family is the worst. The day is all about them. My friends and family weren't allowed to be here because Walter wanted to impress his politician friends and he didn't like the optics of having a bunch of guests speaking Turkish around."

"That's horrible."

She looks at me with wide eyes. "Yeah. I know. It's like I'm a prop in his political career instead of a new family member. This is not how I dreamed my wedding would be. Am I crazy?"

"Not at all."

She offers me the cigarette but I wave it away. *Oh, what the hell.* I take a drag off it and then explode into coughs. Taliah smiles.

"How do you picture your dream wedding?" she asks.

I bite my bottom lip as I think about it. "Honestly, I've never pictured it before."

She's looking at me like she's trying to figure out what species I belong to. "You've never pictured your wedding?"

"Well, I couldn't invite my parents because that would be a disaster. They'd just fight the whole time and I would never be forgiven if I invited one and not the other. So, we'd have to be alone. Somewhere nice and romantic. Like a beachfront villa."

"A beachfront villa?" she echoes.

I'm getting into it now. "Yes, just the two of us. It would be romantic and selfish and pure magic. We'd hire a local official to marry us on the beach." I can see it so clearly now. "We'd ask two honeymooners walking by to be the witnesses and they'd become lifelong friends. After having a delicious picnic on the sand and watching the spectacular sunset, my new husband would make a bonfire on the beach. We'd play some soothing music and dance all night under the bright stars with the magical moon shimmering off the calm warm water. Then, we'd make love on a blanket and I'd fall asleep happy and content, being held by my new husband as the calming sound of the waves serenades us."

I close my eyes as I indulge in the fantasy a little bit longer, tasting the salt water on my lips and the comforting feel of my imaginary man's arms around me. Goosebumps rise on my skin. *Stop it. Big romantic moments aren't in your future.*

When I shake out the frivolous fantasy and open my eyes, Taliah is frantically pointing at me, her tears dried up. Ashes break off the tip of her cigarette as her finger slices up and down. "Yes! *Yes!!* That's *exactly* what I want!"

A sudden and overwhelming sense of dread comes over me as she leaps off the freezer and stands up with determination written all over her face.

"Thank you!" she says as she crushes the cigarette under her foot. "Thank you so much! What's your name?"

A frenetic urge to say Aya flashes into my brain, but I suck in a breath and push it away. "Zoe."

"Zoe," she says as she smiles warmly at me. "I couldn't have decided this without you."

Oh crap. This is not good. She's a woman on a mission now as she starts rattling off tasks.

"I have to get my passport and pack," she rambles on to herself. "We have to find a villa. A minister."

"Wait," I say as adrenaline surges through my veins. "Let's talk this out a bit. I mean a beach wedding? It's kind of cliché, no?"

"It will be *perfect,*" she says, not even hearing me now. "It will be about our love. Our commitment to each other. We don't need anyone else for that."

"But the bugs," I say, grasping at anything to try and turn this crazy train around. "I heard there's an outbreak of sand fleas in the Caribbean and making love on the beach? Have you ever had sand up your hoo ha? It's no picnic!"

She's making plans in her head as my blood pressure skyrockets. *This can't be happening. No, no, no!*

This is why it's a bad idea to think of these fantasies! They cause nothing but trouble.

I'll be ruined if this wedding doesn't happen. What kind of wedding caterer convinces the bride to elope on the morning of the wedding?! The bankrupt kind.

Carter, the groom, comes racing over when he hears his lovely, but a little unhinged, bride's voice. "Taliah! They said you went missing!"

They lunge into each other's arms in a crushing hug. I can feel the love radiating off them. It's heartwarming to see.

"I can't get married like this," Taliah says as she pulls away to look into her lover's beautiful cobalt blue eyes.

I can tell from his pained expression that his heart is shattering to pieces. "You don't want to get married?"

"I do!" she quickly says. "But I want it to be about us. Not about your father's political aspirations."

Carter holds his bride as he listens to her without interruption. It's sweet and attentive and leaves me wondering how his twin turned into a total prick.

"Zoe had a wonderful idea," she says as she smiles at me.

"It wasn't really my idea," I quickly add. "I was hardly involved at all."

"She thinks we should elope."

I shake my head. "I never said elope."

"She said we should take off and get married on the beach. Doesn't that sound romantic? No family around arguing and making it all about them. Just us. The beach. Our love. It would be unforgettable."

She looks up at him with hopeful eyes and I steel my nerves, telling myself that Carter will do the practical thing and talk her down from this ledge. He'll tell her she's having cold feet and that it would be a shame to waste this perfect wedding. He'll do the right thing.

"We can use my boss' villa in Anguilla," he says as his face lights up.

Bloody hell.

"I'll call him right now!"

"I'll book the plane tickets!"

"Hold on," I say as they both whip out their phones and get sucked into the screens. "Let's just take a breather for a second before we do anything rash."

They're not listening. Why aren't they listening?!

"Isn't Anguilla the murder capital of the world?" I throw out like I'm sticking a bandaid onto a burst damn. This is getting out of hand.

"I booked the flights!" Taliah squeals.

"What?" I gasp.

"We leave in two hours. We have to head to the airport now. We don't have time to pack."

Carter kisses her on the lips. Nausea hits me.

"My boss offered the villa anytime I want," he says as he lovingly holds her hand and gazes into her eyes. "I'll call him on the way to the airport, but I'm sure it will be fine. We'll buy whatever we need there."

"My dress..."

"Who needs it? I'd marry you in a bathrobe."

This time she kisses him. "I love you. Let's get out of here."

My stomach drops.

"But..." I cry out. "Plane crashes! Jellyfish! Traveler's diarrhea!"

They leave.

No!! What the hell did I do?!

I grab the sides of my head as I start to hyperventilate.

Luke arrives out of nowhere and shoots me a strange look before calling out to his brother.

"Carter! What's going on?"

Carter turns and his eyes light up when he sees his twin. He rushes over and gives Luke a hug. "Come and meet my bride."

"Isn't it bad luck for the groom to see the bride before the wedding?" Luke asks as Taliah turns around.

"We make our own luck," Taliah says as she hugs him. He stiffens. "I've heard so much about you, Luke. I hope we can see each other again soon."

"We'll catch a drink at the reception. You look like a whiskey kind of girl."

Carter shakes his head. "You'll have to have that drink without us. We're eloping."

Luke stares at him in awe. "Walter will murder you. He has a chainsaw in the garage. I saw it."

"This time it's not about him," Carter says as he slips his hand into Taliah's, entwining their fingers. She grips his forearm and rests her head on his shoulder. "It's about our love."

Everyone's eyes are on Luke as he processes the sudden turn of events. "How can I help?" he finally asks.

Carter and Taliah smile in relief.

"You can break it to Mom and Dad."

Luke shakes his head. "I was thinking more of a ride to the airport or lending you a bathing suit."

Carter lets go of his bride and hugs him. "We'll catch up soon, okay? I hate that it's been so long."

I get startled when Taliah comes over and hugs me. "Oh! Okay."

"Thank you so much for the idea, Zoe," she says in a tender voice. "If it wasn't for you, I'd be getting married here."

"Again, not totally my idea," I say as I glance over at Luke who's giving me the side-eye. "It was just the germ of an idea, really. You're the one who ran with it. All the credit goes to you."

She places her palm on her chest as she shakes her head. "No. This was your idea."

Luke's eyebrows rise as he watches me.

Shit! Why does she keep giving me credit for this? And why are my palms so sweaty?

I rub my hands on my pants as I force out a tight smile. "It's not too late to change your mind! Imagine being wed in this gorgeous venue. Now *that's* romantic!"

I'm chuckling nervously, but it's no use. The couple has made up their stubborn minds.

"Wait!" I say as they turn to go. "You should ride Luke's motorcycle to the airport! Now *that* would be really romantic. Just the two of you riding off into the horizon."

If I'm going down at least I can take biker boy down with me.

Luke turns to me with crazy eyes.

"You said you'd give them a ride to the airport," I say innocently. "Lend them your motorcycle."

"I've never been on a motorcycle," Taliah says, looking interested.

"That would be great, Luke," Carter says. "Thank you."

I'm trying not to laugh as Luke begrudgingly hands over the keys.

"It's parked in the tent," I say as I stare at Luke with a smirk.

We both stand there in shock as we watch them hurry into the tent, hand in hand.

The air gets tense when it's just the two of us. He slowly turns around and glares at me.

"Your idea, huh?"

"Taliah's idea. That's what she said, right?"

"Are you trying to gaslight me?"

The panic comes roaring back. "I don't want to lose my business," I blurt out as I start to feel faint. "Do you think your dad will be mad?"

"Mad?" he says with a laugh. "When my father finds out there's no bride and groom for his precious wedding, he's going to be apocalyptic. I can't wait."

"Oh shit," I mutter as I start to pace around. "This is so bad."

The rumbling of Luke's motorcycle hits our ears and we both watch as the happy couple flee from their perfect wedding.

"At least my brother and his fiancée are going to get the wedding they deserve," Luke says softly. "They'll have you to thank for that."

I look up at him and his blue eyes soften as he looks down at me. He is kind of handsome if you can get past the scruffy beard and long hair that looks like it may have small woodland creatures living in it.

"Where the hell are they going?" Kathleen screeches as she swoops over, sounding like a pterodactyl.

"I should get back to my tent," I say as I side-step away. Luke grabs my wrist and holds me there.

"They left," Luke says. "They're eloping."

"Eloping?" Kathleen repeats with her nostrils flaring. "How could they do this to me?"

Luke turns to me with a shrug. "Now you can understand why they left."

Kathleen whips her head around and glares at me. "*She* knows about this?"

"It was her idea," Luke says.

"Not true," I lie. "I was more of an innocent bystander just trying to put away the strawberry shortcakes. I really should get back to my tent."

I yank my arm out of Luke's grasp, but after three steps, Kathleen grabs my other arm. "Who else knows about this?"

"Just the three of us," Luke says.

"Hmm." The wheels are turning in Kathleen's brain. Why is that so scary?

"Don't tell anyone about this," she says as she releases me. "This wedding is not cancelled yet."

Luke and I watch her as she marches away with her hands clenched into fists.

"It sounds pretty canceled to me," I say once she's gone. "The bride and groom are MIA."

"Who knows what twisted plans her evil mind is concocting right now? It's probably best to leave. Too bad I don't have my bike."

He glares at me. I glare back.

"Thanks for telling on me," I spit out. "What are you six years old?"

"That was for volunteering my motorcycle."

"That was a favor by the way," I shoot back. "You look ridiculous on that thing."

"Are you always this overbearing?"

"Yes. Are you always this cocky and childish?"

"Only on my good days."

We glare at each other for a long heated moment before I catch myself and storm off. "I'll be in my tent. Working."

"Great!" he calls out. "I'll be out here, watching the mess you created unravel."

I really want to turn around and give him a piece of my mind, but I storm off with a *humph* instead. This family is a nightmare. I'm glad I convinced Taliah to escape this wedding, even though it does mean horrible things for me.

I slink back into the tent and Aya looks up at me. "Where have you been? The ceremony starts in—" She looks at her watch. "—an hour and forty minutes."

I slump into a chair and exhale long and hard. "Do you ever think about your future wedding?"

Aya sits down next to me and scrunches her nose up. "I'm never getting married. What if we get divorced and he wants half of my ukulele collection?"

"There's going to be *hundreds* of people here," I say as I look around. "I can't think of anyone who would come to my wedding."

Aya puts her hand on mine. "I'll come to your wedding. Even if it's in fifty years."

"Oh God," I mutter. "I hope it's not in fifty years."

Aya starts looking at me funny when I don't move. Normally, I would be bouncing around the tent nitpicking every detail, but I really don't see the point. There's not going to be a wedding. My chance at impressing new clients will just have to wait.

"Are you okay, boss?" Aya asks.

"I screwed up," I admit. "Big time."

Before she can ask what boneheaded thing I did, Kathleen charges into the tent like a fiery dragon. "*You*," she says with her nostrils flaring. "Chloe."

"Zoe."

"Whatever. Come with me. We're not done with you yet."

I gulp as I get up and follow her out.

CHAPTER Three

"What's this concerning?" I ask as I power walk after Kathleen. The tiny hairs lift on the back of my neck as we walk past the armed security guards and into the gorgeous hotel. I feel like a baby lamb walking into the lion's den.

"What's this concerning?" Kathleen repeats as she threatens me with her eyebrows. "The cocktail napkins in the lounge."

"Oh," I say with a breath of relief. "I'll have them re-stocked immediately."

"I don't care about the bloody napkins!" she hollers. "The bride and groom are missing! And it was *your* fault."

I shake my head as my stomach churns. "This has gotten out of hand. I swear, it wasn't my idea."

She gives me a look that would put Medusa to shame and then charges up the grand staircase with her chin in the air.

"Okay, the beach was my idea," I say as I race up the stairs after her, "but I never told them to elope!"

Kathleen stops and spins on the middle stair. I gulp as she

glares down at me with her finger in my face. "She's gone because of you. And *you're* going to fix it."

What does *that* mean? There's no bride for the wedding. How do you fix the unfixable?

I take a deep breath, trying to calm this crazy situation down. "Mrs. Whitfield. I think if we take a step back and look at the situation for—"

And she's gone. I sigh as I look up at the pink shawl draped over her shoulders flowing behind her as she continues up the stairs. I follow her.

She doesn't say another word or even acknowledge me as we pass through the spectacular hotel. There are enormous flower displays everywhere you look with secret service agents discreetly tucked behind the large vases watching us. They perk up when Kathleen marches past them.

Two massive wooden doors wait for me at the end of the hall and I feel like I'm shrinking an inch with every step I take toward them.

An agent in a black suit with one of those earpieces leaps to attention and opens the door as Kathleen arrives. She doesn't break stride as she charges into the huge conference room.

I follow her in with my heart pounding.

The first thing I notice is Luke sitting at the megalodon-sized mahogany table. His arms are crossed, his face tight, his hair unattractively long as usual. He's sitting as far from his father as possible without climbing onto the window ledge and sitting with the pigeons.

My eyes dart to Walter Whitfield. I can feel the intense authority radiating off him as he sits at the head of the table, talking into the phone with a deep commanding voice.

"Understood, Mr. President. I'll see you later this evening then."

I jump as the door slams closed behind me.

My eyes meet Luke's for a brief moment and then he turns away. The tension is thick in the air as Senator Whitfield hangs up the phone.

"This is her," Kathleen says as she hovers around the table.

Senator Whitfield studies me with an intense stare and then hits a button on the phone. "Kyle, hold my calls."

"Yes, Senator."

He's already dressed up in his tailored tuxedo that fits his broad shoulders and big arms perfectly. It's hard to be intimidated by a man with a bowtie on, but this guy is somehow pulling it off. He's terrifying.

I grew up in rural Vermont in a town I can guarantee you've never heard of. My father was a high school principal and my mother was the editor of the local newspaper. I've never been around powerful people before. People who can pick up a phone and call the President, people who can wage wars in countries most Americans can't pick out on a map, and people who can have troublesome caterers killed for a lot less than ruining their son's wedding.

Senator Whitfield forces out a smile as he waves his hand to a chair. "Sit. Please."

I look at Luke for guidance, support, anything. He twists his hair into a man-bun and stares ahead blankly.

With my pulse racing, I pull out the chair and sit down.

"That was the President of the United States on the phone," Senator Whitfield says as he folds his hands on the table and pierces me with his fierce blue eyes. "He's coming to the wedding tonight."

"Isn't the wedding canceled?" I ask in a small voice.

Everyone is staring at me.

Just as I'm starting to squirm, Kathleen speaks up. "No. It's still on."

"With no bride and groom?"

I can feel the tension in the air getting thicker. Senator Whitfield smiles at me. It's surprisingly warm and feels genuine, which feels strange coming from such a powerful forceful man. "Zoe, is it?"

"Yes, Senator Whitfield. Zoe Fitzpatrick."

"Call me Walter, please." He leans back in his chair with a deep breath and unbuttons his jacket. "Zoe, we have over seven hundred distinguished guests coming tonight. Governors of six different states, dozens of senators and members of congress, the ambassador to Paraguay. Do you know Paraguay?"

"The country? Yeah, I've heard of it."

"Good," he says with a reassuring nod. "Several CEOs of fortune 500 companies are expected to be in attendance, the Secretary of State, and of course, the President of the United States. I know you know him."

Luke rolls his eyes.

"Tonight is not just a wedding," Walter says as he stands and walks to the large curved window. He pauses for dramatic effect and then turns around with a sparkle in his eyes. "Tonight, I will announce that I will be running for the presidency."

"You're going to run to be President?" I blurt out in shock.

"Yes."

"Of the United States?"

"No, of Cracker Barrel," Kathleen says with a roll of her eyes.

"Kathleen," Walter warns with his hand in the air. "Please."

I look at Luke and he doesn't look too pleased. He must be hearing this for the first time as well.

"So, you see," Walter continues. "I'm in a bit of a bind here. Tonight we announce the run for presidency and tomorrow begins a month-long media blitz to capitalize on the excitement. My team has booked the talkshow circuit, late-night appearances, and we have several social media campaigns ready to go the moment after I make the announcement."

Kathleen subtly walks behind Luke and puts her hand on his shoulder. His head is turned away from his father. He's dripping with contempt.

"It's going to be a PR disaster for me if the wedding is canceled," Walter says with a sad shake of his head. "My selfish eloping son and his inconsiderate bride will dominate the news cycle and I will be made to look like a joke. That can't happen. That will *not* happen."

"What would you like from me?" I ask as I wonder why I'm even here. I'm the parking lot caterer. The only way I could be more out of my league was if I was drafted as starting pitcher for the Yankees. "Would you like me to go to the airport and try to talk them out of it?"

Walter's nostrils flare. "No. I already talked to Carter on the phone. When either of my stubborn sons has something set in their minds, nothing can undo it."

I can hear Luke's teeth grinding.

"Maybe this is a sign from a higher power that you shouldn't be president," he says.

"There is no higher power than the US President," Walter snaps.

"It's a sign this girl has total control over your brother," Kathleen says in a harsh tone. "I don't like it."

Everyone's eyes fall back onto Walter as he slowly walks over to the table. This man was born to command a room. He seems to have a sixth sense on how to get attention onto him and shut people up.

"Sir," I say as I glance at the exit. "I still don't understand what you need from me."

Walter takes a deep breath as he pulls out the chair beside me and sits down. I swallow hard as I stare at him.

"Zoe," he says in a soft voice. "We would like you to be the bride today."

I choke out a cough.

"Excuse me," I mutter as my eyes water. "Be the bride? And marry *who?*"

Walter and Kathleen turn to Luke.

"Oh God."

Did I just say that out loud?

"Luke," Walter says in a more forceful tone. "We would like you to cut your hair, shave your beard, and pretend to be your brother for the rest of the weekend."

Luke scoffs. "You can't be serious. Mom?"

Kathleen shrugs. "It will be a PR nightmare for the family if the event was canceled."

My brain seems to be broken because it's not processing any of this. Me? The bride? I'm feeling dizzy and nauseous just thinking about it.

I quickly stand up as I wave my hand in front of my face, trying to get some air. Suddenly, it feels *extremely* hot in here.

"Are you okay?" Luke asks when he looks at me. "You're so pale."

"I'm fine," I lie as a sheen of sweat breaks out on my forehead. Crap, now I'm dizzy. I hold onto the table as I collapse back into the chair.

"Don't bother freaking out," Luke says, "because I'm not doing it."

The warmth melts off of Walter's face as he whips his head around, rearing on his son. "Think of the Whitfield name and the damage this will cause."

"We already know you've done enough damage for six generations, eh pop?"

"Watch yourself, Luke. This affects you too."

"I'm a mechanic in a town of fifteen thousand rednecks," he says with a bitter laugh. "How is this going to affect me exactly?"

"It's the Presidency for fuck's sake!" Walter roars. "This will transform the roots of our family tree into concrete. Your brother can follow in my footsteps, your future children can be President too. If you don't screw them up too badly."

"I can't be worse at being a father than you."

Walter waves a dismissive hand at him. "Save it for your shrink, Luke. We don't have time for your pity party of how you got everything you could possibly want in life and still found endless things to complain about."

"Are you fucking kidding me?" Luke snaps back.

His mother puts her hand on his bicep and whispers something, but he shrugs it off.

The shock wears off me and the need to get out of here comes in hot. I stand up so fast the chair rolls away.

"This is insane!" I say with my eyes squeezed shut. "You want me to pretend to get married? To *him* of all people!"

Luke frowns as I point at him.

"We also need you to pretend to be the bride at the brunch tomorrow morning," Walter adds.

I scoff a little too loud. "In no reality *ever* would I marry an arrogant, childish, pompous ass like *him*."

"We'll pay you one hundred thousand dollars," Walter says in a firm voice.

My jaw drops.

Maybe he's not *soooo* bad.

That's life-changing money. One hundred thousand dollars…

I could move into a new apartment building that doesn't have two broken elevators… A car that's not suicidal… I could pay off my debts… Expand my business… This could change everything for me.

"This is so fucked up," Luke mutters as he stares at the wall.

I agree. But it's also tempting.

"But everyone is going to be expecting Taliah," I say as reality sinks back in.

"Nobody has met the Turk," Kathleen says with a sneer. "Besides us and the wedding party, but we'll take care of them."

"Nobody else knows her?"

Kathleen rolls her eyes. "She snagged my son when he was on a business trip in Turkey and she wisely only stepped foot on American soil a few weeks ago. I would have gotten rid of her if I had more time."

"But some guests must have seen her on social media? On Instagram? Something?!"

Kathleen shrugs. "You both have dark hair and a forgettable face."

"Thanks."

"Your body types are different, but everyone will just think Taliah gained weight from the stress of the wedding."

"Hey!"

"Nobody will know the difference," Walter quickly explains. "You'll pretend you're her, answer by her name, sign a fake marriage certificate, have a few cocktails, shake your butt on the dance floor, have some pancakes tomorrow morning, and go home with one hundred thousand dollars."

I'm speechless as I process this. It could work…

"She won't have a groom," Luke says, "because I'm not doing it."

Walter ignores him and keeps his attention on me. "In two weeks, nobody will remember what you look like."

Ouch.

"I'm the real star of the show," he continues. "During a toast to the bride and groom—"

"*Fake* bride and groom," Kathleen interrupts.

"*No* bride and groom," Luke corrects.

"—I'll make the big announcement. That's what the guests will remember of the night."

My mind races as I pace back and forth. My business really needs an injection of cash. It's been a rough couple of years. Things were going well for the first two years, but just as I leased out a large commercial kitchen, upgraded my equipment, and hired a bunch of staff, Covid arrived and kicked my business in the vagina. It's been hard trying to recover from near bankruptcy. This could really turn things around. I could use this money to pay debts, expand, and grow…

But I'll still be missing the jobs. I need contacts and contracts more than I need money. The money will dry up eventually and I'll be back in this spot. I need long-term change.

My muscles tighten as determination takes over.

I know *exactly* what I want.

"It's a possibility," I say in a non-committal way.

"It is?" Luke and Kathleen say at the same time.

Walter slams his fist onto the table as his face lights up. "Well, alright! Then it's done."

He stands up with his hand extended for a shake. I cross my arms and stare him down. The excitement melts off his face as he takes his hand back and slinks into his chair.

"What do you want?"

My back straightens as I steel myself. "I want the Golden Contract."

They all stare at me in confusion.

"The what?" Kathleen asks.

The Golden Contract might just be a mythical legend amongst D.C. caterers. It's the most coveted, the most prestigious, the most high-paying contract a caterer can dream of. And I'm going to get it.

"I want Catering by Zoe to be the official caterer in Washington D.C., serving all Senate, Congress, and Presidential events."

Walter rubs his chin as he sits back and studies me. He's probably realizing that he underestimated me and is recalculating.

"That's a new one," he mutters after a long moment.

He looks at his wife. "Kitty Kat, who's the head of the event planning committee for the White House and Capitol Hill?"

"Craig Watson," she says without missing a beat. "Don't you have those pictures? The bachelor party in black face."

"Right…" He nods and then thinks about it, probably wondering if he should waste them on me.

"Done," he says in a voice that's final.

My jaw falls open. "Excuse me?"

"If you pretend to be Taliah and pretend to marry my son, I'll give you the Golden Contract."

"*And* one hundred thousand dollars," I say firmly.

"Oh, we're still doing that?"

I grin at him. "Yeah. We're still doing that."

"Might as well make it a million!" Luke shouts as he throws his hands in the air. "It doesn't matter because I'm not doing it."

Walter stares him down with a fierce look that would make a hungry lion cower away. "How much?"

"I don't want your dirty money."

Walter sighs. He takes a few long heavy breaths and then nods. "Fine. I'll do it."

"You will?" Kathleen and Luke both say at the same time, looking stunned.

"Do what?" I ask, but everyone ignores me.

"No joke?" Luke asks, the color draining out of his face. "No tricks?"

"I swear on the Whitfield crest," Walter says as he raises his hand. He has three fingers up with the middle one curled like it's some kind of family gang sign or something.

"Twenty-five years," Luke says.

"*Five* years," Walter counters.

"Fifteen."

"Ten. Final offer."

"Okay," Luke says in a serious tone. "You have a deal."

They shake hands. I notice Luke's hand is trembling after.

"And I get a hundred grand," Luke quickly adds.

"Too late," Walter says.

"Damn it," Luke mutters.

Walter shakes my hand next, nearly crushing it in his powerful grip. "We have a deal, Zoe."

I watch in awe as he pulls out his checkbook and writes a check for one hundred thousand dollars. My name is on the line. It's so pretty.

He hands it to me and then snaps it away when I reach for it. "You'll get this at the end of the brunch tomorrow morning," he says as he folds it and makes it disappear into the inside pocket of his jacket. "This check along with the Golden Contract ready to sign."

I'm shaking. This can't be real.

"Now, I have business to attend to," he says dismissively. "Kathleen will take you to meet the wedding coordinator Heather so you can try on the dress. The wedding begins in just over an hour, so there's no time to lose."

His attention is absorbed back into the papers on his desk as Kathleen walks over and grabs my arm.

"Luke, head to the barber down the street and get all of that cleaned up," she says, waving her hand at his furry face. "I want you looking like a human when you return."

I gulp as she turns to me. "Ready to try on the dress?"

"Dress?"

Oh man. I really didn't think this through. A wedding dress? Seven hundred guests? The freaking President of the United States? What the hell did I do?

"Ready or not," she says as she squeezes my arm and pulls me to the door. "We're going."

CHAPTER
Four

"It's a little small," Heather the wedding coordinator says with a wince when I step into the bridal suite with Taliah's wedding dress on.

"You think?" I respond sarcastically.

It's crushing my ribs. I'm choking out breaths.

The zipper only made it three-quarters of the way up and I can feel it slinking back down.

"Your boobs are exploding out of that thing," Kathleen says with a wrinkled nose. "I feel like I should be throwing plastic beaded necklaces at you."

I walk to the mirror and gasp. "I can't wear this. I'll be on a Buzzfeed list of the top ten sluttiest brides."

It's a gorgeous dress and probably looks stunning on Taliah. She's slim and this plunging neckline would look great with her small breasts and barely visible cleavage. I'm a lot curvier and my curves are out of control in this thing. I'm spilling out of it.

Heather comes over and starts examining it. Her green eyes look intense behind those black-rimmed glasses as she stares at my inappropriate cleavage. I can tell she's a good worker and I like her already. She's pretty, but she's toning it down not to take anything away from the bride, keeping her blonde hair straight and wearing a professional grey pantsuit.

"We need an emergency seamstress," she says as she whips her head around to Kathleen. "I don't think we're going to have time."

"I'll fix it," Kathleen says as she puts her martini on the night table and walks over. "I was a seamstress a lifetime ago."

We both stare at her in shock.

"I didn't always have a rich husband and a full staff, ya know." She starts yanking and pulling at the dress, jerking me along with it. "We have to loosen it up here, and here, and here, and here…"

One more 'and here' and I'll slap her.

"Heather, call the front desk and tell them to bring a sewing machine up."

Heather darts to the phone like an obedient golden retriever.

"I'm not a miracle worker," Kathleen says as she moves behind me and starts loosening straps. "So, don't get your hopes up."

"That's reassuring."

Our eyes meet in the mirror. "At least I'm honest."

"Maybe too honest," I mutter under my breath. She hears. Uh oh.

I swallow hard as her eyes narrow on me. "Too honest would be telling you that if you mess this up, we're going to obliterate your life. It's going to be tragic for you. Funny for me."

A whimper squeaks out of me as she yanks a strap, pulverizing my ribs. I'm trying to tell if she's joking.

She's not.

"Kiss away your food and drink permit," yank, "liquor

license," yank, "business permit," yank. I'm going to have bruises on my wedding night.

An empty feeling hits the pit of my stomach. I knew this was a bad idea, but it's too late to get out of it now. Kathleen will crucify me.

"My husband is a powerful man," she continues. "With powerful friends. How does a long drawn-out business IRS audit sound to you? Sound like fun? Imagine thousands of pages of fine print for you to read every week. Hell, we can even have the police chief show up to every one of your events and make a big scene as they demand to speak to *you*."

A coldness hits me as I stare into her ruthless eyes. "You're evil."

"A necessary evil," she says with another yank. "Behind every great man is a merciless woman. And Walter J. Whitfield will be the greatest man who's ever lived. I'm just doing my part. Heather! Machine?"

Heather puts the handset on her shoulder. "It will be in your room in ten minutes."

"Make it five."

I suck in a glorious breath as Kathleen yanks the zipper down and the dress falls loose. Well, as loose as it can get on my body.

She helps me out of it and bundles it up as I grab the robe on the bed and quickly put it on.

"I'll be back in a bit," she says as she grabs her martini and leaves with the dress.

"That whole family is crazy," I say as I quickly close the door behind her.

Heather creeps up beside me, staring at the door with a shiver. "She's terrifying. She had me so freaked out at the cake tasting that I drank a cup of frosting."

"She's just a bully."

Heather sighs and then lights up again when she looks at me. "We should get started on your hair and makeup. We had a whole team working here but Kathleen sent them home since they already saw Taliah. Everyone is on a need to know basis around here. Top secret stuff. You don't have to worry, though. I'm pretty good."

She sits me down in front of the window and lays out an excessive amount of expensive-looking products on the bed. It's overwhelming. My usual routine consists of mascara and occasionally lip gloss when I'm feeling feisty.

My mind begins to wander as Heather gets to work. This whole thing is crazy. I'm starting to have serious doubts if I can even go through with it.

"Whatever it takes," I whisper to myself. I've been on my own for so long without a safety net that I have no choice but to succeed.

This is a big opportunity and I'm not going to blow it.

I have to do this. I have to make it work.

But I don't know anything about Taliah, except that she's a rich real estate developer and according to this dress, she spends way more time on a treadmill than I do.

"What's Taliah's last name?" I ask Heather.

Heather grabs her clipboard and shows me the name printed out on paper, not even trying to pronounce it. Özüdoğru.

"Ohzo-dog-ru?"

Heather winces. "Not even close."

"What do those dots mean?" I like how they put little hats on their letters. English letters don't have nearly enough accessory pieces if you ask me.

"I don't know," she says as she takes the clipboard away. "Anyway, it doesn't matter. You'll be Taliah Whitfield before you have to speak to anyone."

After the makeup is done, Heather moves on to my hair. She hums Ariana Grande songs to herself as she works.

My mind wanders to Luke and I wonder what he's doing right now. I laugh when I picture him in front of an exhausted hairdresser with a mountain of scraggly hair piled around them.

He really doesn't get along with his father. There's obviously a lot of negative history there. I'm wondering what happened between them when Heather starts talking.

"It's going to be a big wedding," she says as she brushes my hair and squirts something into it. She starts telling me about the extravagant ceremony and the reception after and I start to feel dizzy with nerves. My heart is threatening to pound out of my chest as she tells me all about the prestigious guest list.

After some more poking and hair pulling, I'm finally ready for my big reveal. With a deep breath, I walk over to the mirror and gasp when I see a stunning girl in a bathrobe staring back at me.

I look beautiful. I've never looked this good before. Ever.

I'm always dressed so practical. Never dolled up like this. Ponytail, comfortable shoes, crisp formal clothes. That's my dress code. Professional and functional.

But this is... unexpected. I look like I should be on the cover of a magazine. I can't look away.

My focus has always been on survival. I never had the time, the interest, or the disposable income to focus on my looks. It was always my last priority. How can you justify spending money on beauty products when you have trouble keeping the fridge stocked and the lights on?

"Thank you, Heather." I'm still in shock as I turn to her. "You outdid yourself."

"All part of the service," she says with a smile.

She hands me Taliah's shoes and then leaves to freshen up in the bathroom. I gulp when I look at them. I've never worn shoes like these before. Nothing even close to them. I like flats. Comfortable, professional, functional. These are anything but.

They're sexy and beautiful. All straps, no support, and arched like a terrifying waterslide. *And* they're two sizes too small.

Holy crap, they're so tight my blood suddenly stops at my ankles and reverses back up my legs. I can't wear these.

I take two steps and tumble into the dresser. The lamp falls over, but thankfully it doesn't break.

"How are the shoes?" Heather asks as she pops her head out of the bathroom. "Beautiful aren't they? Special order Jimmy Choo. Cost over ten grand."

"For that price, I wished they came with more shoe. They're a little tight."

"You'll have to make do. You can't walk down the aisle in those things." She frowns as she glances at my work shoes by the door.

"I'm worried my baby toes are going to fall off by the end of the night," I say as I rub my ankle. "They're being crushed."

Heather shrugs. "At least you'll still have eight more."

She disappears back into the bathroom while I practice walking around the room. I stumble a few times, but I'm starting to get the hang of them at least.

I spot my reflection in the mirror as I walk by and smile. I can't wait to see the look on Luke's face when he sees me walking down the aisle looking hotter than the hell that's waiting for him.

"Seriously," I whisper as I turn away with a shake of my head. "What do you care what he thinks?"

Kathleen returns with the altered dress and I squeeze it back on. It's a bit better. I can breathe, but there's still way more cleavage than I'd like to show. Especially at a wedding. Especially at *my* wedding.

"It's not going to rip apart and explode off me, is it?" I ask while checking it out in the mirror.

"Impossible," Kathleen says between sips of her martini. "I sewed it tighter than my husband's wallet at a youth charity dinner."

She pulls some jewelry out of her purse and my eyes widen when I see the size of the sparkling diamonds on them.

"This will distract from the cleavage," she says as she puts the necklace on me.

"It's stunning."

"It's been in the Whitfield family for generations. Although, I did have it remodeled a few years ago to help bring it into the twenty-first century. We're not barbarians after all."

I put in the earrings and slide on the fake engagement ring whose diamonds are anything but fake.

"You look lovely," Kathleen says as she takes me in. "Strikingly beautiful."

"Thank you," I whisper as I stare at myself in awe. A heaviness hits my chest. A lump forms in my throat.

This unexpected yet striking woman in the mirror is swirling up all sorts of long-buried emotions and desires in me. Whenever I think about the future, I picture myself alone. Eating breakfast by myself, coming home to an empty apartment night after night… I like my life, but seeing myself like this… I start to wonder… Can it be different?

I swallow hard as my eyes start to water. I never thought this kind of life could be for me, but now, I don't know. A husband… A family to come home to… A toddler sitting at the table munching on Fruit Loops… Could that ever be an option? Could that ever be my life?

Maybe I could see myself wanting that.

But that would just lead to disappointment when it inevitably doesn't happen.

I fight back the lump in my throat as I turn to Heather and Kathleen with a smile.

A child? A husband? Where did that come from?

It's the first time I've seen an image like that in my mind and I already know it's one that will stay with me for a long time.

This stupid dress. It must be cursed.

First Taliah and now me. It's like whoever wears it is suddenly filled with discontent.

"The maid of honor fled in an Uber when we told her the plan," Kathleen says with a laugh. "Can't blame her for that one. She called us deranged."

"There's no maid of honor?" I never even thought of who would be in my bridal party.

"Do you have a friend who can fill in? Preferably a size eight? We'll pay her ten thousand dollars."

A friend…

I have friends. *A lot* of friends. There's my high school friend Jenna who lives in Atlanta. She sends me a Christmas card every year. And the girl with the short black hair from the coffee shop. She always draws a smiley face on my cup. I'm also friends with my dentist, although I don't have her phone number and I doubt she would be interested in being my pretend bridesmaid anyway. She's probably with her kids. I think she has kids…

Aya pops into my brain and my body relaxes. "One of my employees, Aya Zhao can do it. She's the beautiful Asian working in the service tent. I'll go get her."

Kathleen stops me. "You're a Whitfield now, dear. We have staff for our fetching. Heather!"

Heather's head pops out of the bathroom.

"Go to Zoe's tent and get Aya the Asian."

"Yes, Mrs. Whitfield!" she says as she runs out of the room, an unplugged straightener dangling from her hair.

Kathleen wanders over to the bed and sits down. I swallow hard as I sit in the chair by the mirror.

The room fills with awkward silence.

Both of us are sitting here, slowly dying.

"So?" Kathleen says. "Where are you from?"

"From a little town in Verm—"

"I can't do this," she says with her hand in the air, interrupting me. "I don't care." She takes the remote off the nightstand and turns the TV on while getting comfortable on the bed.

So much for bonding with my new pretend mother-in-law.

Forty-six minutes to go before showtime. I keep feeling sicker every time I see the clock move.

A knock on the door interrupts the gameshow Kathleen is watching. Her feet are on the bed and she doesn't look like she answers the door for anybody, so I get up and look through the peephole.

My heart swells in my chest. "It's Carter! He's back!"

"Carter is back?" Kathleen says, sitting up.

I yank the door open, filled with gratitude that I won't have to go through with this after all, and smile when I see the real groom standing there.

He's so handsome, unlike his twin. These two brothers look the same but are drastically different. Like buying two identical apples where one is delightfully sweet and delicious, and the other is rotten inside.

Taliah is a lucky woman to marry this stunner of a groom. If I were her, I'd get married in a junkyard if it meant I could cuddle this perfect specimen of a man all night. I'm glad to see that she's come to her senses and they came back for the wedding.

"Come in! Please!" I step to the side and Carter walks into the room. Kathleen's excitement fades when she sees him and she drops back onto the pillows with a sigh.

"Is Taliah here too?" I ask, peeking into the empty hallway. She's going to be furious about the dress, but at least we can call this crazy idea off.

"Twins, remember?" Carter says. It takes my brain a second to click. *Damn it.*

It's not Carter. It's Luke. A freshly made-over Luke.

I feel nauseous, realizing I thought *he* was actually handsome for a minute.

"I never understood why you hide that flawless face with a hideously scraggly beard," Kathleen says, turning back to her show. "It's a crime against humanity."

"I don't like to shave every day," he says with a shrug.

"Neither do I, but you don't see me with braided armpit hair."

Luke can't seem to take his eyes off me. Is he breathing?

He's talking to his mom, but his eyes keep darting over to me. They're flitting up and down my body before he catches himself and tears them away with effort.

"What are you looking at?" I ask, feeling self-conscious. Heat blooms in my cheeks.

"Nothing," he says as he jerks his head away. "You look nice."

Nice. What a jerk.

"Your husband wants us all to meet in the conference room in ten minutes," he says to his mother. "The entire bridal party."

Kathleen gets up and downs the last drop of her martini. "Escort your mother to the bar first."

"As long as I don't have to carry you to the ceremony," Luke says before glancing at me one more time on their way out.

The empty room is paradise. I sit back in my chair, close my eyes, and breathe in and out slowly.

A wave of calm washes over me as I focus on my breathing. This is just what I needed. A few minutes of—

Heather explodes into the room, holding Aya's wrist. She's practically dragging her in.

"Zoe, where have you been?" Aya asks as she rubs her wrist. "Alex dropped a tray of—why are you wearing a wedding dress?!?"

"Long story." I fill her in as quickly as I can and she bursts out laughing when I get to the part about me being the replacement bride. "I need your help. Will you be my maid of honor?"

"I'll do it," she says without hesitation.

"You haven't even heard the best part! You'll get ten thousand dollars."

"Ten thousand dollars?" she repeats in awe. "I'd marry you for that price."

Heather lifts up a shimmering blue dress that was hanging over a chair. "Put this on," she says. "We have to get to the meeting in eight minutes."

Aya looks at me as she pulls off her shirt, not even bothering to change in the bathroom. "There's going to be free booze at this thing, right?"

Maybe I should have tried calling my dentist after all…

CHAPTER
Five

"I'm really glad you're here," I tell Aya as I squeeze her hand, trying not to break her fingers. She looks radiant in the blue bridesmaid's dress, which of course fits her perfectly.

"It's going to be so fun!" she says with a bounce in her step as we hurry to the conference room. It's taking a lot of focus not to fall in these shoes, and even then, I still stumble a few times.

"Fun?!" We turn the corner and I stop, staring at the big closed wooden doors of the conference room looming down on us. I take a deep breath as my stomach flutters. "We have to pretend we're other people in front of seven hundred of the most powerful people in the world. Some were actual CIA agents. They'll be able to tell that I'm lying. I'm the worst liar."

"That's true," Aya says with a laugh. "Remember when Alex dropped all those appetizers and you made up a huge ridiculous story about a pack of wild dogs running into the kitchen when the client asked what happened?"

My jaw clenches as she bends over laughing. "I don't quite remember it that way, but yes. I'm bad at lying. I can't do this!"

Aya hooks her arm around mine and pulls me to the intimidating doors. "Chill out. It's just a wedding. Weddings are fun!"

"Not when you're the bride!"

Heather catches up and barrels past us. "Ready?" she asks as she grabs the door handles.

I'm about to say no when she opens them both with a dramatic push. "Presenting, the bride!"

Luke and his family are sitting around the table with a few new faces and a short balding priest. Heather is the only one clapping at my pathetic grand entrance.

Everyone is dressed up in their wedding gear, looking anything but festive in the conference room.

Walter stands up from the head of the table. "Zoe, come on in."

Aya bounces in with an enthusiastic wave. "Hi, y'all! I'm Aya."

They just stare at her as she takes a seat. *Damn it.* The only remaining seat is next to Luke. My feet are already killing in these shoes that are two sizes too small, so I head over and reluctantly sit beside him, keeping my body as far away from him as I can.

"Why is that lady wearing Taliah's dress?" a twenty-something girl with the same hair color as Luke and Carter asks. She's wearing the same blue bridesmaid dress as Aya and looks like she could be their sister.

"Zoe, this is my daughter, Victoria," Walter says as he sits back down. "And these are the two groomsmen, Ryan and Owen. Younger cousins of my children."

Ryan is grinning at me in a way that says he's definitely typed 'bride' into his Pornhub browser, and Owen, who is maybe thirteen, has barely looked up from his phone.

"There's no easy way to say this," Walter says with a frown. "Carter and Taliah have eloped."

Victoria gasps.

I swallow hard when he points at me. "This is her replacement."

Victoria looks appalled. "You can't be serious. *Dad!*"

"Under no circumstances can the wedding be canceled," Walter says as he raises his hand.

Kathleen jumps in. "You know how hard your father has been working for this. Believe me, none of us are going to want to live with him if this goes badly."

"Thanks, Kitty-Kat," Walter says with a bitter look. "But she's right. I'll be horrible."

Luke scoffs, his arms crossed over his chest. "So, it will be an improvement from awful is what you're saying?"

Walter's fierce eyes narrow on him. Luke glares back and the air in the conference room charges up a few degrees.

"Luke will be taking Carter's place as the groom," Kathleen says before the heated tension boils over. "And Zoe will be taking over for Taliah. Nobody will know. The ceremony will be pretend."

The priest sitting next to Kathleen starts squirming as he listens. "You want me to perform a fake wedding in the Lord's home?"

"You'll still get your five grand, Father Cliff," Walter answers in a tight voice.

"I must say," Father Cliff says as he stands up with an affronted look on his face. "I'm highly offended. I don't feel comfortable with this arrangement at all. The Lord—"

"Ten grand," Walter grunts.

"I guess it's not *that* bad," Father Cliff says as he casually sits back down. "And if this is God's plan, who am I to interfere?"

"That's very noble of you, Father Cliff," Walter says flatly. He doesn't look impressed.

Ryan won't take his perverted googly eyes off me. What is this kid, like nineteen?

"So, *she's* single?" Ryan asks as he shifts excitedly in his seat. "I'm Ryan Wooten. Girls go woot woot when they see me."

Aya tilts her head as she watches him from across the table. "Do they, though?"

"Nah," he says, looking unfazed. "But it would be dope if they did!"

"Am I the only one who thinks this is a horrible idea?" Victoria says in a near-frantic voice. "Won't people know it's not Taliah?"

"They're both females," Kathleen says with a dismissive wave. "It's close enough. Who looks at the bride at a wedding anyway?"

"Everyone," Victoria says as she stares at her mother in disbelief.

Kathleen scoffs before taking a sip of her fresh martini. *Where does she keep getting those?* "Everyone is busy looking around for a suitable second spouse."

We all stare at her.

Walter lets out a long breath and shakes his head. "Thank you for that wonderful insight into our relationship, Kathleen. But regardless, it doesn't matter. In two months, no one is going to remember the bride's name or that she's showing too much cleavage."

My cheeks burn as I try to pull up my dress.

"As long as she acts like Taliah and everyone treats her as such," Walter continues, "we'll be fine."

The guests might not have seen Taliah before, but they've probably heard some things about her. Even I know that she's a very successful real estate developer. It would probably be a good idea to know some more basics in case someone brings something up to me.

"What is she like?" I ask.

They all stare at me.

Kathleen frowns. "Who?"

"Taliah. The bride."

"Oh, her." Kathleen rolls her eyes. "I don't know. She's a Turk."

Nobody has anything to contribute. What is wrong with these people? I always hated not having a family, but if this is what families are like, then I'm better off on my own.

"Really?" I snap, getting annoyed. "She's going to be a part of your family in like an hour and you don't know anything about her?"

These people don't realize how lucky they are to have an amazing girl like Taliah join their family. No wonder she left. I would kill to be related to someone like her. To have a new sister to call or go out to lunch with.

"We know she's a real estate developer," I say, trying to jog their memories. "What about her past? Where does she live? Where did she go to school?"

More blank stares.

"Seriously?"

"It doesn't matter what she's like," Walter says in his deep booming voice. "We're going for a boring and forgettable bride. Not memorable in any way. Smile. Thank everyone for coming. Sit at the table and chew with your mouth closed. That's it."

"And what about me?" Luke asks. "Everyone here knows Carter and will be expecting him. I don't know his finance friends from work or his swim team friends from college."

"You have the same brain," Kathleen says as she fishes for an olive in her martini with her finger. "How hard can it be?"

"Keep it simple," Walter says. "Talk about the wedding. That's it. If something else comes up, excuse yourself and move on. No long conversations."

"This is so messed up," Victoria says as she massages her temples.

I knew there had to be at least one sane person in the family.

"Ryan," Walter continues, "you'll step in and be the best man since Luke is now the groom."

Ryan flashes me and Aya a toothy grin. "Hear that, ladies? Want to get with the best?"

"Don't tell your parents about this," Kathleen warns Ryan. "Randy won't last five minutes before he grabs the microphone and blurts it out."

"One more thing," Walter grunts. "You two." He points at Luke and I. "Can you two pretend to be an affectionate, loving, newly-married couple?"

A sour taste hits my mouth as I look at him.

"Yes," I say, but I'm not really selling it. Ugh. Just… does it have to be him?

Kathleen sighs. "If you two lean any further apart, you're going to tip over."

Walter leans forward. "Show me."

"Excuse me?" I say with a gulp.

"Hold hands."

I cringe as I glance at Luke's hand. Touching it must feel as gross as putting your hand inside of a pumpkin or reaching into someone's pocket and grabbing a used Kleenex.

With my eyes closed, I reach over and—actually, that's kind of nice. *No, it's not! It's Luke. Gross.*

I yank my hand away and rip my eyes open. "I'm sorry, but

he's the worst! He parked his motorcycle in *my* service tent and then called *me* overbearing when I asked him to move it!"

"*Ordered* me to move it," he corrects. "Remember, Captain?"

I shake my head in disgust. Will he ever let that go?

"And for the last time," he says, raising his voice. "Your tent *is* the parking lot!"

Father Cliff does the sign of the cross. Even Owen is looking up from his phone and staring at us with his jaw hanging open.

"This is not going to work," I say as I fold my hands on the table and fight down my anger. "Are you sure you don't have triplets? By any chance was there a third son given up for adoption or something? Maybe mistakenly given away by the hospital staff?"

"I think I'd remember a third human passing through my loins," Kathleen says in a flat voice.

I'm desperate as I look around the room, trying to think of any solution that doesn't involve me pressing my lips against Luke's.

"What about Victoria?"

"Me?"

I nod, panic taking over. "We could cut her hair. She kind of looks like her brothers."

"Where did you get this woman?" Victoria asks as she stares at her parents in horror. "A mental institution?"

"I'm not crazy," I tell her. "I'm the caterer."

"Of the parking lot," Aya helpfully points out.

"Thanks, Aya," I answer through gritted teeth.

"I should get going," Father Cliff says as he stands up. "The ceremony starts in thirty minutes."

"Thank you, Father Cliff," Walter says with his eyes narrowed on him. "And not a word to anyone. Even to the big man."

Father Cliff nods nervously and quickly leaves. Heather is hanging by the door, looking anxious to get on with things.

"I should go too," Luke says, standing up.

"Sit," Walter barks. "We're not done yet."

He sits back down and the tension hovering over the table returns with a vengeance. *Are they always like this?*

"I want to see you two kiss," Walter says in a serious tone.

I cross my arms and shake my head. "*Pfff*. Yeah, right."

"You're going to have to kiss at the altar," Victoria not-so-helpfully points out. Geez, since when is she on their side?

Okay, let's give it a shot. I take a deep breath and shake my hands out as I turn to him. He's handsome enough, but I can't stop my face from scrunching up in disgust.

"It's just kissing a stranger," Aya says with a shrug. "It's easy. Look."

She leans over the table, grabs Ryan's tie, yanks him forward, and crushes her lips to his. His cheeks are bright red and his eyes are glazed over when she pulls away and releases him.

"Woot, woot," he squeaks as he slumps into his chair, looking a little unsteady.

"Yeah, I'm not doing that," I say firmly. "We'll kiss cheeks. That's as far as I'm willing to go."

"I'm sorry," Walter says in a sharp tone. "I was under the impression you wanted the silver contract."

"Golden contract," Kathleen corrects.

"Whatever."

Oh, crap. That contract would change everything. I do need it. Desperately.

Whatever it takes.

"Fine," I say as I steel myself. "I'm a professional."

I turn to him and look at his lips.

His mouth is much better without the scraggly beard. Kind of nice even.

Luke suddenly stands up and shakes his head at me. "Let's save it for the audience."

My mouth drops open as he walks out of the room.

Hey! I *reject* him, *not the other way around!*

This guy really is the worst.

"We should all be going," Heather says nervously from where she's hovering by the door. "The limos are waiting downstairs. It's time to go to the church."

Everyone looks at Walter. "This better go well," he grunts. "I'm relying on all of you to pull this off and I'm not a man you want to disappoint."

He gets up and then so does everyone else.

Ryan races around the table with his eyes locked on Aya. "Aya! Want to share a limo?"

"Don't fall in love with me, kid," she warns. "You'll never recover."

Ryan swallows hard. "Is it bad that I want it even more now?"

They head out, followed by Owen and Victoria.

My heart is pounding as I walk to the door, but it's not from the wedding, it's from Luke. He turned me down when I was about to kiss him.

I'll make him pay for that.

I'm going to kiss him so hard. He won't know what hit him.

Yes. When Father Cliff pronounces us pretend husband and fake wife, I'm going to rock his world. I'm going to kiss the shit out of him.

I leave with a grin on my lips.

CHAPTER *Six*

Heather is spitting out the itinerary as I slide onto the leather seat in the limo. She's talking so fast I'm getting a headache trying to keep up.

"So, it's the ceremony, you're married, yay yay, next scene celebratory champagne on the steps outside of the church, waiters will be waiting with silver trays and crystal stemware. Next scene we immediately move you and Luke to the water for pictures."

She's flipping through the pages on her clipboard as my head spins. This is going to be okay, right? I can do this. Can't I?

"Oh, good," Heather says when she looks out the window. "There's Luke. *Luke!*"

"No, don't call him ov—oh shit."

He spots her and comes over with his younger sister Victoria beside him. Why did Heather have to go and do that? Maybe there's another limo I can take...

I'm looking around as he opens the door and climbs in.

His face sours when he sees me sitting inside.

"I'm going over the itinerary with Zoe," Heather says as

she shifts down the leather bench, letting him and Victoria in. "So, for the church, remember the three C's. Ceremony, champagne, and click click."

"Isn't that four C's?" Victoria asks.

Heather looks down at her clipboard with her forehead scrunched up.

"You sure you want to marry into this shitshow of a family?" Luke asks me with an incredulous look on his face.

"It's too late now," I say as I fidget with my dress. "I shook your father's hand. We made a deal."

"Oh, believe me, he would rip that deal to shreds if it benefitted him even in the slightest way."

Victoria looks up at her older brother with defeat in her eyes. She has the tired weary look of a normal person trapped in a dysfunctional family.

"Well, if someone is going to break the contract, it's not going to be me. No matter how tempting it sounds."

The limo starts moving. I take a deep breath. This is happening. I'm actually going through with this.

"Great," Heather says, getting back to her itinerary. "Kiara is going to be taking the pictures of the happy couple by the water and there will be more photographers and a videographer at the reception."

"Why so many pictures?" Luke asks with a sigh. "It's fake. Is a photoshoot really necessary?"

"Senator Whitfield wants them for his ad campaign," Heather says.

Luke shakes his head. "Of course he does."

"And the video will be used as B roll for his commercials when he runs for President."

Victoria and Luke glance at each other. Something passes between them, some unspoken language between siblings that goes over my head. I don't have any siblings, so I don't speak the language.

"Next scene is the reception line," Heather continues in her rapid-fire tone, "a short break while the guests find their tables, next scene the newly married couple have their first dance."

I dart upright as a sudden sense of dread overwhelms me. My body goes cold. My fingers dig into the hard leather seat.

"Dance?" I whisper, teetering on the edge of panic.

My chest is crushingly tight. It feels like I'm choking.

"Yeah, the first dance," Heather says like it's nothing.

It's dancing in front of seven hundred plus people. It's not nothing!

"Are you okay?" Victoria asks as she looks at me funny.

I must be the color of my dress because they're suddenly all focused on me.

"Is there a problem?" Heather asks.

"I don't dance."

"Like… ever?"

"Not since I was six."

Victoria scoffs. "Where did you say you found this lady? In the parking lot?"

"I'm the caterer thank you very much." I liked her better when she was on my side.

"You don't dance?" she says with her voice rising. "At all?"

I think the events of the day are catching up to Victoria because she's suddenly bubbling with frustration. Either that or she gets really triggered by people who don't dance.

"I hate nightclubs."

"So do I," she says, "but don't you dance around sometimes when you're on your own? Around your room or around the kitchen?"

"No!" I say with a sudden burst of laughter. She's not

laughing… Wait. Is she serious? "You do that? People actually do that?!"

Victoria turns to the window. "Oh, my God."

"It will be fine," Heather says as she gets back to business. She bats her eyelashes at Luke. "Just grab onto these gorgeous muscles and enjoy the ride."

Luke's eyebrow raises as she runs her hand along his bicep for a few seconds too long.

"The dance won't be a problem," I say, sounding more confident than I feel. I'll just hold onto him and sway from side to side for the length of a song. I can do that.

I'll ignore the seven hundred plus people in the room staring at me, filming me, judging me, and I'll look into his eyes and pretend that I'm not nauseous. It will be a piece of cake.

"Oh, that reminds me," Heather says to Victoria. "Are you, Ryan, Owen, and Lily still performing your song for the bride?"

Victoria's eyes begin to water as she stares out the window. "No. It was a song to welcome Taliah into the family. We're not doing it for a stranger."

She turns and her wet cobalt blue eyes bore into mine.

I shift in my seat.

"What were you going to sing?" Luke asks her softly.

Her chin trembles and she takes a deep breath. "A song. It doesn't matter," she says with a crack in her voice. "Owen was going to be playing the spoons, Ryan on guitar, Lily on tambourine, and I was going to sing and play. We've been practicing for over a month."

"I didn't know they all played instruments," Luke says, looking impressed. "So, you're still singing?"

"Every Friday at the pub." She shoots him a look. "I play too. I'm better on the Gibson than you now. Maybe you'd know all this if you ever came around to family events anymore."

"You know how it is with me and our father…"

"Yeah, but that's you and Dad," she says in a harsh tone. "I thought *we* were still cool. I guess I was wrong considering I haven't seen you since Christmas two and a half *years* ago. And thanks for not calling me on my birthday. That was really nice."

Luke crumples back into the seat with a heavy breath.

"I hate this family," she says as she crosses her arms and turns back to the window. "You've cut me out of your life and now Carter and Taliah kick me out of their wedding and elope? I was so happy for them and so excited to watch them commit to one another and recite their vows. I helped Mom pick out the flowers and the cake. I was looking forward to it all summer. But they just left." Tears finally break through and slide down her cheeks. "I was so thrilled to finally get a sister and she couldn't care less about me. She ditched me immediately. The worst part is, they didn't even say goodbye. I didn't do anything to them. Why do you guys hate me? What did I ever do to deserve such horrible brothers?"

Luke drops to a knee in front of her and takes her hand. She won't look at him as she stares out the window, trying to hide her tears.

"You're right," he says in a calm soothing voice. "I have been a shitty brother."

She finally looks at him. Her eyes are wet and puffy, but at least the tears have stopped.

"Just because I don't get along with our father," he continues, "doesn't mean we can't have our own thing. You've grown up into a smart, beautiful, capable woman and I'm an idiot for shutting you out. I'm so proud of you, Victoria. You're the best of us. The only good one."

She wipes her eyes as she looks down at him. Heather hands her a tissue and takes one for herself. Geez, even Heather is crying?

"I'm sorry I didn't call you on your birthday. That wasn't cool. I'd like to make it up to you. How about I watch your show on Friday and then I'll take you out to a late dinner?"

She smiles as she wipes her nose. "Okay. I'd like that."

"As long as you don't mind me sitting in the front row and loudly telling everyone we're related."

She laughs.

"And as for Carter and Taliah," Luke continues. "I know it's hard, but they were right to leave. This is not a place to celebrate their love. It's a place to celebrate our father's colossal-sized ego. They deserve a secluded beach and a romantic night to themselves."

Victoria looks down at her lap and nods.

"But they were wrong to not say goodbye to you. They should have explained. They should have gotten your blessing. It was shitty and I'm sorry that happened. You didn't deserve that."

She sniffs as she looks up at him. "Thank you, Luke."

"You are stunning," he tells her as my heart pangs. "And I'm glad you're going to be our bridesmaid tonight. And fake wedding or not, we're going to have some fun together. It's long overdue."

She wraps her arms around him and he whispers something in her ear. I turn away, wanting to respect the private moment, but Heather doesn't. She's eying Luke like a hungry chihuahua eying a chalupa taco.

I can't help but get a little jealous—Luke is supposed to be mine for the day—and look back to admire the sweet way he's whispering to Victoria and making everything alright.

Maybe he'd be a good boyfriend.

I can picture coming home after a long hard day and having those big comforting arms wrapped around me like that. One sweet whisper from him telling me everything is going to be okay and I could see all of my troubles melting away.

He sits back down and Victoria gets herself together. "I am glad they're getting the wedding they want."

Luke smiles as he looks at me. "I guess our beautiful bride was right after all when she suggested it."

Victoria rears on me, the touching moment over. "*What?!* It was *your* idea?!"

Panic rushes back in as I sit up straight. "Not my idea," I spit out defensively. "Well, technically it *was* my idea, but it wasn't meant for her. It was meant for me."

"We really should finish going over the itinerary," Heather says nervously as she rifles through her papers.

"What do you mean it was meant for you?" Victoria asks while giving me the side-eye. "You want to get married on the beach?"

"It would be nice, I guess. Taliah was really the one who ran with it. I didn't even—"

"Do you have a fiancée?" Victoria interrupts.

I bite my bottom lip as I suck in a breath. This is going to look so bad. Dreaming of a wedding and I'm not even engaged. I don't even have a boyfriend.

They're all looking at me, waiting for me to answer.

"Not currently."

Victoria won't quit. "Is your boyfriend going to propose soon?"

"Yes," I blurt out. I immediately regret it. I'm the worst liar, but this is a day of lying so I might as well start trying to get comfortable with it.

"Congratulations," Heather says. "If you need a wedding

coordinator, I'd be happy to offer my services." She pulls out a card and hands it to me.

"Oh," I say as I awkwardly take it. "But it's… complicated." My panicked brain is racing to come up with something. "He's always away for work in the… forest. He's a lumberjack! From Canada. British Colombia, actually."

I'm nodding my head confidently even though I'm dying inside.

"A hot lumberjack from Canada," Luke says with a skeptical smirk. "Does he ride a moose to work?"

"No, a… horse."

Damn! Why couldn't you just say a car?

"A hunky Canadian lumberjack who rides a horse to work," Luke says with a chuckle. "Sounds legit."

"I didn't say he was hunky."

"Is he?"

I shrug. "Well, yes…"

If I'm going to be making up boyfriends, I might as well make them hot.

"Getting back to the itinerary," Heather says in a more forceful voice. "First dance. Next scene, we all sit down to eat. Next scene, Senator Whitfield will announce his Presidency. Next scene—"

"What is that?" I interrupt with a gasp when we turn a corner and see a mob on the street.

The limo driver has to stop with the mass of bodies blocking the way. There are people *everywhere*. Onlookers, reporters, protestors with an alarming number of grammatical errors on their signs, police officers, secret service agents, wedding guests dressed up in their finest suits and dresses, all blocking the way to the church.

They swarm the limo, shoving their faces and cameras against the window, trying to catch a glimpse of who's inside.

I flinch back, the tightness increasing in my chest. Adrenaline surges through my veins as a man knocks on the window and shoves his camera against it.

What the hell have I gotten myself into?

These aren't just friends and family of the bride and groom.

That painful fact becomes abundantly clear when I spot the familiar logo on the camera.

"Is that TMZ?!"

CHAPTER Seven

"It's showtime," Heather says when she gets the signal from Father Cliff. "Does anyone have any questions?"

"When does the bar open?" Aya asks.

"How can I get a new family?" Victoria mutters to herself.

We're all standing in a line, waiting to walk into the crowded church. The limo driver backed up and sped into an alley that was being secured by the secret service. They let us through and held everyone else back. We raced into the church through the priest's private entrance and then split up to take our places.

I'm guessing Luke is standing at the altar right now, pretending to be Carter in front of hundreds of guests. I wonder if he's feeling as nervous as I am. There's a mob of butterflies in my stomach fighting for supremacy. I'm so nervous. I'm so everything. Overwhelmed, intimidated, panicked, terrified. Emotions are ripping through me like a category five hurricane.

I'm full of regret, self-loathing, desperation, fear. My heart is racing. My palms are sweaty.

If my shoes weren't two sizes too small, I might just run out of here and not stop until I hit Canada.

I close my eyes and focus on my breathing for a couple of long slow breaths. *Whatever it takes.*

Whenever I'm feeling overwhelmed, I must remember what I'm doing this for. My future, my security, my survival. I have no one else to rely on. No hands to catch me if I fail. I can't fail. I *won't* fail.

The organ starts playing, echoing through the cavernous hall of the church like the entrance song for the grim reaper.

"Where the hell is the flower girl?" Heather says as she looks around in a panic. "Has anyone seen Lily and Tammy? Oh, thank God. Lily! Hurry please!"

A cute little blonde girl about seven years old in a baby blue dress and holding a basket of rose petals comes running over with her mother.

She takes one look at me and her face twists up in confusion. "Who are you?"

My mouth gets all dry as she stares up at me with these big blue eyes. "I'm, uh… Taliah."

"I saw Taliah this morning. You're not her."

"Actually, yeah," the mother says, looking at me funny. "You look different. Your nose looks bigger."

"Could be the makeup," I say with a nervous laugh.

The mom looks me up and down with a frown on her face. "Did you change your dress or something? I don't quite remember this much cleavage."

"This is the one and only Taliah," Heather says, swooping in to save the day. "Love of Carter's life. Bride for the day. Places, people. Please."

The poor mother looks so confused. Heather takes her arm and ushers her away. "Thank you, Tammy. Please take your seat in the church."

She glances at me over her shoulder as she leaves, trying to make sense of all of this.

Heather walks along the line of us for one last inspection before it's go time. Lily, then Victoria, then Aya, then me.

Heather stops and plucks at a few white roses in my bouquet. "It's going to be great!" she says, but her wrinkled brow and forced tight smile are saying the opposite.

Aya is all loose and carefree like she's done this a million times. I hate her.

"Are we allowed to dance down the aisle?" she asks.

Heather looks like she's on the verge of a migraine. "Please don't."

The organ hits a high note and Heather rushes to the front. "Okay, that's our cue! Go, Lily! Remember, spread the flowers *evenly.*"

Lily is staring me down with the force of a Terminator. "I'm watching you," she warns before switching into an adorable flower girl smile as she turns the corner and disappears into the church.

I can't even fool a seven-year-old. I'm never going to make it.

This is actually happening. This is my last chance to back out. I look around for an exit.

My heart feels like it's going to explode out of my body.

Can someone open one of those stained glass windows? There's not enough oxygen in here. I'm choking down breaths into my tight chest.

I need to sit down.

My head whips around from side to side, desperately looking for a seat before I pass out.

Heather puts her hand on Victoria's shoulder and holds her there as she pokes her head into the church. "Okay, go!"

You can tell that Victoria is enjoying this as much as I am

by the way she's crushing her bouquet of flowers with that white-knuckled grip. She forces out a smile as she rounds the corner and disappears.

This is like being in a small plane twenty thousand feet in the air with a parachute strapped to your back and watching the other passengers disappear out the door. In a second it will be my turn and I don't know if I can actually take the leap.

Aya and I take a few steps forward as Heather peeks around the corner.

I'm so focused on the back of Aya's head that I don't notice a random man creeping up next to me. I nearly scream as he hooks his arm around mine.

I gasp as I look up at him. He's about fifty-five or so with scruffy salt and pepper hair and a tan on his face in the shape of sunglasses. He's wearing a cheap black suit with a mustard stain on his lapel.

"Who the hell are you?"

He clears his throat as he looks down at me. "Limo driver. You?"

"Caterer."

He nods and we both look forward like two shell-shocked soldiers about to enter the battle of their lives.

"Aya! Go!" Heather says with a wave.

Aya doesn't dance, but she does skip out like a carefree kid on a warm summer day. Surprised laughter mixes with the screeching of the organ.

"Why is she skipping?" Heather says with a frown as she watches Aya go. She shakes her head and turns to me. "It doesn't matter. You're going to be okay. Walk straight to Luke. Remember to smile. You're happy. Joyful. This is your wedding day!"

"I'm ecstatic," I hiss through gritted teeth, my lips twisted up in a crazed killer prom queen smile.

The organ changes tunes and the sound of seven hundred plus people standing up sends a cold shiver racing down my spine.

"I can do this," I whisper to myself. "I can do this."

I grip my pretend father's arm and we start walking.

"Holy shit," I gasp under my breath when I turn the corner and see the terrifying sight in front of me. I almost take a step back, but somehow my feet move forward, my fingertips digging into the handle of my bouquet.

The church is *huge*. A big domed ceiling with a never-ending row of benches packed with hundreds of people staring at me. There are balconies on each side, crammed with people looking down at me, filming me, taking pictures of me.

All eyes are on me as I take one shaky step after another, trying not to fall in these crazy tight shoes.

I'm suddenly feeling very grateful to have this man with the sunglass tan by my side. He's keeping me steady. Keeping me going. It clicks that my pretend father has done more for me in the past ten seconds than my real father has done in the past ten years.

Every cell in my body is screaming at me to escape, to turn around and flee, but I keep a smile plastered on my face and focus on one step at a time.

I glance into the crowd every few steps and real smiles greet me back. Tilted heads and blushed cheeks. Some people are even crying.

One woman has her head on her husband's shoulder, smiling as she dabs her wet eyes with a crumpled-up tissue.

These are the people I wish I could be like. They love love. They don't know me, or that this guy—who really smells like parmesan by the way—is a complete stranger. Yet, they're still crying. It's that touching to them.

They must really love love to shed a tear over the love of strangers.

It makes me feel guilty for lying to them.

I'm not one of those people. I don't love love. I'm more skeptical, reluctant, hardened by it. I don't cry at weddings or during sappy movies.

I'm not like that man in the blue tie who's trying to hold back a tear, or like that woman with the giant hat who's on the verge of sobs. I'll hand out the tissues, but I'll never use one.

I snap back into reality with a jolt and get a fresh wave of nausea as my pretend father pulls me toward the altar where my pretend fiancé is waiting.

My eyes dart up to the gigantic stained glass window over the priest's head, vibrantly lit up by the afternoon sun.

I don't want to look at him.

At my groom. At my nemesis. At Luke.

I don't want to see him standing there in his fitted tuxedo, smiling back at me with that smirk in his eyes. I'd rather watch the horrific torture scenes on the stained glass windows thank you very much.

Finally, the organ dies down, we reach the steps that lead up to the altar, and I'm forced to look at my groom for the night.

I hate to admit it, but he is really handsome.

He walks down the steps and my eyes roam over him, taking in his broad shoulders and muscular form. His arms are slightly bigger than Carter's, so his biceps are strained against the tight coat. I feel the pace of my heart picking up when he reaches out and offers his arm to me.

Maybe I have been too hard on him. He was really sweet back in the limo when he was talking to Victoria. I'd like to see more of that side of him.

An image of him laying under a broken motorcycle,

looking smoking hot in a stained undershirt and ripped jeans flashes into my mind. I'm sitting on a stool, watching his muscles tighten and ripple as he twists a wrench with his dirty hands, knowing those same strong hands will be on me later.

I push it out as fast as it comes and wrap my hand around his arm with a tight smile.

Luke shakes the hand of my pretend father. "Who are you?" he whispers as he leans in.

"The limo driver," he whispers back as he wipes his eyes, pretending to be emotional.

He kisses my cheek, lets go of me, and sits down in the empty seat in the first row.

Please don't fall. Please don't fall.

Luke guides me up the six steps and I arrive safely at the altar despite my deadly shoes trying to kill me. Being with him is making me feel a bit better. I'm not alone anymore. He's as deep in this as I am. Maybe even more so. After tonight, I never have to see any of these people again if it goes horribly wrong. Not so for him. It's his family.

Ryan and Owen are standing behind Luke. Owen looks bored, but Ryan looks thrilled, his eyes never leaving Aya. Photographers are running around the outer aisles with their gear, clicking away, not wanting to miss a single second of this abomination of a wedding.

The crowd sits as I take Taliah's place in front of the groom with Father Cliff between us. There are a million eyes on me and I'm suddenly very aware of every microscopic movement I make.

I glance back at my bridesmaids as Father Cliff clears his throat into the microphone. Aya gives me an encouraging smile. Victoria stares at me with dead eyes.

"Thank you for joining us today as we bless Taliah

Osadogroom and Carter Whitfield into the covenant of Holy Matrimony."

Luke and I are staring into one another's wide panicked eyes as we both try to keep it together.

It's unnerving, staring at him like this, so I turn away and glance at the first row on the groom's side. Lily the flower girl is sitting between her mother Tammy and a man with a Bruce Springsteen t-shirt under an old faded sports coat.

Another older lady—tall, short hair—who must be Luke's aunt is viciously texting something into her phone. I'm not sure if she's looked up from her screen once. Beside her are Kathleen and Walter, staring back at me with an intensity that keeps my eyes quickly moving along the line.

The last person on the row, sitting next to the aisle in the best seat in the house, is glaring at me and Luke like a shopkeeper studying someone with a candy bar in their pocket, knowing they're up to something, but not quite knowing what it is. She's an elderly lady with alert, observant eyes and a stern stare that announces she's the alpha in the room, no matter who else is in it. I want to ask Luke who she is but now is hardly the time. We're in the middle of getting married.

Father Cliff is rambling on, earning his ten thousand dollars and basking in the trapped attention of everyone in the room.

The bride's side of the church is also filled, although they're all here for Walter and not for me, or the real Taliah.

It's embarrassing to think that my side would be pretty much empty if I ever did get married. Maybe I could scrounge up a dozen people. Maybe I could hire a few people off of Craigslist so my future husband won't think I'm a total loser.

"Please head over to our Facebook page at w-w-w-dot-facebook-dot-c-o-m slash Cathedral of the Sacred Heart," Father Cliff says slowly. The look Luke gives him nearly makes me laugh out loud. I bite my tongue and swallow it down. "And join the two hundred and twenty-seven people who have already hit the thumbs up button!"

My mind zones out as he goes on with the ceremony. I stare at Luke and pretend there aren't seven hundred plus people staring at me at this very moment. Staring at my cleavage that is popping back out, at my face that's hiding behind a few layers of makeup, at my hair that has never looked so good.

I get so lost in his cobalt blue eyes that the aggressive butterflies in my stomach settle down to a rumpus roar.

Unfortunately, it's not long before I'm jarred back to reality.

"It's now time for the vows," Father Cliff belts into the microphone.

I turn to him in shock. *Vows?!? Heather never said anything about vows!*

Father Cliff lifts his arms and opens them wide, which in his black and white robe makes him look like a giant penguin.

As I'm repeating *vows?* in my head for the third time, an overeager choir boy saddles up beside me and shoves a hot microphone in my face. He stares up at me—wide-eyed, freckled cheeks, excited innocent smile. I could kill him.

I suck in a sharp breath as the microphone sits there, waiting like a grenade with a pulled pin.

Seven hundred people in the room and the only sound is the hum of the microphone feedback, a cough in the back row, and Aya softly chuckling behind me.

Say something! Everyone is waiting!!

"Um… Lu—Carter."

Whoa. That was close.

Walter and Kathleen are on the edge of their seats as they watch me, either praying that I'm not going to mess this up for them, or contemplating what hell they'll put me through if I do.

I shake that terrifying thought out of my head and turn back to my groom. He's biting his lip, trying not to laugh.

"I… love you." *Ugh. Why do I feel so dirty now?*

I'm trying to think of all the romantic movies I've seen for ideas, Hallmark cards I've read, even sappy commercials. I'm desperate for anything.

"You are my soulmate, obviously. Otherwise, we wouldn't be getting married. Which we are."

My pathetic incoherent words reverberate around the church and back into my ears. This is bad. What would Taliah say?

Whatever she'd say, it would be articulate and intelligent, not the gibberish that's coming out of my mouth.

"Umm…"

Oh no. Say something.

Fuck.

It's been so long since I've spoken.

Fuck. Fuck!

What do lovers talk about? Love? Bills? Sex?

Fuck, say something! Now!

"I love, sex with you."

Luke's eyes grow absurdly large as hushed laughter fills the church.

My eyes dart to Walter and Kathleen. Their faces are burning a hellish red. They look furious.

Nervous laughter bubbles out of me. Real laughter bubbles out of Luke.

"I mean…" I spit out, trying to get back on track. "What I'm trying to say is, I love you, Carter. Even without sex, I love you. Not that you're bad at sex. No, you're good at it." I turn to Father Cliff in panic. "Actually, we haven't had sex, obviously. Saving myself for tonight!"

Aya snorts behind me.

Stop saying sex! Please stop saying sex! You're in a church for fuck's sake!

I close my eyes, shake my head, and turn back to Luke.

People are really paying attention now—even Luke's aunt has turned her phone off—so I have to finish strong.

Just be honest.

"Umm..." I say as I open my eyes and look at him. "I like that little dent in your cheek when you smile for real. It's not quite a dimple, but it's adorable nonetheless. I love how you always know the perfect thing to say and that mischievous smirk that I'm not sure if I want to slap off or kiss."

The crowd laughs, and not in a mocking way this time.

I'm turning this ship around. Time to land strong while I got them.

"You're my heart and my soul. And I'll love you forever."

I try to hand the microphone back to the choir boy who is creepily staring up at me, but he doesn't take it. How do I end this thing? With an amen? With a mic drop? Will someone please start clapping?

The harsh sound of my throat clearing reverberates through the vast church. "That's the end of my vows. I'm finished."

Luke's lip curls up as I awkwardly hand him the microphone, my ears turning a hot red.

That was more awkward than the time I opened a champagne bottle while working in the middle of a huge gala and it sprayed in my face like a bubbly firehose.

At least now it's Luke's turn to make a fool of himself. I'm going to relish this.

"Taliah," he says in that smooth suave voice of his. He takes my hand and stares into my eyes. My breath quickens with the captivating way he's looking at me. "I don't know if I'm the man you deserve, but I'll strive to be that man every blissful day that I get to call you my wife. I promise to be everything for you. I'll be an ear when you need to talk, a shoulder when you need to cry, a comedian when you need to laugh, a caretaker when you're sick, a chef when you're hungry, I'll be whatever you need. I'll be anything, do anything, as long as I get to hold this hand and wake up to your beautiful smile every morning."

He gracefully hands the microphone back to the choir boy, who this time takes it (jerk), and releases my hand, leaving me with a fluttering in my chest and a kind of lightheadedness that I'm not sure I've ever felt before.

It's all pretend. This is just a show.

I don't know why I have to remind myself, but I do.

Father Cliff takes the floor once again and then brings us behind the altar to sign some papers while the photographers move in.

"Luke," I whisper as I bend over and pick up the pen.

He looks at me with his eyebrow raised.

"Our real names are on the paper."

He leans over and sees Luke Whitfield and Zoe Fitzpatrick written in permanent black ink.

"Sign the papers please," Father Cliff impatiently says when we both hesitate.

I smile nervously as I look around the room at all seven hundred plus people staring at me. The photographers have me in their crosshairs, the cameras waiting for me to sign. I grip the pen with white knuckles and sign the line above my name, hoping that this document is as fake as our love.

Luke signs as well and minutes later, we're back in front of the altar placing rings on each other. They're the real rings, which I'm going to happily give back to Taliah at the end of the night. She's slimmer than I am, so the only finger that it can get past the knuckle without baby oil is my pinkie. Luke shoves it on there with a grunt. So romantic.

I grab his hand and slide the ring on his finger. He's a motorcycle mechanic so I'm expecting oil stains in the lines of his skin and blackness under his nails, but they're very clean and surprisingly soft to the touch.

Father Cliff turns to me and asks if I'll take this man to be my husband. I croak out an "I do." He turns to Luke and asks him if he'll take me to be his wife.

He looks right at me and smiles. "I do."

A charge fills the room. I can feel the excitement crackling in the air.

Father Cliff puffs out his penguin chest. "I now pronounce you husband and wife. You may now kiss the bride."

Luke leans in slowly, but I grab the back of his neck and crush my lips to his. His lips are softer than I expected. Warmer. Tastier.

I moan into his mouth as my lips part. *Mmmm*. He tastes good.

My toes curl in my shoes as he slides his hot tongue against mine. Hot shivers race down my skin as I tilt my head to taste more of this hot frustrating man.

The crowd stands up and roars their approval.

His big hand flattens against my lower back and he pulls me into him. Having my body pressed up against his makes me sink into the kiss for a moment longer than I had planned.

Finally, I rip my lips away from his and stare him straight in the eye. "For the audience," I say with a grin.

For the first time since I've met him, he doesn't have a sarcastic retort or a witty comment. He's dead silent as he stares back at me with his cheeks reddening and his breath caught in his throat.

A rush of adrenaline surges through my energetic veins. I

feel like I could run a marathon, even in these painfully small unbalanced shoes.

He's still silent. I won this battle and I couldn't be happier.

I turn away from his blushing face, feeling victorious as I take a step, and then promptly fall down all six stairs before landing *hard* on the floor.

CHAPTER *Eight*

I'm on the floor.

I'm a bride, at a wedding, on the floor.

Somewhere in the crowd, looking at my cheek plastered against the red carpet is the ambassador of Paraguay. I don't know why that's the first thing to pop into my head, but it is.

I swear my bouquet hasn't even landed before Luke swoops down the stairs like a stylish superhero, grabs my armpits, and hoists me up to my feet.

I'm dizzy, the room is spinning, my knee is burning, and—

Holy cleavage!

I quickly yank my dress up before anyone can snap a picture and I'll be immortalized on the Internet forever.

Luke wipes the rose petals off my cheek and wraps his arm around me. "Let's go."

I let my new pretend groom get me out of here. He's ninety percent carrying me, ten percent dragging. He doesn't stop past the rows and rows of strangers trying to be the first one to congratulate us until he Rambo kicks the huge wooden doors open and carries me into the fresh air.

The cool breeze hits my hot sweaty skin as the big heavy doors slam shut behind us.

It's just us out here.

No crowd of strangers staring. No unwanted eyes judging.

The secret service has managed to clear the block of all the busybodies who showed up with no invitations.

I close my eyes and take a deep breath, feeling like it's the first time since I met this man that I can breathe.

I can hear cars, and seagulls, and a lawn mower somewhere far away.

It's a glimpse of heaven. A moment of respite.

It doesn't last long.

"What the hell did we agree to?" Luke says in a strained voice. It's the first time I've heard an edge in his tone, like he's as freaked out as I am.

I open my eyes and turn to him, shocked to see a practically feral look in his eyes as he violently rubs his temples.

My knee is killing and I have my own issues to worry about. I don't have the time or the mental energy to soothe him.

"I knew I shouldn't have worn these toddler-sized shoes," I say with a wince. I pull up my dress and yes, my knee is bleeding from a fresh new gash.

Luke immediately drops to a knee, pulls out the handkerchief from his jacket pocket, and dabs it. It's easy to not focus on the pain when his big strong hand is gripping the back of my calf. The feel of his skin on my leg grabs all of my attention.

His brow furrows as he focuses on trying to stop the bleeding.

I glance at the big wooden doors, knowing they're about to burst open any second and we'll have to slip back into character.

There's something bothering me that I have to get out while I can.

"Why were our real names on the papers?"

Luke looks up at me. *God, those eyes…*

"I'm sure they're fake. My father wouldn't do that."

I tilt my head as I look down at him. "Are you sure?"

He sighs as he turns his attention back to my knee. "No."

The doors explode open like a monster breaching our peaceful oasis and fancily dressed guests pour out like an invading army. Dozens of champagne corks pop like artillery as the servers arrive. We're doomed.

Luke releases my leg and stands up with a welcoming smile as we're ambushed by men in tailored Italian suits and women in thousand-dollar gowns. Servers in tuxedos mount the steps holding silver trays with champagne flutes teetering on them. A string quartet quickly sets up on the grass and begins to play.

I inch beside Luke as the crowd swarms around us, smothering and constraining us in a mass of perfumed bodies, everyone talking at us at once. Our hands find each other and our fingers entwine. We may not get along, but we're all we have in this messed-up situation. Between having him and nothing, I'll take him.

A few young couples surround us, enclosing us in the thick crowd. My back straightens and I'm feeling suffocated as the girls compliment my dress. The black-haired one is eying my cleavage with a disapproving look on her face. I try to pull it up, but the dress won't move. I swear this thing is shrinking as the day goes on.

"Congrats, Carter!" judgy girl's boyfriend says as he slaps Luke on the shoulder. "Can't wait to catch up with you over a few Hollywood Stingers! For old time's sake!"

"Okay!" Luke says as he awkwardly gives him a thumbs up.

"What's a Hollywood Stinger?" I whisper to him once they've moved on down the steps.

"I have no idea," he whispers back. "I've never seen that guy in my life."

He reaches through the crowd and grabs two champagne flutes off a tray and I swear, I've never tasted anything so good as alcohol in this moment. I just wish it was something stronger.

A few more strangers squeeze by to congratulate us. I'm feeling trapped and imprisoned on these steps, but I'm still relieved that no one is bringing up my fall. That was humiliating—everyone gasping and standing up to see. I guess we're all just pretending it didn't happen. A consensual non-verbal social contract that we've all agreed to—

"What a fall!" Aya shouts as she pushes her way through the crowd with a wide grin on her infuriating face.

"Will you—*shhh!*"

Aya grabs a champagne flute and downs half of it. "I saw some people filming so you'll be able to watch it on the Internet later."

"Shit," I mutter under my breath. "Do you think it will go viral?"

"Probably," she says with a shrug and then downs the rest of her drink. "The Internet loves falling brides."

"Thanks, Aya."

"Especially ones showing a lot of cleavage."

I wiggle my body as I try to pull my dress up. "I'm not showing that much cleavage, am I?"

Aya glances down at my chest and laughs as she melts away into the stifling crowd.

What a nightmare.

Luke's family starts making their way out of the church. Walter grabs a champagne glass and raises it into the air, arms out like he's the star of the show. "Here's to the new couple!" he hollers and everyone raises their glasses and cheers.

I'm forcing out a smile to everyone as I feel a drop of blood rolling down my leg, wet and warm.

The man in the sports coat over the Bruce Springsteen t-shirt pushes his way up to us. He doesn't quite have a mullet, but it's pretty darn close. For some reason, he's holding a can of beer.

"My uncle Randy," Luke says when he arrives. "My father's brother."

This is Walter's brother?! If those two apples fell from the same tree, then Randy's apple must have rolled into the trailer park down the street.

"Congratulations, Carter," he says as he shakes Luke's hand. "She's a knockout."

Geez, I'm standing right here. But I'm not sure if I'm more annoyed or flattered. Mullet or not, no one has ever called me a knockout before.

"I heard Luke didn't come," he says with a frown and a shake of his head. "What a leech-headed thing to do. I never liked him, you know?"

The vein on Luke's temple has joined the party and it's throbbing.

"I mean, what kind of son punches his own father in the face?"

"With all due respect, *Uncle Randy,*" Luke says with a tight jaw. "Some people deserve to get punched in the face. Fathers included."

Randy shrugs as he finishes off his can of beer and crushes it in his hand. Classy. "I never liked him."

"Luke really wanted to come, but unfortunately it was an

impossibility," I say, stepping in. "He's been a huge help in the planning of our wedding and has been nothing but supportive. He's a great brother and Carter here is *very* lucky to have him."

Randy looks at me for a long moment. I lock eyes with him. "Taliah, right?"

"That's right."

He shrugs before leaving. "Welcome to the family."

"Did you just stick up for me?" Luke whispers with an eyebrow raised.

I can't help but grin back.

I'm not sure why I felt compelled to do it, but Luke is mine for the day and I got a little defensive. I'll be damned if I'm going to let a guy who showed up in a Bruce Springsteen t-shirt to *my* pretend wedding badmouth *my* pretend groom. Not on my watch.

Heather elbows her way over and starts pushing us into the middle of the stairs as even more people crowd around, telling me how beautiful I look, how nice my hair is, how happy they are for me. I try to thank each one, but Heather is strong and she's got her fist digging into my lower back as she pushes me through the cramped mob of guests.

"Remember the four C's," she says. "Ceremony, champagne, click click."

Heather is really earning her paycheck as she tries to get everyone lined up for the group photo. The photographer, a nerdy-looking girl with long braids, round glasses, and a t-shirt that says Intellectual Badass, is standing in the road and holding a camera, patiently waiting for everyone to line up on the stairs.

"Kiara!" Heather yells, frantically waving at her. "Just take it. This is the best we'll get."

After Kiara snaps a few pictures, Heather grabs me and

Luke and pulls us down the stairs and over to the water for some more bride and groom photos, just the two of us.

I'm thrilled to be away from that hot sticky crowd. The breeze is nice and cool as we head to the water.

"I have to jet back to the hall to make sure the DJ arrived and to prepare a few things," Heather says as she scratches something off her clipboard. "Kiara will take some pictures. A few by the water, Kiara. Maybe that weeping willow over there. Then, you two will hop back in the limo and go to the reception. DO NOT get out of the limo until I come and get you. Oh crap, the guests are already leaving. I gotta go! Big smiles, happy day!"

The three of us watch her as she sprints back to the parking lot.

"So, let's start by the water," Kiara says as she adjusts the lens on her camera. "Congratulations by the way!"

"Thanks, we're thrilled," Luke answers in a flat voice.

We set up by the water and both force out smiles.

"Maybe stand a little closer?" Kiara says, hesitating to bring the camera up.

We both reluctantly take a step toward each other.

"Even more. You're going to have to touch."

Luke and I look at each other. We're going to have the only wedding photos styled after American Gothic, you know the old painting with the unimpressed man and woman with a pitchfork.

We're going to have to do better than this.

I take another step toward him and Luke answers by putting his arm around my shoulder like a brother being forced to take a picture with his younger sister.

"Okay," Kiara says, staring at us with a frown. It's clear she's trying hard to comprehend what's going on. How our marriage has already descended into cringe town. She's probably wondering if we've been married for ten minutes or ten years. "*Hmmmm.*"

"Just put your arms around me," I snap at him. I grab his wrist and yank his arm around my hip.

His cologne hits my nose and I hate that it sends a small thrill through me. It smells like the nervous excitement of being on a first date, which makes me wonder what a first date with Luke would be like. Probably awful. I bet he'd offer to pay and then skip out on the bill while I was in the bathroom.

"Now we're getting somewhere," Kiara says as Luke awkwardly holds me with his body leaned out like elementary school kids at their first dance. She's pinching her bottom lip as she stares at us, but at least she's no longer frowning. "Closer. That's it. Even closer. Don't be afraid."

His hard chest touches my back and my heart skips a beat.

Kiara starts taking pictures quickly like she's afraid we'll explode away from each other at any moment.

"Would your hot Canadian boyfriend have a problem with this?" he whispers in my ear.

"No," I fire back.

Because he doesn't exist.

"He'll understand that this is just a job. He'll know you mean less than nothing to me."

"What about you kissing me like my tongue had the antidote to a poison you ingested? That wasn't in the job description."

"We had to kiss," I say, feeling my voice getting louder and my face getting hotter. "So, I kissed you. I was merely playing the part."

"The part of horny bride?"

"Less arguing, more smiling please," Kiara says as she peaks out at us from behind her camera.

We shift places and this time, I'm curled up in his embrace

against a tree. Kiara drops to her knees in front of us, pointing the camera up.

"What's your boyfriend's name?" Luke asks.

Kiara's lips mouth *'boyfriend?'*

Luke must notice too because he directs his next words at her. "She has a Canadian lumberjack boyfriend. He rides a horse to work. Or, was it a moose?"

My body is all rigid and tight as I smile at the camera. "It was a horse."

Kiara glances around like she's wanting to know if anyone else is watching this crazy train of a marriage. "Coooooool," she says stiffly as she turns back to us. "Maybe one by the water. Next to those ducks."

We head over, but I stay a little far from the ducks. I'm not a big fan of birds. They freak me out. I'm not getting close to anything that has a sword sticking out of its face. I'd rather appreciate them from afar where the chances of them getting caught in my hair are slim.

We settle into a clumsy embrace as Kiara watches and wonders what went wrong in her life. She only lets out two impatient huffs, so I guess we're getting better.

"What's your boyfriend's name?" Luke asks again.

Geez, why won't he let this go?

Kiara lowers the camera for a second and looks at us, probably hoping at least one of us is sterile.

"It's... Donald."

He snorts out a laugh.

"What?"

"Oh, come on! You're single. You were looking at the ducks when you said his name. Sorry, *made up* his name."

"So what!" I snap. "I'm single! Is that a crime? I work hard. I do my job. I recycle and pick up the occasional piece of garbage off the sidewalk. I contribute to society. Who cares if I don't have a boyfriend? I don't have to justify myself to you or to anyone."

It just explodes out of me. I'm just tired of all the bullshit pressure from society to be attached to some man, like that determines my worth as a person.

Luke has his hands up. "No judgment here. I'm single too."

Kiara is openly staring at us with her jaw hanging down. She's not even trying to hide her confusion now.

"Oh shit," Luke says as he turns away and drops his eyes to the ground. "My parents are coming over."

Dammit. That's the last thing I need.

A sour taste hits my mouth as I watch Walter and Kathleen march over, looking like they're about to demand to speak to a manager. Behind them, most of the guests are caught in a traffic jam of shiny Bentleys, Rolls-Royces, and limousines. Only a few people are left on the church steps.

Kathleen charges up to me and immediately starts adjusting my dress. I brace myself, waiting for her venomous words. As usual, she does not disappoint.

"Brides are supposed to lie on the floor on the honeymoon, dear. Not at the ceremony."

Walter shoots me a stern look. "Do we owe extra for the gymnastics show?"

"It's my shoes," I try to explain. "Taliah has ridiculously small feet!"

He waves his big hand dismissively at me. "You two need to get it together."

"It wasn't that bad," Luke says defensively.

Walter points at me as he rears on Luke. "She talked about sex like nine times!"

"I agree. That was bad," I say with a firm nod. "I'll do better."

"Good," he barks as his vicious eyes dart to mine. "Don't fuck this up for me."

His whole demeanor changes when he sees an older man walking by the water in the distance. "Governor Kasker!" he says with a jolly wave. "So happy you could make it!"

The anger and tension eases out of Luke after his father leaves.

"The seams are ripping here," Kathleen says as she inspects the back of my dress. "Suck everything in."

I suck in my stomach and hold my breath as she runs her fingers over the material. "For how long?"

"All night, preferably."

"No problem," I gasp. "Oxygen is overrated anyway."

I let out the breath before I pass out. She frowns.

"It will hold."

"Are you sure?" I keep hearing creaks and groans coming from it like a bending tree before the trunk snaps and the whole thing comes tumbling down.

"I'm sure," she says as she releases me and heads over to her son. "You looked stately up there. Like a young Marlon Brando. Like a true Whitfield." She runs her hand along his cheek. "If you ever grow that beard again, I'll haunt your dreams once I'm gone."

"You already do that now, Mother."

She lets out a cackling laugh and gently slaps his cheek before heading back to Walter.

Once again, it's just me, Luke, and an even more confused Kiara.

"Would you like to take some more photos?" she asks. "Maybe this time lying down in the grass?"

Our emphatic answers come at the same time.

"No!"

CHAPTER *Nine*

Luke loosens his tie and slips the top button of his shirt out as he sinks into the leather seat of the limo. The window is open and the cool breeze is ruffling his hair. I'm sitting across from him, trying not to look.

We're parked in the back of the reception hall waiting for Heather to come and fetch us.

"Tell me about Carter," I say as I rub my bare feet on the carpet, trying not to moan in ecstasy at how good it feels to have Taliah's shoes off.

He looks at me like his brother is the last thing he wants to talk about. "Why?"

"Because I just married him, so I should know some of the basics."

He sighs. "He says his favorite movie is Citizen Kane, but it's really Step Brothers. He's allergic to marshmallows, is afraid of frogs, and he accidentally burned down the shed when he was fourteen."

"I don't think any of that will come in handy unless there's a campfire planned. That's it?"

He shrugs.

"I met him a couple of times," I continue. "He seemed very sweet."

Luke exhales long and hard.

"What?"

"That's what everyone thinks."

"He's not?"

Luke takes a deep breath as he glances out the window. "Yeah. He's great."

"So, you don't get along with your brother either," I say with a roll of my eyes. "Shocker."

"You try living with him for eighteen years and see how you do."

"What, did he steal your Playboys and not give them back?"

"No," he says with his eyes hardening. "He's a chip off the old man. A winning smile and kind word to say—always distracting from the fact that he's putting himself first. And I'm a Penthouse kind of guy by the way."

"Not everyone is out to get everyone else," I tell him, feeling my voice rise despite my effort to keep it steady. "Maybe if you took that chip off your shoulder, you could find the good in people."

His body tightens as he looks at me for a long moment. I hold his intense gaze.

"You know what I can't stand about people like you?"

I laugh. "Oh, please tell."

"You think your positivity is a gift. That it's noble to find the good in people. To ascribe honor and integrity to people you've just met."

"I give people the benefit of the doubt. What's wrong with that?"

"Everything. Expecting good from people leaves you open to getting blindsided by their greed. This chip on my shoulder is here to protect me. It allows me to keep my distance from all these fake people with their nefarious intentions."

I know it couldn't have been easy to grow up in his family, but he's carrying a lot more than annoyance. There's a deep hurt there that he's protecting with a surly outer shell.

"Just because your dad is an asshole, doesn't mean everyone else is."

He looks out the window.

"What happened between you two?"

"Nothing."

"Oh, please," I say with a laugh. He finally looks at me. "You two are so toxic, when you're around each other you glow green."

He smiles. Barely.

"Why did you punch him?"

"We're not talking about this."

"Fine. We don't have much time anyway," I say, looking around for Heather, but seeing nothing but a few guests wandering around. "Let's get back to Carter. What college did he go to?"

"Yale. He was captain of the swim team."

"Wow. That's impressive."

"My grandmother made a large enough donation that assured he got in," Luke says dismissively. "Still impressive?"

"Well, where did you go?" I ask, my voice a little on edge. It's starting to get to me that he keeps putting everyone down. Can't he be happy for his brother?

"I didn't go to college."

My brain scrambles to understand. "What?"

I can't fathom having the opportunity to go to college and not taking it. I would have killed to go. My parents bankrupted each other through their divorce. The lawyers took their fair share during the long drawn-out process. Then came the one-upmanship. When my mom bought a huge house, my dad had to upgrade his. The fancy cars came next, the vacations to brag about on Facebook, the designer clothes and jewelry—all stuff they couldn't afford. It was petty, vindictive, and just plain stupid. Not productive at all. My college fund vaporized in the smoke of their mutual destruction. My future was the collateral damage of their competitiveness.

When I was finally able to move away from it all, I had nothing. No money, no job, no education, and no chance to go to university without getting saddled by loans that would follow me to my grave.

And this man could have had an all-expenses-paid trip to Yale. And he said no. Un-freaking-believable.

"I got away from my parents as soon as I could," he says.

"You would have gotten away from them in college," I say with a huff. "And gotten an education at the same time."

"Why are you getting so bent out of shape?" he asks, eying me with those frustratingly blue eyes.

"I would have done anything to go to college."

He shrugs. "So go."

"Easy for you to say," I shout a little too loud. "That's such a rich person point of view. I can't, Luke. Okay? I don't have three hundred dollars, let alone three hundred grand! I think it was selfish of you not to go."

He shakes his head in disbelief.

"You think everyone is so selfish, huh?" I say, getting on a roll now. "What about you? Dysfunctional or not, you were born into a special family, Luke. A family that can get things done. That can do some good in the world. You had that opportunity and you just threw it away. And what did you do instead? You ditched your sister and went to live in some crappy small town where no one will ever try to push you out of your comfort zone, or challenge you, or say that you could be more than you are. You live there and do the absolute bare minimum and call it selfless. Please. Give me a break."

He loosens his tie even more as his eyes narrow on me, nostrils flaring. "Oh yeah? And what about you?"

"What about me?"

"You're wound so tight, I'm afraid you're going to unravel and spin away like a top. Do you ever have fun?"

"Yes!"

"When was the last time you had fun?"

"I don't know… last week I got a new lamp for my home office."

His laugh is so grating. "I'm not talking about getting a new lamp. I'm talking about *fun*. You know fun? Laughing until tears pour out of your eyes and your sides hurt. Feeling like the universe has made this special moment just for you. Having your heart so full of joy it feels like it's going to explode out of your chest. Fun?"

I cross my arms, wishing that Heather would hurry the hell up.

"Fun is the last thing on my list of things to care about."

"Yeah, clearly."

The nerve of this guy, talking like he knows me or knows what's best for me. He doesn't know a damn thing!

"When you have been through—"

Just as my tone rises, the photographer Kiara walks by and sees us fighting through the open window.

"Hi," I say with an awkward wave. She hurries away without waving back.

We both laugh and I let the anger fade out of me. So far, this has been a wild, emotionally exhausting day. And it's just starting. I have to pace myself.

"Think she's had a crazier couple than us?" he asks with a grin.

"I sure hope not. Better close the window. Some of the guests are bound to hear us fighting."

"And you're worried they're going to think we're married for real?"

Another laugh bursts out of me. One thing I'm learning about Luke is that he has his moments. He can always surprise me.

"There's my happy newlyweds!" Heather says as she arrives at the limo. "I'm thrilled to see you two getting along!"

"Enjoy it while it lasts," I mutter.

"We have to move now," she says as she opens the door. "The guests are getting rowdy."

Luke climbs out and then Heather helps with my dress as I get out too, shoes in hand. "These don't go on until absolutely necessary."

"Hot pavement is not necessary?" Luke asks.

I shake my head. "Walking on lava is more comfortable than these shoes."

"We don't have time to discuss footwear," Heather says as she turns and starts hurrying toward a back door. "Let's go."

We follow her as she charges through a maze of hallways, yelling at the serving staff we pass.

"Bride coming through!" she hollers when a chef carrying a large tray of appetizers walks toward us. He practically leaps into a stockroom and nearly drops the whole thing.

She pushes a door open and guides us through a huge kitchen. "Bride present!" she bellows. "Hands in the air!"

A young dishwasher flattens against the wall with his wet hands in the air as we pass.

Cooks are popping their heads out and watching curiously as we hurry by. It smells good in here, like fresh fish cooking. The sizzle of the grill makes my stomach growl. *When was the last time I ate?*

"Watch the dress!" Heather shouts as we pass the sauce station.

Heather seems very stressed and overwhelmed. Every time she snaps at a chef or server walking by, I cringe.

Is that what I sound like?

God, I hope not.

Maybe Luke was a tiny bit right. Maybe I do need to have more fun.

It's just there's never any time. I'm always working. Always grinding it out.

As a caterer, I'm around fun, I'm just never the one having it.

I'm the fun giver, not the fun haver.

I make a mental note to schedule some fun time in my daily planner. I'll show Luke. I'm going to have so much fun on Monday morning that he's going to eat his words.

Heather guides us the rest of the way to where Kathleen, Walter, and my pretend father slash limo driver are waiting to start the reception line in front of the entrance to the hall.

"Look everyone," Kathleen says with a martini in her hand, "our new daughter-in-law is here. Quick. Put a baby gate on the stairs."

"Let's see how well you walk down the stairs after that drink," I mutter under my breath as I take my spot between Luke and the limo driver.

"I'm your father, Frank," he says with a laugh.

I sigh. "I'm your daughter, Taliah."

"We're just waiting for Mrs. Whitfield," Heather says, looking around nervously.

"Mrs. Whitfield?" I repeat. I thought she was already here. She just insulted me for the tenth time.

"My grandmother, Eleanor," Luke clarifies.

Oh. It clicks. The old lady in the front row who was glaring at us all throughout the ceremony. This should be fun.

"Heather," Kathleen says. "Send the low-status guests in through the other door. I'd rather not have to touch them."

"Each one is a potential vote, Kitty-Kat," Walter says.

"And a potential case of ebola." She grimaces as she pulls out a mini bottle of hand sanitizer from her purse and squirts it on her hands.

"Why were our real names on the marriage documents?" Luke asks his dad.

My heart starts thumping.

Walter shrugs in disinterest. "Father Cliff wrote them up. Don't worry about it, he probably just mixed up the names."

I take a breath of relief. One less thing to worry about.

"Here she comes!" Heather says as Luke's grandmother charges around the corner like an angry lioness who's well past her prime but still very much in charge.

"Walter Harold Whitfield," she shouts. "What kind of tomfoolery bullshit are you playing at?"

For the first time ever, I see Walter squirm. He stands straighter with a nervous smile as his mother charges right up to him, finger pointing in his face. "I may be past my best before date, but I'm not expired yet. What in tarnations was Luke doing up there? Where's Carter?"

Walter swallows hard. "That's Carter, mother."

"Bullshit!" she shouts. I lower my head and bite my bottom lip to stop giggling. "Do you seriously think I wouldn't recognize my own grandson?"

She charges over to Luke, grabs his shirt, and yanks it out of his pants.

"Three freckles!" she says in triumph. "I knew it."

There are three tiny freckles beside Luke's navel on his very hard, very defined abs. Abs that I'm totally not looking at. Nope. Not interested at all.

Oh, look. That's a nice plant over there by the window.

"What the hell is going on here?" Eleanor demands as she walks up and down the line like a drill sergeant inspecting a fresh batch of rookie troops.

Everyone is afraid to speak. This lady is small but terrifying. The only sound is the crunching of Frank eating nuts from a tiny bag.

The sound grabs her attention and she rears on him. Frank munches away, completely unfazed.

"And who are you?"

"I'm Frank."

"Frank who?"

"Frank the limo driver." He offers her some nuts.

She looks at the bag, takes some, and then throws them at Kathleen and Walter.

"Somebody better tell me what is going on here!" Everyone is looking down except for me and Frank. She locks eyes with me and marches over.

"Who are you? And don't say Taliah!"

"This is Zoe Fitzpatrick," Walter quickly interjects. "Luke's girlfriend."

This is getting beyond ridiculous. First I was his fiancée, then I was his wife, now I'm his girlfriend? Don't they realize we hate each other?

"Girlfriend, huh?" she asks as she looks me over with her sharp blue eyes. "And why the hell are you in my granddaughter-in-law's wedding dress?"

I explain how Carter and Taliah eloped, leaving out my involvement of course, and how they asked me to step in.

She can barely believe it as she looks at her family.

"I thought you were the smart one, Luke," she says with a shake of her head.

Carter went to Yale, but Luke is the smart one? I guess I can see that. He is pretty quick and perceptive.

"This will be an epic scandal for our family if your ridiculous plan blows up," Eleanor warns Walter.

"It won't," he answers, giving his winning politician smile.

She's his mother. It doesn't work.

"It better not, Wally. I won't let you drag the Whitfield name through the mud again. I trounced your ass for driving my Jaguar into our inground pool thirty-five years ago, and I'll do it again!"

Walter looks at us with an uncomfortable smile. "That was a… never proven in court."

"The tire marks are still on the diving board!" Eleanor shouts.

"The doors open in three minutes," Heather announces.

"Nuts?" Frank asks, offering me the bag.

I sigh. "Sure."

I take a couple and toss them into my mouth as Eleanor stares Kathleen down. Even Kathleen looks rattled by this woman.

"Did you at least have these three sign an NDA?"

Kathleen curses under her breath.

"What about the Asian girl and the wedding coordinator? The photographers? The priest?"

"It happened so fast," Walter desperately explains. "Carter and Taliah left at eleven this morning!"

Eleanor rolls her eyes as she pulls a phone out of her purse. "Fucking amateurs."

She calls someone who answers on the first ring and orders them to prepare a dozen non-disclosure agreements and have them shipped to the reception hall as soon as possible.

This lady is *very* impressive. I love how she stormed in here, probably in her eighties, and is taking charge like she owns the place. Maybe she does. She's my kind of woman.

"One minute!" Heather shouts.

Eleanor looks me up and down one last time. "Are you sure you're up for this?"

I look her dead in the eye. "Yes, ma'am, I am."

"Good. Let's hope you shake hands better than you walk down stairs. Heather! Open the doors!"

I hold my breath as Heather pushes the doors open and a tsunami of guests surges forward, about to drown us.

CHAPTER Ten

"I understand you're a real estate developer," the elderly man shaking my hand says. "What sort of real estate do you specialize in?"

"Oh, you know," I say with a nervous shrug. "All kinds. Houses and buildings and… schools."

"Schools?" he says, nodding in interest as his eyes narrow on me. "Interesting. I thought schools were exclusively developed by the state."

"Schools for… dogs."

Crap.

He looks at me funny and then moves on to congratulate Frank.

"If you're into real estate," Frank says as he leans in while shaking his hand, "my cousin has a lot in a trailer park for sale. It's a bit pricey at seventeen thousand, but it's walking distance to Mudskipper Lake. Trout the size of a newborn baby in there."

This is torture.

We must have been shaking hands for about two hours now. I glance at the clock and—*eleven minutes?!*

I'm never going to make it.

At least Luke is getting it bad too.

"So disrespectful of your brother not to show up," a man says as he shakes Luke's hand. "There's no excuse."

"I'm sure he had a good reason," Luke says as a little bead of sweat drips down his temple. "My brother is a stand-up guy."

"Your brother is an ass."

Luke sighs as the man moves on, shaking my hand and then Frank's.

"Seems like I'm not the only one who's immune to your charm," I whisper.

He grins back at me. "You think I have charm?"

"What? No, that's not what I said!"

He laughs as he shakes the next hand. "Zo—Taliah, this is my aunt, Janet. My cousin Owen's mom and my father's sister."

I'm so confused with all the names, but I recognize the tall lady. She's the one with the short hair who was texting throughout the ceremony. She even has her phone out now.

"Nice to meet you," I say as I put my hand out.

She's about to shake it, but her phone rings. She puts her index finger up as she answers it and then leaves, yelling something about logistics in Hong Kong.

"She runs a pharmaceutical company," Luke whispers. "She's a bit of a workaholic."

A few politicians trickle by in the steady stream of guests and then some of Carter's friends from college. It's hilarious to watch Luke pretending to know what they're talking about.

"The Bulldogs are lit this year," a guy with a dimple on his chin and too much gel in his hair says. "They got Hawkins ripping through the fifty fly and Maddox on the five hundred breast. The cup is ours this year for the taking!"

"Totally," Luke says, looking dizzy.

"Are you going to be at Razzi's for New Year's?" another guy with even more gel in his hair asks. "Bring your girl. I'm bringing the Jaegermeister!"

"We'll be there," I say with a smile as I grab Luke's hand and squeeze it.

They move along and Luke looks at me as I release him. "I didn't take you as the Jaegermeister type."

"There's a lot of things you don't know about me. I love Jaegermeister,"—that's a board game, right?—"and I'm a *ton* of fun."

"I didn't mean it like—"

"Shake the hand, Carter."

He turns and shakes the hand of a few gray-haired politicians that I probably should know, but don't.

A few minutes later, someone is asking Luke about Carter's new car, and it's clear that he has no idea what kind of car it is. I have to hold back a laugh when the guy asks 'how fast is it?' and Luke answers 'super fast.'

"Smooth," I whisper to him once the friend is shaking Eleanor's hand.

Walter is talking to someone for extra-long and the line holds up. It's a nice break, but it won't last long.

"Who is that guy?" I whisper to Luke.

Walter is schmoozing him pretty hard as Kathleen compliments his wife's pearls.

"That man once lit a gas station on fire with a cigarette," Luke whispers back. "Now he is the governor of Texas."

I look down the long line of people waiting and spot an older man who looks very familiar. He's hunched over in a wheelchair with a blanket over his legs.

"Who's that old man?"

Luke laughs when he sees him. "My great uncle. Ninety-three years-old. He's famous. Maybe even more famous than my father."

"An actor?"

Luke shakes his head. "Better."

He turns as he pulls out his phone, hiding it. I watch as he opens the YouTube app and pulls up a video from three years ago.

"I've seen this!"

"You and half a billion other people. Look at this. Six hundred and thirty-nine million views."

"Wow," I whisper as the video starts. It's the dance floor of a wedding and he's swaying in his wheelchair to Billie Jean from Michael Jackson. Suddenly, he gets up, does a spin, loses his balance, and then takes off, landing head first into the wedding cake. The video ends after someone pulls his head out of the cake. He's covered in it.

Luke looks at me with a grin. I'm trying not to laugh. That poor old man. But it is kind of funny. He had frosting eyebrows.

We're both giggling like naughty school kids when the teacher comes over. "Put that phone away," Eleanor snaps as she pushes past Frank to stand beside me.

Luke makes it disappear real quick as I pull up my dress.

"Back straight," she tells him.

Her face softens when she looks at me. "I can't imagine what you think of my family."

"Everyone has been so nice," I answer with a smile.

She's looking at me with a flat expression like her bullshit detector is ringing off the hook.

"It has been a bit of a weird day," I admit.

"You can say that again. How did you and Luke meet?"

"How we met?" Oh crappers. I was ready to come up with lies about being Taliah, but not about being Luke's girlfriend. My mind races trying to think of something. Where do romantic occurrences happen? "At the... a... carnival."

Shit.

"At the carnival?" she says, looking up at me with a tilt of her head.

Why did I pick the carnival of all places? Maybe that would be a good choice if we were living in a rom com from the 1920s. Do they even have carnivals anymore?

I swallow hard.

"Yup," I say, grabbing Luke's hand. "On a rollercoaster. We were both alone and we got sat together."

"Luke, why were you alone at the carnival?" she asks.

"I was with a date and she got sick."

"And you left her alone to ride the rollercoaster?" Eleanor asks with an unimpressed look. "Charming."

"I know, right?" I say, shaking my head. "That's what I told him."

Luke crushes my fingers.

"And why were you alone, dear?"

I'm thinking as quickly as I can, but my brain always muddles up whenever I'm put on the spot like this. "I uh... was working there."

"You're a carnie?"

Luke chuckles as Eleanor stares at me, waiting.

I can feel my face reddening. My skin tingles as beads of sweat pop out.

What the hell was I thinking? I work there?! *You're trying to come off as classy, not as a mullet-having redneck carnie!*

"I *used* to work there... but I don't anymore."

"Why not?"

"Yeah, Zoe," Luke adds. "Why not?"

"The clowns... um, died... in a... airplane crash. We were

all so sad and couldn't go on, so we disbanded the whole carnival."

Silence.

I force myself to look at Eleanor. She's watching me skeptically.

I stare back at her, not quite believing that I actually spat that out.

"I see," Eleanor says, watching me with her eyes narrowing. "A plane full of clowns dying. That's tragic. It must have been in the news, a story like that."

"Yup," I say with a hard swallow.

"So, I could just Goggle it and find the article?"

I can feel my eyes widening as we look at each other. "Probably. Although, Google is so unreliable these days. It wasn't what it used to be."

Clowns? Airplane crash? Oh god… Why the hell did I say that for? I told them this would happen! I'm no good at lying. What a debacle.

The line starts moving again and my forced smile is back as one sweaty palm is thrust into mine after another.

"Congratulations," they all say. "What a lovely ceremony." Not one of them brings up the fact that I took a nosedive down the stairs, which I'm counting as a win.

It's not long before the line gets held up with another high-profile guest. Walter gives the man a big warm hug.

No! Damn it! Don't let her talk to me again…

"The Secretary of State," Eleanor whispers to me. "A friend of the family. Also a complete and utter twat."

I look at her in shock.

"Non-stop lying that one," she continues as she glares at him. "He tried to pass a fast one on me once, but I'm a human lie detector. I'm not to be trifled with."

"I'll keep that in mind," I say with a gulp.

"Good. Keep that in mind if you're going to remain attached to my grandson. Unless of course you're planning to run off with the next carnival that comes to town. Secretary Evans! It's been too long!"

The Secretary of State smiles at Luke and me before kissing Eleanor on the cheeks. "Eleanor," he says warmly. "When are you going to have lunch with me?"

They're chatting like old friends as I lean over to Luke. "Your grandmother thinks I'm a fraud!"

"That's surprising," he says in a flat voice. "Your carnie backstory was so believable."

"Shut. Up."

"Why didn't you say literally anything else?"

"I told you I'm not good at lying!" I whisper-scream at him. "I hate this!"

"Just be cool," he whispers. "Keep it simple. Act natural."

"I'm trying!"

Ugh. This is the worst.

A large imposing man with a big bushy mustache and matching eyebrows shakes Luke's hand. "Congratulations, Carter Whitfield," he says in a thick accent I can't quite place. "I am Fevzi Karakaş, the Ambassador of Turkey."

Oh fuck.

"Nice to meet you, Ambassador," Luke says, glancing sideways at me. "We're pleased to have you here and I hope you enjoy the wedding."

My body goes cold with dread as the man turns to me.

"Birliğiniz güçlü olsun!" he bellows with his arms in the air.

My eyes are open so wide I can feel them drying out.

Just be cool. Keep it simple. Act natural.

"Oh, yes," I say with a frantic nod. "It was a lovely ceremony and I'm so happy you could be here with us."

His big bushy eyebrows drop down into a frown. "Amerika'da yaşarken ana dilinizi mi unuttunuz?"

We stare at each other for a long awkward moment as I imagine the world opening up and swallowing me into a blissful darkness, never to be seen again.

"Right. Okay. So, enjoy your dinner. The bar is open."

He looks to the man on his left and frowns hard. "Vatanından utanıyor. Kendi dilini konuşmaktan utanıyor." His voice is loud enough that everyone in the room can hear him.

What is happening? What is he saying?

He's getting more and more flustered, his big hairy hands gesticulating wildly as he unleashes another string of consonant heavy words I don't understand.

That's when Luke swoops in and saves me. In the most embarrassing way.

He grabs my nose and pushes my head back. "Nose bleed!" he yells. "Watch the dress! Out of the way please!"

I'm staring at the ceiling, my nose in his hand, as he guides me away from everyone and down a few winding halls.

We turn one corner and then another, safe from prying eyes.

"Where are you taking me?" I ask in a Kermit the Frog voice.

I push his hand away when he laughs.

"In here," he says as he opens a glass door and slips inside. I'd rather be anywhere than in that reception line—even alone with Luke—so I follow him in.

CHAPTER Eleven

We hurry into the fitness center of the inn and Luke slams the door closed behind me before anyone can see where we escaped to.

The Whitfields rented out the entire inn, so the small gym is empty. Just a few unused treadmills, stationary bikes, weight lifting equipment, and dumbbells staring back at us. The sharp tang of antibacterial cleaner hits my nose.

I take a complimentary water bottle from the small fridge and twist it open as I sit on a bench that's attached to a big metal rack.

"Next time you save me," I say to Luke as he grabs a bottle of water too, "can you perhaps not do it in the most embarrassing way possible?"

He sits on a Bowflex and twists the cap off his water so hard that it makes me think this may not be the first time he's been on a Bowflex.

"Are you incapable of just saying thank you?" he says with a look of disbelief.

"Oh please. You were saving your own ass too."

He shakes his head. "You're unbelievable."

This is a game he's playing and I'm not going to fall for it. I'll feel bad and say thank you and then he'll grin and have the upper hand. Not going to happen.

"I'll say thank you when you apologize," I tell him with a challenging stare.

Neither of us break eye contact. Turning away is a game of chicken at this point and I know I'm not going to be the one to lose.

"I'm sorry."

My head jerks back. Mouth open. I'm speechless.

Those are the last two words I expected to hear coming out of Luke's mouth after 'you're right.'

I take a deep breath and move slowly. Cautiously. Seeing Luke apologetic like this is like seeing a baby deer in the wild: one wrong step and it will bolt, disappearing forever.

"What are you sorry for?" I say softly like I'm trying to coax a butterfly into my palm.

He sighs as he leans back on the Bowflex and looks at his hands. Post-haircut Luke has looked good all day, but remorseful Luke is really doing something for me. I shift on the bench as a ripple of warmth flutters through my chest.

"I've been cold to you," he says as his blue eyes meet mine. "And rude. I get a little frayed around the edges when I'm forced to interact with my parents."

"I get that," I say with a nod. "But what exactly are you sorry for?"

His forehead scrunches up as he looks at me. "What do you mean? I just told you."

"Which specific instances are you sorry for?"

He laughs. "Are you serious?"

I just stare at him.

"Fine. I'm sorry I was short with you, that I told my mom it was your idea that Carter and Taliah eloped, that I refused to kiss you in the conference room, and for calling you Captain, Captain. That was the last one, I promise."

My eyes narrow on him. "And for parking in my tent?"

"No, it's in the parking lot."

"Ugh!" I say as I whip my head to the side, frustrated that I can still see him through the mirrors.

He smiles. "You're cute when you're mad."

"Then I must be fucking adorable right now."

He laughs as I glare at him. It's all an act now. I'm not really mad. Not anymore.

"I'm sorry I parked in your tent," he says with a smile that draws my eyes to his lips and won't let them go. "I initially thought it was allowed, since it was in the parking lot."

"Is this an apology or…"

"But the way you charged up to me, so full of fire and passion…" he says, his breath quickening as he pictures it in his mind. "You were so compelling. I had to say something to keep you focused on me."

My body leans closer as I hold in a breath.

"I could tell you were frustrated and needed to release it on someone. I didn't mind being that person at all. Sometimes I use my assholeness for good, you know."

"I was pretty frustrated," I say with a soft laugh. "Mario and Luigi didn't like my food. Maybe it was too fancy."

"It looked good to me."

"You're in luck because I'm sure there will be *a ton* of leftovers," I say as a pink flush heats my cheeks. "And you're not an asshole, Luke."

He looks like he wants to believe me.

"You're the most frustrating man I've ever met, but spending time with you is not so bad. It's been kind of fun. Wild and terrifying, but fun."

The air in the gym charges with something as we stare at

each other. I'm not sure what it is, but it causes my lips to part and the tiny hairs on my arms to rise.

"So, we're good?" he asks.

"We're good."

"We don't need marriage counseling?"

I shake my head with a smile. "You're off the hook, for now."

My breath catches as he stands up. He walks over and sits on a giant bouncy ball, close enough that I can smell his cologne. This time it doesn't make me want to gag. "Start over?"

He puts his hand out and I glance down at it. It's a nice hand. Strong, stable, and softer than it looks. I'm about to shake it, but I abruptly pull my hand back.

"Want to drop one more Captain in there before we shake?" I ask with a grin.

He smiles. "Why, are you starting to like it?"

"I was wrong. You are an asshole."

I shake his hand firmly.

Now that we're no longer mortal enemies, we relax in the room, avoiding the fact that we should probably be getting back out there. There's soft instrumental music playing through the speakers, but it's not loud enough to fully erase the sporadic clinking of plates, the Aretha Franklin song playing in the hall, and the murmur of hundreds of guests conversing around the inn.

"This is way more intense than I thought it would be," Luke finally says as he rubs his jaw with his hand.

"I have so many threads of lies going, I feel like I'm drowning in a sea of yarn."

"I said 'nice to meet you' to one of Carter's ex-girlfriends," Luke says, staring straight ahead with dead eyes. "She was not impressed."

"Your grandmother knows I'm lying. She probably thinks I'm a Turkish spy."

"A Turkish spy who doesn't speak Turkish?"

"Which would be the perfect cover for an actual Turkish spy. I'm so getting arrested by the end of the night."

He smiles as he lightly bounces up and down on the ball. "At least you'll get to leave early."

I smile. "Prison does sound pretty tempting compared to this. Your family is *crazy*. How did you grow up around these people?"

"Very carefully."

"Are they always like this?"

"Always," he says, looking exhausted. "That's why I left. I couldn't take it anymore. They're getting worse with age. My family thinks they're American Royalty. My father thinks he's the king and the presidency will be his crown."

"They're certainly ambitious. I normally respect that, but with them…"

"It's not a virtue."

"No, it's not."

"My family is ambitious in the way a virus is ambitious: it infects everything it touches and won't leave until it's sucked out every last drop of life it can get its greedy hands on."

I'm ambitious too and it's something I value about myself, but ambition is a scale that if you tip too far onto either side, things will get ugly.

"My grandfather was a senator for decades," Luke continues. "He ran for president and lost, and now my father is determined to succeed where he failed. It's an obsession with the Whitfields. If my father fails, it will be Carter's turn one day, and *his* child after that."

"Did he expect you to get into politics?"

"Of course," Luke says with a humorless laugh. "But he

learned pretty quickly that was never going to fly. So, he pretty much ignored me and focused all his energy on Carter. I was just relieved he finally left me alone."

"Do you think he would make a good president?"

Luke sighs as he thinks about it. "Better than the rest of those gray sharks out there? Maybe. Probably. Would he be what the country really needs? Not at all."

"Let's vote for his opponent," I say with a conspiratorial grin.

He smiles. A real genuine smile that makes me realize I made a new friend.

"What's your family like?"

"Mine?" Just the thought of my family sends a jabbing pain through my chest. "It's non-existent."

"What do you mean?"

"I mean, it's just me. No brothers, no sisters."

"But you have parents?"

"I guess technically they're parents," I say with a sigh. "Biologically they are."

"Are you from around here?"

"I grew up in Vermont. In a really small town. My mother was an editor at the tiny local paper and one day, when I was fourteen years old, she ran an article on the front page stating that my principal was having an affair with Mrs. Marshall, the tenth-grade teacher."

"Ouch," Luke says with a wince. "It couldn't have been easy to go to school after that."

"It wasn't. And what made it worse was that my father was the principal."

"Wow..."

"Yup."

It was so humiliating. I hated both of them for it. I had nothing after that. No social life, no friends, no future in that town and I knew it. I was counting the days until I could escape.

I became obsessed with it. All I wanted was to start over somewhere new.

"They got divorced, obviously," I continue. "A long, vicious, drawn-out divorce that I was smack dab in the middle of. They split custody of me and I spent one week at my mother's house where she complained about my father non-stop, and then one week at my father's where he pretended like nothing happened by avoiding me completely. I left as soon as I could. When I was eighteen, I took the few thousand dollars I had squirreled away, got on a train, and came to Maryland."

"Why Maryland of all places?"

"It's silly, but my favorite book takes place in Maryland. It was also far. It seemed to be as good a place as any."

"It's not silly, it makes sense. Which book was it?"

"The Sisterhood of the Traveling Pants," I say, feeling a bit embarrassed. I just loved how four friends came together and loved each other like family. I always wished for friends like that. I thought if I came to Maryland I might find that, but of course, that's just fantasy. It doesn't quite work like that in real life.

"So, you're all alone here?" Luke asks with a look of pity on his face. That look irks me. "No cousins or other relatives?"

"I have two cousins in Florida but I never met them. But I'm not totally alone. I still see my mother about once a year. She goes to Las Vegas on vacation and then stops by for a day or two on the way home."

And it always goes horribly.

"But this is boring. Let's talk about something else. Do you think your mom will put up our wedding photos or are they going straight into the fireplace?"

Luke still has that look on his face. *Ugh.* Can't he realize that I'm *fine* without a family? They don't need me and I don't need them.

"You can always make your own family, Zoe," he says softly. "All you need is love, respect, and a commitment to stay together."

"And someone who can stand being with you for more than ten minutes."

"I doubt you'll have a problem finding that. You're one of a kind, Captain."

Luke smiles, only this time it has none of the cockiness or arrogance I've gotten used to. It's warm and welcoming and I want to sink into it like a hot bath.

It's also unnerving.

I'm not used to this kind of thing.

So, instead of finding out where this leads, I chicken out and change the subject.

"I can't stop freaking out about the dance."

"Still?"

I nod. My stomach is in knots just from thinking about it.

"You really haven't danced in twenty years?"

"Wait, that's not true! I had to do a synchronized dance with three girls when I was in grade nine."

It went horribly. They hated my hair and when I turned the wrong way, I bumped into Angie and she fell off the stage.

Luke rolls his eyes. "That doesn't count. I've never met a cook who didn't dance around the kitchen."

"And I've never met a mechanic with clean hands."

"Other mechanics don't have my mother to worry about," he says with a laugh. "I made the mistake of coming home with grease-stained hands once. You should have seen her freak out. I had tinnitus for a year with all the screeching. After that, I started wearing gloves at work."

We both look down at his hands. If the mechanic thing doesn't work out, Luke can always be a hand model.

"Just hold onto me during the dance," he says with a confident nod. "We'll keep it slow. Nothing crazy. I'll lead you the whole way."

"Thank you," I say, feeling better already. I'm probably freaking out over nothing. It's hardly even dancing. It's more swaying while I hold onto his biceps and gaze into his eyes. When I put it like that, it doesn't sound too bad at all. Kinda fun even.

Just me, Luke, and seven hundred plus people staring at us…

The nerves start to come roaring back, so it's time for an abrupt subject change. "So, what happened between you and your dad that made you punch him?"

His smile dissolves and the warmth in his blue eyes extinguishes like a dying star. "Nothing."

His back straightens, his body tightens, eyes dart to the door. This is the Luke I'm used to. We're back to square one.

I don't want to be back at square one. I liked it better when we were friends.

"I'm sorry," I say, feeling flustered. "I just thought since I told you about my family…"

"It's not something I want to talk about." His tone is all short and choppy. Cold and distant. "Ever."

"Okay," I say, leaning back. "Noted. I'm sorry."

A few awkward seconds pass between us and then he exhales long and hard. "This is why I don't like being around my family. This is the monster they bring out. But it's not the real me."

"Should we start over again, again?"

He smiles as his shoulders slump down. "How about I just apologize? Again."

"I don't think I'll ever get tired of that."

His head tilts as he looks at me. The warmth comes raging back into his eyes like someone poured gasoline on the dying embers.

"Once again, I'm sorry, Zoe. For being a jerk and a terrible husband."

"While you're at it," I say with a grin. "There's one more thing you should say sorry for."

"And what's that? For bringing you into an old sweat-filled gym while you're in a wedding dress?"

"No. You don't tell a bride she looks *nice*. You might as well have pulled a brown paper bag over my head and stabbed me in the heart."

He slowly stands up and walks over. My heart does a gymnastics routine in my chest as he grabs my hands and gazes into my eyes.

"You're the most gorgeous woman I've ever seen," he says, not breaking eye contact, not sounding sarcastic at all. "You make a stunning, elegant, classy bride."

I swallow hard as those mesmerizing cobalt blue eyes drop to my mouth. My lips part. My skin tingles.

The air charges with heat between us.

And with a hard knock on the door, the spell is broken. We separate as Heather explodes into the room. "Where the hell have you two been?! It's time for the first dance!"

She whips around and storms off, heels clacking on the floor, ponytail bouncing aggressively off her back.

She doesn't wait to hear our excuses. She's in no mood for our shit.

Luke offers his hand once again. "Can I have this dance?"

I slide my hand into his and let him pull me up. "Let's get this over with."

CHAPTER
Twelve

T*his is the job.*

You're a professional and you always *get the job done.*

I have a good track record so far, but the job has never simultaneously been my worst nightmare. And dancing in front of a room full of people is definitely my worst nightmare.

I keep my eyes locked on Heather's bouncing ponytail as Luke and I follow her down the hall and around the corner.

I'm ignoring the sound of my heartbeat thrashing in my ears and the intense primal urge to turn around and flee.

This is going to be okay. I'm going to do great.

My hands squeeze in and out of fists.

I got this.

Heather walks right up to the big scary doors that lead into our reception room. There are a ton of people inside waiting for us. I've been so freaked out by that room, I haven't even peeked inside.

My stomach lurches.

I don't got this.

My legs wobble back and Luke catches me. I look up at him

and shake my head, my eyes telling him that I can't do this. His eyes tell me that I can.

His eyes are stupid. They've never been more wrong.

"They're here," Heather grunts to the guy waiting outside the door whose white teeth are shockingly bright against his dark skin. He's wearing a shiny suit and holding a microphone, which must make him the DJ.

Heather disappears inside as the DJ runs up to us. He holds out a paper with *Taliah Özüdoğru* written on it. "How do you pronounce your last name?"

"I have no idea."

His mouth drops in confusion as we walk right past him and through the big doors. The crowd erupts in cheers so loud you'd swear Beyonce just entered the room.

I jerk my head back, shocked and unable to move as hundreds of people leap out of their seats and give us a thundering standing ovation.

"Make some noise for the Whitfields!" the DJ hollers through the sound system as he bounds into the hall behind us. "First time as husband and wife!"

My cheeks burn as the guy with the spotlight finds us. Luke raises our hands and the crowd goes nuts.

I squeeze his fingers as we start walking through the crowd, not ready to release my lifeline. I'm never letting go of this hand.

Everywhere I look people are smiling, cheering, clapping, filming. It's ear-piercingly loud. It's overwhelming. Every sense I have is overloaded. My ears are ringing, my skin tingling, the smell of thousands of flowers and hundreds of different colognes and perfumes hit my nose all at once. I don't know where to look.

I long for a quiet chair and a good book. A silent room with a hot cup of coffee. Solitary confinement in Guantanamo Bay. Anywhere but here.

Heather is standing on the edge of the empty dance floor, waving us over like an airport marshaler guiding a 737 to the runway. All she's missing are the orange batons.

Luke goes to her. I'm along for the ride at this point. My brain has malfunctioned in this environment. I don't know how my legs are still moving.

"Let's get the party started!" the DJ shouts into the mic as he races ahead of us to get to his booth. "I'll be your MC tonight, DJ Brain Damage. Just a name I trademarked when I was sixteen and haven't changed yet. Don't worry, I do *not* have brain damage. But enough about my cranial fluids, the stars of the show Mrs. Taliah and Mr. Carter Whitfield!"

People clap and cheer as Luke leads me onto the dance floor under the giant chandelier. There are so many lights focused on my face. The place is packed and all eyes are on us. It feels like the entire universe is watching this moment.

DJ Brain Damage is behind us in his booth which is a few feet away from the dance floor.

"Everyone please gather around for the first dance," he hollers into the mic.

No, don't gather around! I want to yell. *Stay at your tables. Talk amongst yourselves. Don't even bother paying attention to what's happening up here!*

"Everyone come on over," the DJ shouts, not knowing when to shut the hell up. "Yes, you people outside. I see you. Come on in and enjoy the show!"

I glance over to the huge wall of open glass doors and gulp when I see even more people coming inside. There's a huge patio and grass section with a gorgeous view of the water behind it. It must fit three hundred people and right now, all those people are coming in to crowd around and watch me make a fool of myself.

"Pull out your phones," DJ Brain Damage says, "you're going to want to record this!"

I turn and glare at him. "Dude, shut up!" I whisper, hoping he's the only one who can hear it.

I reach down and pull off my shoes before the music starts. Heather rushes over and grabs them as I turn to Luke.

He takes my hand. A hand that's no longer part of my body.

He whispers something to me but I don't hear it. The sound is muffled like I'm underwater and can no longer breathe. The pressure is crushing my lungs. I'm flailing inside even though I'm motionless.

I watch his hand wrap around mine as he puts his other arm around me, his palm sliding onto my lower back like we've done this a million times.

With his hands on me, I start to drift back into my body. I can feel my heart pounding, his warm skin, breaths start coming.

I swallow hard, trying to ignore the crowd around me as I look up at him. He smiles and for the first time, the smile travels up to his eyes. I instantly feel better. Still shaky and panicked, but better.

"You got this, Zoe," he whispers just for me.

Man, I hope he's right.

The soft music begins playing. I recognize it immediately and exhale in relief. *Can't Help Falling in Love* by Elvis Presley. I know this song. It's simple. Easy. I can get through this.

Luke takes a step to the side and I let him guide me. Our eyes are locked, our bodies moving around the dance floor as one. I'm trusting him to get me through this. Considering where we were this morning, that's saying a lot. Our relationship has come a long way in a few hours.

He lifts me and suddenly turns. The crowd cheers as I glide over the dance floor, my dress twirling around me. We're actually pulling this off. I'm dancing and not making a fool of myself. I never would have bel—

The record scratches with a cringing screech. Luke and I stop and turn to the DJ in shock. He has the microphone to his mouth.

"Oh yeah!" he shouts as he throws his arm in the air. "Because the Whitfields do it right, we got an epic synchronized mashup first dance for you!"

My stomach drops. *You've gotta be fucking kidding me.*

I slowly look around and *all* the phones are out now. *All* recording.

My body seizes with panic. I'm so far past my fight or flight reaction that I'm deep into full fucking frozen territory. I'm a baby deer facing down a hungry lion. I've lost all bodily functions except for my wide bulging eyes.

Luke turns to me and laughs. He's actually laughing! Not dying of dread and horror, laughing!

"I'm not doing this," I whisper to him in a panic as a song from Grease begins to play—the one where Sandy embraces her leather fetish.

"It's going to be okay," he whispers back. "Just follow me."

I shake my head. He doesn't understand. This is not going to happen. I'm incapable of this.

My blood pressure skyrockets.

"Luke, I *can't* do this."

He grabs both of my hands and leans in close to my ear. "You can do anything, Zoe Fitzpatrick. Even boogie that nice little ass off."

I want to tell him that he's never been more wrong in his

life, but he darts off and is suddenly strutting around the dance floor like a young John Travolta. The crowd roars.

What do I do?

I look at Heather for help. She mimes smoking a cigarette.

Right.

I snap my hip back and forth to the beat as I smoke an imaginary cigarette, watching Luke steal the show.

He yanks off his jacket, tosses it into the crowd, pops his collar, and shakes his hips, giving every hot-blooded woman in the place an image they won't soon forget. His head whips around and he dances up to me, lip-syncing about how he's losing control. He's not the only one. A smile curls up my lips as I watch him come.

At 'electrifying' he mimes a seizure and drops to the floor.

I drop my imaginary cigarette in front of him and crush it with my bare toes as he looks up at me with an encouraging grin.

He's gone all-in. My competitiveness kicks in and I know I can't let him show me up.

An internal battle rages within me. My need to avoid embarrassment versus my need to beat Luke at everything.

When I realize I won't be making a fool out of myself, I'll actually be making a fool out of Taliah, something in me snaps. It flicks on like a light switch.

I'm fucking doing this.

Luke rises to his knees and I push him back down with my foot. He falls as I strut away, lip-syncing and warning his ass that he better shape up because I need a *real* man.

He follows me like a lovestruck puppy and I turn and guide him backward across the dance floor as a girl hollers and more people cheer. Just as we're getting into it, the beat changes to *Baby Got Back* by Sir Mix-A-Lot.

Oh god.

Suddenly, I'm twerking in front of Luke's relatives while he's behind me air smacking my ass. I wonder if Luke still thinks I'm an elegant classy bride now…

The song doesn't last long, thank god.

It's Not Unusual by Tom Jones comes on and Luke breaks into a perfect Carlton dance. I don't even try to compete on this one. I just laugh my ass off as I watch him swing his arms from side to side with a big goofy grin on his face. He wins this round.

The song switches again and my heart is pumping as I try to recognize it. This time it's not pumping from terror, it's from excitement. I'm actually having fun.

Thriller comes on and Luke spins around in his best Michael Jackson impersonation. He's pretty good too and almost has the moonwalk down perfectly.

I'm not going to let him beat me again. I grab my head and grab the place where my belt buckle should be and start popping back and forth, copying MJ's iconic move.

I kick my leg up and twist it around, landing on my toes, and feeling more alive than I've ever felt as the crowd erupts like we're performing at Madison Square Garden.

I throw out my hand, shuffle my feet, circle to the side. I'm MJ reincarnated. I feel his spirit flowing through my veins. And the crowd is here for it. They scream as Luke spins like a top.

The record scratches and polka music starts playing. Luke and I look at each other and burst out laughing, but we don't stop moving. He slaps his knee as he bounces it up and down, playing what I think is an air accordion. I don't even know what I'm doing, but it involves a lot of jumping, twirling, and wild awkward elbows flying all over the place.

Next, we're Uma Thurman and John Travolta (again) dragging peace signs across our eyes as we do our best Pulp Fiction impersonations.

We're bouncing around, getting all hot and sticky, but I'm having too much fun to care. The self-consciousness is gone. Is this what I've been missing all these years? Is this what it means to cut loose?

Speaking of loose, *Footloose* comes on and we start kicking our feet out and throwing our hands in the air as we try to hold in our laughter. We turn to each other as we move and he catches my eye, grinning as if to say 'I knew you had it in you, Captain.'

Luke does the running man and I strut around rapping like a gangsta when Kanye West's *Gold Digger* comes on.

The crowd is loving it. They're getting louder and louder. Some are dancing along with us and the ones who are too shy are bobbing their heads and cheering.

We dance through quick cuts of *Gangnam Style,* which has us bouncing around like we're riding imaginary horses, N'Sync's *Bye Bye Bye,* which has us bent over with our arms out like marionettes, and Elvis' *Hound Dog,* which has Luke gyrating his hips to the sound of screaming women.

It's like two decades of songs and dancing and fun I've let pass me by, all crammed into one epic, crowd-cheering dance.

The upbeat part of *(I've Had) The Time Of My Life* from Dirty Dancing cuts in and Luke looks at me from across the dance floor. His hair is a mess and he's huffing out breaths. There's a sheen of sweat on his forehead, his shirt is half untucked, and the smile he's giving me makes him look like a little kid. It's unrestrained joy. I've never seen him like this.

I laugh as I smile back at him, my body emptying of all tension and unease. There's no more panic. No more insecurities or embarrassment.

Just me and Luke having the time of our lives.

The title of the song checks out.

With a mischievous grin, Luke drops to his knees and does the Patrick Swayze move when he's between the chairs while Jennifer Grey watches from the stage. I grab my dress and sway from side to side as a warm weightlessness fills my body.

I'm not doing this for the money anymore. I'm doing this for Luke. For me. I've never done anything crazy like this before. This is so not me.

And I like it.

"Put your hands together for the big jump!" DJ Brain Damage shouts into the mic.

The breath catches in my throat as everyone flips out, hollering so loud I can't even hear the music.

Luke is biting his bottom lip, grinning at me as he gets to his feet.

I shake my head. "No," I mouth.

He nods his head and puts out his arms.

"Come on," he mouths. My eyes bulge. He laughs and nods.

Screw it.

This is the day for taking chances. I'm in too deep to back out now.

And if Luke drops me, then I'll always have that to hold over his head, so it won't be all bad.

I close my eyes, take a deep breath, and run.

There's a collective gasp and then silence as Luke's big hands grip my waist and I jump in the air. He hoists me up, extends his arms, and I'm suddenly flying over all the guests, able to see all the cheering people standing on their chairs in the back.

We bring the fucking house down.

It's so loud I can barely hear myself think, which is good because I'm wondering if anyone can see up my dress...

Luke slowly lowers me down into his embrace as the deafening applause turns to a thunderous roar. It's real legitimate cheering, not the half-assed cheering of a bunch of moms watching a crappy sixth-grade flute recital. It's energetic and alive.

We're rock stars. We're pop idols. We're gods.

Just for a moment.

My feet touch the floor. Luke's big arms are still around me and I've never felt so weightless. My breath catches in my throat. Every cell in my body is vibrating as I look up at him, the music slowing to an end.

His hands slide up my body and cup my cheeks. I don't pull away. I don't want to.

For him, it's part of the show, but I'm not so sure it is for me anymore.

I close my eyes as he leans down and kisses me.

The crowd roars their approval. My heart does too.

When he pulls away and I look into his warm blue eyes, I know this night has gotten even more complicated.

Didn't think that was possible, but here we are.

Complicated with a capital C.

CHAPTER
Thirteen

"That was incredible," Heather says with an approving smile on her face. "You were the star of the party!"

I've never been the star of the party before. I've been the cleaner of the party and the person who didn't get invited to the party and is at home going to bed at a reasonable hour, but never the star.

"Where's Luke?" she asks. "It's almost time for the mother groom dance."

"He's over there getting hammered," I say, nodding to the bar with my head.

Heather does not approve.

After the dance, some of Carter's ex-frat buddies grabbed Luke and dragged him to the bar, bellowing something about Hollywood Stingers. I smile as I look over and see his contorted face after downing a shot. I'm not sure what causes the sting in a Hollywood Stinger, but I can see the pain on Luke's adorable face as he tries to refuse a second one. Carter's buddies aren't having it and are ordering more.

"After the dance with Kathleen and Luke, it's going to be you and Frank."

"Do I have time to go to the bathroom?" I ask, squeezing my thighs together. I've had to go pee for the last hour, but I've been too scared to try in this wedding dress. My bladder is done patiently waiting and is starting to sound alarm bells.

"You're going to need someone to help you with that dress," Heather says, looking at my train.

"No, I'll be fine," I insist, although I'm not quite sure I can maneuver this thing in a tiny stall.

"I just have to talk to the DJ and I'll take you," Heather says as she glances at her clipboard. "Give me five minutes."

"Five minutes? What do I do until then?"

"It's your wedding," she says like it's completely obvious. "Mingle."

Mingle. I gulp as she marches away with her clipboard, leaving me standing here all alone.

I can mingle. I can do that.

My hands squeeze into fists at my sides.

I take a deep breath as I look around at closed circles of conversation, wondering how to break into one. If I try, everyone is going to stop talking and stare at me with exaggerated smiles. I'm not a human today. I'm a bride. It would be as natural as a giraffe trying to enter a conversation. They'd just stare. Or worse, they'd compliment me non-stop.

I spot some easy pickings and head over. Luke's great uncle, the famous viral YouTube star, is sitting alone in his wheelchair.

He doesn't even look up at me as I stand in front of him.

"Hi, there," I say in a friendly tone. "You're Carter's great uncle, aren't you?"

His head lowers.

"Are you enjoying the wedding?"

A low snore rumbles out of him.

Great, he's sleeping.

Kathleen walks by and scowls at me. "Try not to put the guests to sleep, will you?"

I bite back a growl as she continues over to a rich-looking couple and lets them shake her hand.

As fun as it sounds, it's not the time to give Kathleen dirty looks behind her back. It's time to get my wedding coordinator so I can go to the bathroom.

I have to go *sooo* badly. I frantically look around for Heather and spot her behind the DJ booth, flirting with DJ Brain Damage. *What the hell?*

She's playing with her hair and laughing exaggeratedly at whatever he's saying. Meanwhile, he's leaning on the wall, completely ignoring his DJ duties. The song has switched on its own and an inappropriate gangster rap song is blaring through the gorgeous hall. By the fourteenth 'bitch' and the ninth 'ho' he realizes and puts on something more appropriate for a fancy wedding.

Come on, Heather…

I don't need her to pee, do I? I think I can handle this dress by myself and as a card-carrying member of the shy bladder society, I really don't want her standing over me while I'm trying to go.

Screw it.

I hurry to the bathrooms, but Aya intercepts me halfway. She has a big pink fruity drink with a huge chunk of pineapple on the rim. It looks ridiculous. I want one.

I was hoping she'd be a loyal maid of honor and stick by my side, but I should have known better with Aya's work ethic. It's the first time I've seen her since the ceremony. I'm afraid to ask what she's been up to.

"Wow, boss. Loved that wild dancing! I didn't think you had it in you with that big stick up your a—"

I grab her arm and yank her away when I spot the Turkish Ambassador staring at me from across the room.

Oh crap! I forgot all about that guy…

"Aya, look at that big man by the window," I whisper as I duck behind a confused elderly couple. "Is he still watching me?"

"The one with the giant caterpillar eyebrows?"

"Yes."

"Yup, and he's coming over."

"Shit!"

I hurry away, dragging her along… right into Luke's grandmother, Eleanor.

"You're right," she says as she looks up at me.

I swallow hard as I force out a smile. "About what?"

I glance longingly at the bathrooms. I don't have time for this right now…

"Google must be unreliable. My assistant couldn't find anything about a plane full of clowns dying."

I cross my legs and gulp. "He couldn't?"

"Nope."

"You never know with Google," Aya chimes in. "I was looking up my grandfather Hung Wang, but that's not what Google showed me at all."

Eleanor looks her up and down and then turns back to me without a word. "Why don't you tell me who you really are, Zoe Fitzpatrick, before I have the Director of the FBI—who is enjoying a bloody caesar over at the bar—dig into your past like an Adderall addicted archeologist?"

It's no use lying to her. She's a human lie detector and I'm the world's worst liar. Plus, I kind of like her.

"I'm the caterer," I tell her. "For the drivers and the secret service."

"In the parking lot," Aya adds.

Why is that detail so damn important to everybody?!

"The caterer?" Eleanor repeats.

"Yes," I say, trying to unclench my jaw. "When Carter and Taliah left, Kathleen and Walter asked me to step in."

"Which makes sense since you're dating Luke."

Aya's head tilts. "What?"

"Exactly," I quickly jump in. "Because I'm dating Luke."

I turn to Aya and widen my eyes. You never know what's going to come out of her mouth, but she seems to get the point and sips on her drink without another word.

"It's your company?" Eleanor asks.

I nod, smiling proudly. "Catering by Zoe."

"Well, I'm glad my grandson is dating a working girl," she says with a nod. "And an entrepreneur on top of it all. Very good."

All sorts of emotions are tugging at me. The pride of a maternal figure finally commending me on my accomplishments mixes with the guilt of lying to her face (with the intense urge to urinate thrown in there for good measure). I wish it didn't have to be like this. Eleanor is someone I could see myself looking up to and bonding with. I've always wanted a strong accomplished mentor like her. Someone to offer an encouraging word when business has kicked me down and to tell me that everything will be okay in the long run if I keep my head up.

"That reminds me," I say. "Aya, I need you to check on the tent. Make sure everything is running smoothly."

"But I was just about to get another drink."

"Work comes first," I say, sliding back into a familiar skin. "Make sure Carlos isn't burning the kale cakes and bring some ice from the freezer to Jason. I want the oysters served on freshly crushed ice and *not* directly on the tray like he tried to pull last time."

I catch Eleanor looking impressed as she watches me.

"Make sure Sarah is cooking *real* bacon for the salad," I go on. "The smell will bring people in and the fake stuff is just disgusting. Don't let her pull her vegan guilt trip on you."

I make Aya repeat everything back to me. "Kale cakes, ice for the oysters, real bacon. Anything else, boss?"

"That's good for now," I tell her. "Make sure everyone knows I'm going to be checking up on them later."

The groomsmen Ryan comes slinking over with red cheeks and his hands in his pockets. He smoothes his hair out as he heads straight to Aya.

"What do you want?" Aya says in a flat voice.

He looks so sheepish as he drops his eyes to the floor and drags his toe in a circle. "Do you want to have a drink with me?"

Aya can be absolutely brutal when it comes to shutting down guys. "No."

"I'll pay!" he says, desperation oozing out of him.

"It's open bar."

His face drops. "Oh… I'll give you my cherries!"

Aya shakes her head. "The last thing I want is your cherry, little man."

He sighs, looking crushed.

"I'll tell you what," she says. His face lights back up like a gas station slot machine. "I'll let you carry some bags of ice for me."

"Okay!" he says as if she just made every dream he had come true. "I'd love to!"

"Come on, boy," she says as she leaves. Ryan follows her like one of those high energy yappy dogs.

Eleanor shakes her head as she watches them leave. "I swear the Whitfield males get dumber with every passing generation."

"Must be all the inbreeding."

She snorts out a laugh. "Incest joke at a wedding? Ballsy. I like ballsy. Luke finally did something right when he landed you."

"Really?"

"I think so. I'm impressed with you, Zoe."

"You are?"

"I like your work ethic. You remind me of myself when I was your age. You're running your own business, standing up to my son and his Disney villain wife, and so far, you're pulling this hoax of a wedding off. You've got moxie, kid."

Moxie. I love that word and have always wanted to be thought of as having it.

"And it's obvious my grandson is utterly in love with you."

"What?" I say stepping back, completely thrown by her comment.

"I've never seen Luke look at a girl the way he looks at you."

"Really?"

I look at Luke over by the bar. I'm always aware of where he is in the room, but this time he's aware of me. He smiles—a little drunkenly—when we meet eyes. A flush heats up my cheeks.

He's never looked at a girl like this before? Is this part of the act, or…

It's part of the act, Zoe. Get a grip.

"So," Eleanor says with a stern glare. "What's in this for you? What are you getting out of playing bride for the day?"

"I just wanted to help out," I lie. "If you'll excuse me, I really have to go to the bathroom…"

She sees right through my lie and laughs. "Go skip back to the playground with that bullshit. How much?"

I grin. I like this woman's style. She's moxie incarnate.

"One hundred grand and contracts for my catering company at the White House."

She nods, impressed. "You negotiated that?"

I hold my shoulders back and grin. "I did."

"Pretty good," she says, nodding. "Although, you could have gotten two hundred and fifty thousand. You have a lot to learn, kid. Luckily, I have some time left to teach you."

We both smile at each other and for the second time today, I've made a new friend.

"Is that really the director of the FBI?" I ask her as I uncross my legs and bounce on my feet.

She laughs. "No, that's my cousin Rick. The only thing he's directed is an AA meeting."

Now that the pressure is off and we're both relaxed, my bladder urgently waves its hand again, demanding my attention.

I really had to go an hour ago. Now, we're creeping into emergency territory. So, unless I want to throw the bouquet in a yellow dress, I have to go now.

I excuse myself and practically sprint to the bathroom. Some people turn their heads and watch, but I don't have a choice at this point. The time to play it cool is over.

I explode into the bathroom like my dress is on fire and meet eyes with Victoria.

"Ugh," she grunts, rolling her eyes as she continues washing her hands at the sink.

I rush over to a stall and push it open as a drop or two comes dangerously close to leaking out. I'm in pain now. This is *911* territory.

"Come on," I whisper through gritted teeth as I hold up my

dress and quickly wipe down the toilet seat. My dress practically fills up the whole stall. This is much harder than I anticipated. I'm not mobile at all.

I close the door and catch my dress in it. Damn it! I quickly re-open the door, pull my dress in, and try to turn and maneuver myself onto the toilet seat. I can't even pull my dress all the way up.

Where the hell is Heather?!

I'm pretty sure in the list of wedding coordinator's responsibilities, making sure the bride doesn't pee herself comes above flirting with the DJ.

I have seconds until blast off.

Every time I close my eyes, I see waterfalls, geysers, broken faucets, raging rivers. I have to go *now!*

I'm desperate and I'm stuck.

With my core clenched and my frantic eyes as wide and round as ping pong balls, I swing open the door. "Victoria! I need your help!"

"Get lost," she says as she looks at me through the mirror. "You're a liar."

"Yes, I am," I tell her. "But you walked down the aisle too, so you're as much a liar as I am."

She frowns as she drops her eyes.

"Look, I'm sorry your brother and his fiancé eloped and cut you out of their wedding. It was a shitty thing to do and I hope you stand up to them and tell them how you feel."

"I could never talk to them like that," she says with a heavy sigh. "I'm just a baby sister to them."

I squeeze my thighs as I clench the door so hard the metal groans under my grip. "What I see in front of me is a strong, smart, confident woman who is a total knockout in that dress. It's time your brothers see it too. Not the knockout part, the other stuff. Be that woman and they'll see that woman."

She looks at herself in the mirror—eyes watering—and takes a deep breath.

"Tell them they suck for bailing on you, but please realize that has nothing to do with me. I'm just helping your mom and dad because they asked me to."

And because they're paying me a hundred grand...

"You have no reason to be mad at me. I did nothing to you, except help your family out. So, for fuck's sake, please help me pick up this dress so I can pee for the next twenty minutes!"

She turns and looks at me for a second.

"Please..."

She rolls her eyes and then hurries over, grabbing my dress off the bathroom floor.

"Thank you," I gasp as the dress lifts up and my butt hits the cold toilet seat. I've never felt a more pleasurable feeling in my entire life.

She closes the door and I let loose.

I'll have to return my membership to the shy bladder society. It sounds like a firehose is hitting the bowl. And it's not stopping anytime soon.

It feels too good to be embarrassed.

I look up at Victoria and she turns away.

After about seven minutes, the stream slows to a trickle and Victoria starts to reposition herself.

"Hold on," I say. I push out again and there's a second burst, the firehose roaring back to life.

Victoria's stoic face cracks and she starts to giggle. It's contagious and I giggle too.

The longer I go, the more the giggles build until we're both laughing so much that tears are leaking from our eyes. Victoria falls against the bathroom stall, bent over laughing as my never-emptying bladder continues to go.

We're still laughing when I'm finally done and we're trying to get this huge monstrosity of a dress out of the stall.

"This is what I wanted," Victoria says with a warm smile as she looks at me. "To have a sister moment like this with my new sister-in-law."

"I've been wanting a sister moment like this for my entire life," I tell her as a warmth fills my chest. "It's funny that I got one from the one girl who hated me five minutes ago."

"Isn't that what sisters are like though?" she asks with a smile as she wipes the tears from her cheeks. "Hating each other one minute and then best friends the next?"

"I guess you're right."

We smile at each other for a moment and then she guides the rest of my dress out. I catch my reflection in the mirror and am shocked by the amount of cleavage I'm showing. I yank it up as much as it will go, which is only about an inch.

"Are we cool?" I ask as I try to turn the water on with those stupid sensors that never work for me.

She reaches over and waves her hand under it. Water pours out. "We're cool."

I wash my hands while she hops up on the counter and watches. "So, how would I tell Carter and Taliah how I feel?"

"Just be honest."

"I couldn't do that," she says as she looks at me through the mirror. "I hate conflict."

"Conflict is the first step toward reconciliation," I tell her. "It's not a bad thing. It's better than keeping it bottled up where it will slowly poison your relationship. Just tell them how you feel."

She breathes in and out as her eyes wander to my dress. They widen.

"What is it?" I ask in a panic.

She hops off the counter and inspects the back of my dress.

"This seam is tearing. Oh no! Did my mother sew this?"

My blood goes cold. "Yes… She was a seamstress…"

"A seamstress? My mother was born a Carmichael."

"So?"

"You've never heard of them because they don't want you to know who they are. But they're the fifth-richest family in the country. My mother was never a seamstress."

"Oh. Shit."

Victoria looks over the rest of my dress and points out a few more areas of concern.

"What do we do?" Victoria asks, looking flushed.

"Heather will know what to do."

"And if she doesn't?"

I pull up the front of my dress as I look myself over in the mirror. "Then I guess I'll be showing a lot more than an inappropriate amount of cleavage by the end of the night."

CHAPTER
Fourteen

"Mrs. Whitfield," the bartender says with an incredulous look on her face, "you don't have to keep doing this!"

"Yes, I do," I answer curtly. Every caterer instinct in me is blaring like a fireman parade. There are dirty glasses and empty bottles everywhere. It's insulting.

I place the three empty glasses on the bar and then take the four empty beer bottles tucked under my arm and hand them over.

"It's your wedding day," she says, looking at me like she thinks I should be in a straitjacket rather than in a wedding dress. "Please, leave that to our staff and try to enjoy yourself."

I am enjoying myself, I want to say. This is how I enjoy myself. By cleaning.

"Your staff needs to step up their game," I say, spotting another cluster of empty glasses around the large fountain in the lobby. "This is a premier wedding hall, charging premier prices. Start acting like it."

Her brow furrows as I turn and charge away.

A bunch of Carter's swim team friends are sitting on the

couches near the fountain and the first thing I notice is the glasses and bottles gathering on the table.

"Hi, Taliah," one of them says when I make eye contact. "Lovely wedding."

"Those glasses and bottles go to the bar when you're done with them," I say, giving him a look that has him quickly nodding.

"Yes, ma'am."

I huff out a breath and keep walking. I hear laughter behind my back, but I don't turn around. I don't care.

Luke has been gone for so long. Thirty minutes at least, and I'm starting to get stressed out without him. I always clean when I'm stressed. Luckily, the staff here is mediocre at best, so I have a lot to do.

Kathleen slithers over to me while I'm rearranging the few remaining cards with the guest names and table numbers on them.

"You're at the head table, dear," she says in a voice that sends cold chills snaking down my spine. "Probably for the first and last time in your life."

I spin around and glare at her, teeth clenched, body tight. My eyes can melt metal. I'm done playing nice with her. I'm doing everything I can for this fraudulent hoax of a wedding and she's done nothing but put me down. I've given up my dignity by dancing to *Gangnam Style* in front of seven hundred plus people, my integrity by lying to every single person here, and I've taken years off my bladder because of this stupid dress.

"Stop talking to me like that," I snap.

She looks amused, like someone smiling at a puppy who's trying to take on a full-grown pit bull.

"You weren't even a seamstress!" I whisper scream at her. "Are you even capable of not lying? What is wrong with you people?"

"Watch your tone, missy," she warns.

"No! I'm not afraid of you! Get a professional seamstress here, right now!"

My heart is thundering through my body. Adrenaline is surging through my veins as I take on this powerful woman.

She looks around and forces out smiles at the few people nearby who are starting to turn and watch the show. Her steel fingers wrap around my arm and she squeezes *hard* as she drags me to a quiet corner where she can chew me out in privacy.

Her voice is like venom. "Who do you think you're talking—"

"I don't care!" I snap back, my voice like TNT. "Get a seamstress here before my dress explodes! I keep hearing tears and rips. You *have* to call one."

"I don't have to do a damn thing," she fires back. "I'm a Whitfield, don't you forget. *I'm* in charge here."

"You think you have all the power in this situation?" I say with a deranged laugh. "How about I go on 60 Minutes and tell the American people that the next major presidential candidate threw a fake wedding with the wrong son and the caterer?"

"Of the parking lot."

I huff out a breath. "Even worse for you!"

She stares at me, trying to see if I'm bluffing.

"I wonder what kind of book contracts I'd get… Probably big ones…"

"You can't say a thing," she hisses. "We'd sue you into oblivion."

"I didn't sign a non-disclosure agreement," I say with a gloating smile. "Remember? *You* forgot to give me one."

For once she doesn't have a thing to say. I can't believe it. I made the great Kathleen Whitfield speechless. I wish Luke was here to see it.

"Seamstress," I say as I cross my arms and raise my chin. "Call one."

"Do I look like I'm friends with any seamstresses?"

"Your husband paid my deposit with a black American Express card."

"So?"

"So, that card comes with a twenty-four-seven worldwide concierge service. Call them. They'll find you one."

Kathleen looks at me for a long moment and then nods her head, impressed. "Pretty good, Chloe."

"It's Zoe," I say as she walks away. "Oh, never mind."

I need some air.

My bad mood dissipates as I walk around the spectacular inn. It's hard to be mad when you're surrounded by thousands of gorgeous flowers in a luxurious venue that belongs on the cover of every wedding magazine in the world.

I stop in front of a table of cocktails and admire the huge ice sculpture of an angel smiling down at me. She's carrying a banner with *LOVE* carved into it. I wonder how much this thing cost. Probably more than my car and it's already melting away, her brow sweating and dripping off her chin onto the white table cloth.

Poor girl. She was brought into this world to celebrate commitment and love, and she got this abomination instead. No wonder she's sweating. They should have carved out the four horsemen of the apocalypse instead. That would have been more fitting.

I run my finger over her slick foot and head outside. People everywhere smile at me and compliment my dress. "Thank you," I say, feeling like a queen as they lower their heads while I pass.

I slip outside and spot my groom by the water surrounded by a bunch of strangers our age. He says something and they all laugh.

I smile too even though I didn't hear it. He's looking good by the shore with the breeze in his hair. It's flopping at a weird angle, but it makes him look cute. My fingertips tingle with the desire to run my hands through it to fix it.

I keep feeling his hands on me when we were dancing, the way he was watching me, the heat in his eyes. I shiver from the memory of it.

Maybe he's not as bad as I initially thought. Of course, he's frustrating, but he's also—*oh fuck!*

I yank up my dress and dart out of the way, hurrying around groups of people chatting. *Is he still there?* I duck my head and—*shit! He's still staring at me.*

By the tree is the Turkish Ambassador, looking meaner and Turkisher than ever. His horrible eyes are fixated on me. He's like a character from a horror movie, except instead of wanting to kill me, he wants me to speak Turkish in front of everyone.

I hurry over to Luke. He saved me last time, so maybe he has a few more tricks up his tuxedo sleeve.

Luke turns and gives me a smile that nearly brings me to my knees. The Hollywood Stingers must have put some color in his cheeks because they're an adorable shade of pink. He looks relaxed and calm and cool and a little bit tipsy. It's a combination that suits him well.

"Hey, beautiful," he says softly as he puts his arm around my shoulder. It's so casual and natural, you'd swear we were actually a real couple.

I step on my toes and plant a soft kiss on his cheek. It's very important to maintain the image that we're together, so I also wrap my arm around his back, feeling the hard muscles under his suit. It's all for the show, obviously. I even rest my cheek on the side of his chest for a few seconds and breathe in his cologne. I'm professional if nothing else.

"Mind if I steal him for a second?" I ask the six people he's talking to.

"You locked him down!" a woman with a floral dress says in a 'you go girl' tone. "He's all yours now!"

I smile as I pull him away toward the water where we can have a few seconds alone.

"Thank you," Luke says with a long exhale. "They were asking me—well, Carter I guess—where he was living."

"You don't know where your brother lives?"

"Nope."

"Are you two fighting? Do you get along with anyone in your family?"

His eyes narrow on me. "Do you?"

"Good point."

He smiles sadly as he looks around. "We don't keep in touch too much."

"You're identical twins," I say in disbelief. "Aren't you guys like telepathic?"

"No, but we're both allergic to guinea pigs. Our psychic connection ends there."

Two women walk by and smile at us. I take a step closer to Luke as I smile back. Thankfully, they keep walking.

"I'm so bad at this."

"At what?" he says, looking at me with amusement in his eyes. Sometimes he watches me the way you watch a puppy, wondering what they're going to do next. I'm not sure if I hate it or love it.

"At lying! At making up stories. Can you not leave me ever again?"

"Lying is not that hard," he says. "Didn't you ever lie to

your parents when you got a bad grade or snuck out of the house?"

"I got all A's."

"Big surprise there."

"And I only snuck out of the house once when they were already sleeping, so no lying necessary."

"Big party?"

"My favorite author was giving a reading and signing books after."

"That's the saddest thing I've ever heard."

"It was pretty sad. I was so nervous I forgot to bring my books."

"That's not what I meant… Never mind. Lying is easy. The trick is to give *specific* information. It makes the story more believable with precise details."

"Specific information…" I roll it around on my tongue as I think about it. I can give details. Is it really that easy?

"Those are some old family friends over there," he says as he glances at a group of six or seven people talking on the dock. "We spent a few summers with them in Big Bear when I was a teenager. They're very nice. Let's try it out."

"Okay," I say as I shake out my hands. *Specific details…*

"Hey, guys!" Luke says with a big delicious smile on his face. I try to match it, but I bet I look like a serial killer trying to pretend she's normal.

"There's the bride!" a girl with red hair says, laughing nervously as we approach the group. Some of the guests in the circle smile at me, but some are keeping their eyes on her.

"You make a beautiful couple," the redhead says with a high-pitched laugh. She can't stop blinking nervously as she smiles tightly at us. "Tell us, Taliah. How did Carter propose?"

"Yes!" another girl in a bright yellow dress says, smiling

warmly at us as she clasps her hands together. "Tell us the story!"

"I bet it was romantic," the redhead says, looking at Luke longingly. "Carter was always so romantic. He bought me a diamond necklace after the third time we slept together."

"Cindy!" yellow dress girl snaps. "Inappropriate!"

Everyone frowns at Cindy as her cheeks turn the color of her hair.

"I'm sorry," she says, on the verge of tears as she plays with the diamond necklace that she's *still* wearing. "I didn't mean to say that. You're a beautiful bride. I'm so happy for you!"

She bursts out crying and runs away.

Everyone is staring at her in shock as she bumps into a waitress on the way inside.

"So," yellow dress says, trying to smooth things over. "How did Carter propose?"

He grins as he looks down at me. "Taliah tells the story so well."

"No," I quickly say, feeling the now familiar sensation of panic rising up in me for the twelfth time today. "You should tell it. You're the one who planned everything!"

"But you *love* telling it," he says, grin widening.

Yellow dress gets impatient and takes it upon herself to get the story out. "Where did you propose?"

"Maui," Luke says at the same time I say, "Seattle."

Eyebrows raise around the circle.

"Seattle was the name of our villa in Maui," Luke says without hesitation. "It was actually named Seattle on the Beach, but we called it Seattle for short."

He's a natural at this. I can picture a teenage Luke sweet-talking his teachers as he lies about why he was absent or why his term paper is late. Making up details off the top of his head and sprinkling them into his story.

"What a fun name for a villa," yellow dress says with a laugh. "Were the owners from Seattle?"

Specific Information…

"They were from Madagascar," I say, throwing out random details that are sure to make the story more believable. "The villa was on a long street called Apple Lane and there were big McIntosh apple trees in everyone's yards."

"McIntosh apples?" one of the guys with spiky hair and a thin beard asks, looking confused. "In Hawaii?"

"Did I say apples?" I ask with a swallow. "I meant mangoes. Obviously."

Luke is looking at me like I'm hopeless. I think he may be right.

"Anyway," he continues, taking over again. "We were walking along the beach and the setting sun was casting the most spectacular shades of pink and purple across the evening sky. It was magnificent. The white sand was like flour under our feet and the gentle waves were slowly easing onto the shore. Taliah was wearing a white dress and it was flowing in the warm breeze. I remember looking into her stunning hazel eyes and knowing that I wanted to spend the rest of my life with her."

He turns to me and my shoulders sink, every muscle in my body losing tension under that loving stare. This time I can't stop myself. I reach up and fix the fluff of hair, running my fingers through it. His hair is otherworldly. It's bewitching.

"It was perfect," he goes on in a soft, soothing voice that has me under a spell. "Except for the guy in a Speedo, but I couldn't do anything about that."

They all laugh and it snaps me out of my daze. I'm supposed to be contributing details here. I really want to show Luke that I'm not completely incompetent.

"The Speedo was green," I add. "The man's name was Magnus. He was from Iceland."

"You talked to the guy in the Speedo?" spiky hair asks with a laugh. "After getting engaged?"

I'm about to make up a whole story on the fly about a shark attacking Magnus and Carter jumping in to save him, but luckily, Luke goes first.

"He was our neighbor," he says simply. "We met him later. Weird guy. So, I took her hand, got down on one knee—"

He takes my hand and drops to his knee as he narrates it. My heart goes into overdrive with this beautiful man kneeling in front of me. I can't look away.

"—and I told her that she makes life exciting. That she makes my heart race. My soul sing. I told her that I wanted to be with her forever and asked if she would be my wife."

Swoon.

"Did you have a ring on you?" yellow dress asks.

"I bought it the day I met her," he says as he stares into my eyes. "I knew immediately."

"Awww," the other girls say like a swooning chorus.

Shut up, he's mine.

"And the rest was history," Luke says as he stands up.

We chat for a bit longer and then yellow dress glances back at the inn. "I better go check on Cindy."

She leaves and Luke and I sneak back to the water. "Who's Cindy?"

"Some girl we knew growing up," he says with a shrug. "I didn't know Carter was into her."

"Apparently, he wasn't *that* into her."

"I guess not. Oh, by the way, I meant normal-sounding details. Not ridiculous outlandish ones."

He laughs. I glare.

"Not everyone has your comfort with deception," I say with my chin in the air. "I like to be honest when I—"

Shit! Not again!

"That guy keeps following me!" I say as I hide in front of Luke.

"Which guy?" He looks around, his blue eyes full of something. Is that protectiveness? Jealousy? My lips curl into a grin seeing him like this.

"The Turkish Ambassador. He's over by the dock. It's like he's following me or something. Why can't he just leave me alone?"

Luke scans the waterline. His eyes narrow when he spots him.

"Can your dad kick him out?"

His eyebrow raises. "Not unless you want the US to go to war with Turkey over this fake wedding."

I think about it for a few seconds and then sigh. "I guess not. Maybe we can put something in his food so he gets sick and has to go home?" I throw out. That could work.

Luke sighs as he looks at me. "We're not poisoning a foreign diplomat. I don't want to be thrown into Guantanamo Bay for the rest of my life and trust me, neither do you."

"I was just thinking a laxative," I mutter, feeling slightly abashed, "not *real* poison."

Heather comes rushing over and I give her a look. "Five minutes, eh?"

"Oh, shit!" she says, grabbing her forehead. "Did you make it okay?"

"Barely."

"Good." She looks Luke up and down and then leans in close to him while she fixes his corsage. I want to claw her face off. "Are you ready for the mother-son dance?"

"I need a few more Hollywood Stingers for that," he says, glancing longingly at the bar in the distance.

"Easy, Hollywood," I say with a grin. "I don't want a drunk groom."

Poor brokenhearted Cindy is probably just waiting for an opportunity to get him hammered and steal him from me. Not on my watch.

Heather brings us inside and up to Kathleen who's waiting at the edge of the dance floor.

"Are we ready?" the DJ asks as he shoots a flirtatious smile at Heather.

"Something classic," Kathleen snaps at him. "None of that Josh Groban bullshit. And if at all possible, keep your mouth shut while the song is playing this time. We don't need a narrator."

"Okaaay," DJ Brain Damage whispers as he backs away like a scolded child.

"Let's get this over with," Kathleen says as she marches onto the dance floor. Luke turns to me and grins.

"Have fun," I say, grinning back as I give him a little wave.

"Please put your hands together for the groom and his mother…" the DJ says through the speakers as the soft music begins to play, "…who is a total bitch."

All eyes dart to the DJ, but mine are on Kathleen. She looks like a dragon about to turn a village into ash as she glares at him.

"Technical difficulties," the DJ says as he blushes so hard his dark skin practically turns pink. "The microphone was supposed to be off for that last part. Kathleen Whitfield is not… a bitch. She's a wonderful person."

He swallows hard, looking like there might be a bit of throw up in his mouth.

Luke and Kathleen begin the most awkward, uptight

mother-son dance in wedding history as Luke's aunt, and the flower girl's mother, Tammy comes over to join me.

"This is nice," she says as her head tilts to the side. "Whenever I begin to think this family is beyond dysfunctional, there's a sweet moment like this that keeps me hopeful."

I look at Luke's straight back and the way he's holding in his breath, and wonder what kind of shit this woman has seen over the years that qualifies this as a 'sweet moment.' Her bar is disturbingly low.

"What's Luke like?" I ask, shamelessly fishing for details. "I still haven't met him."

"It always makes me so sad whenever I think of Luke." She sighs as she watches who she thinks is Carter and his mother awkwardly step around the dance floor like there are minefields hidden underneath it.

"Why?" I'm all ears now. "What happened?"

"You're family now," she says, smiling sadly at me. "I guess I can tell you. Luke always had the biggest heart and he wore that heart on his sleeve. Even from a young age, he could light up your insides with a smile if he liked you, and if he didn't, well, he'd let you know that too."

My body is still, my breath caught in my lungs as I hang on every word.

"The problem with big hearts is that they're easy to break and not so easy to put back together. Luke's father broke that soft tender heart a long time ago and it never healed. Unfortunately, it's all sharp edges and jagged corners now."

"What happened? How did Walter break it?"

"Oh, that's not for me to say."

"But nobody will tell me."

And it's driving me crazy!

"You'll find out soon enough," she says softly. "You're one

of us now and even if you haven't met Luke, you're still his family. He might not see it that way, though."

"What do you mean?"

"He doesn't come around much anymore, but I'm still hoping one day that big sentimental heart of his will heal and he'll fill it with forgiveness. Just give it time and don't give up on him. He's worth it. But you better know that having a brother-in-law like Luke is going to be like having a sister-in-law like Kathleen: it's going to require a lot of patience."

We watch in silence for the rest of the song. I can't take my eyes off him.

A big tender heart…

Patience…

I can have patience.

For some reason, I feel like I could wait forever for this man.

I mean, I could… if this was real.

Which it's not.

Why do I keep forgetting that?

CHAPTER
Fifteen

"Everybody stops what they're doing," I say as Luke hangs on my every word, deep laughs bubbling out of him. "Talking, dancing, eating their slices of marble cake. They all stop, turn, and stare at me as champagne pours down my face and flows out of my hair. I was *soaked*. Champagne shot up my nose, which burns like crazy by the way, and it went into my eyes. They were bloodshot for three hours after. It was horrible."

"I'm sorry to laugh," he says as he unsuccessfully tries to hold it back. I don't mind. I love the deep rumbling sound of it. "What did you do?"

"The show must go on," I say with a chuckle. "I poured the two glasses of champagne, excused myself, got in my car, treated myself to a nice little scream session, and then I pulled myself together, went back in, grabbed the mop, and cleaned up my mess."

We both laugh as we watch each other. He's got such a nice smile. I don't think I'd ever get sick of it.

"That's a funny story," he says as he wipes his eye.

"Yeah," I answer, even though I never saw it that way before now. This is the first time I've laughed when I told it.

The waitress comes by and fills our wine glasses. She doesn't spill a drop. Finally, a professional in here.

We're finally getting a bit of a break from everyone now that we're sitting at the head table for dinner. Everyone is focused on the guests at their tables, so I'm able to chat with Luke in privacy. People are still looking at us, but they can't hear what we're saying so we can be ourselves. It's nice.

What's even nicer is that my shoes are off under the table. I nearly moan as I rub my feet together. I'm going to hike up an active volcano after this just so I can throw them into molten lava and watch them die.

I had my father-bride dance which was terribly boring, which is good, I guess. Most of the guests didn't bother to come inside to watch. It was a lot of awkward touching of Frank's dandruff-dusted shoulders. His parmesan smell seems to be growing stronger and more fierce throughout the day. My cat would love him.

After the dance, DJ Brain Damage announced that it was time to get seated. I'm on full display at the head table along with the rest of the wedding party. It goes Owen, Ryan, Frank, Aya, me, Luke, Victoria, Kathleen, and then Walter at the far end.

Poor Aya is stuck next to Frank. I heard her ask him if he just ate a caesar salad. I should include her in our conversation, but I kind of want Luke all to myself. I should get to know him better. It's easier to pretend we're married that way. I am getting paid a lot of money for this, so it's important to do the best job I can.

"It must be hard being an entrepreneur," he says as he takes a sip of red wine.

"It is," I say, feeling my insides light up with excitement.

"But it's also thrilling. I left my mom's house and moved to another state when I was eighteen. I had no opportunity, so I made one. I made my own way."

He's almost completely turned in his seat, focused on me. I keep thinking he's going to get bored and turn to talk to Victoria, but it's like we're the only two people in the room.

"How did you do that?"

"I started by selling sandwiches at construction sites. Grilled cheese or peanut butter and jam. Two bucks a pop. It was all I could afford and all I knew how to make. Three weeks in, I was selling turkey for six and roast beef for seven."

Luke smiles at me and it makes me feel like the most interesting woman in the world.

"I worked my way up, got bit by several dogs, and next month, I'll be catering for the President of the United States in the Rose Garden. So, don't screw it up!"

My tone is harsh, but the smile on my face eases the blow.

"That's quite the journey," he says as he holds my eyes. "I know it must have been a lot harder than you make it out to be."

"Maybe a little…"

"And look where you're ending up," he says as he looks around. "The White House. That's amazing. But can I ask you? Aren't you disappointed that you're getting it through… nefarious means?"

"Nefarious?"

"Okay, maybe that's a strong word. Dishonest."

"Not for a second."

He laughs.

"I'm serious," I say firmly. "When you come from where I come from, you take *every* opportunity you can get. Sometimes even the *nefarious* ones."

I throw him a flirty smile as I say it and he starts to blush a bit.

I made Luke blush?

Crap, now *I'm* blushing!

I take a big sip of wine and turn back to him. "That reminds me. What are you getting out of this?"

He takes a sip of his wine too and turns away from me a bit. "I'm just helping out my family."

"Bullshit. What is it? A new jet?"

"A new *jet?*"

"Something even more obnoxious like a yellow Lamborghini? Bicep implants?"

"Bicep implants?" he says with a laugh. "That's not even a thing that exists."

"And you know because you looked into it?"

He shakes his head, laughing.

"Are you getting millions of dollars? Is your father going to buy you a soul?"

"You're ridiculous."

Some pervert out there starts clinking their glass and soon the entire room bursts into a clinking orchestra. Luke and I look at each other, wondering what to do.

"Kiss!" Luke's uncle Randy shouts, putting our confusion to rest. "With tongue!"

Suddenly, there's a literal spotlight on us and there's no getting away.

The crowd roars as Luke stands up and offers his hand. He's looking down at me, hand extended, a slight flush in his cheeks, a devastating smile on his face. I can't resist. He's the type of handsome that women obsess over, that they willingly ruin their life over.

I swallow hard as I slide my hand into his, feeling every cell in my body come to life. I'm breathless and lightheaded as he guides me to my feet. I'm even shorter than him with my shoes off, so I have to stand on my toes to reach his mouth. He meets me the rest of the way and the crowd roars as I taste the wine on his soft lips.

Aya belts out a 'woo hoo' and Frank whistles.

"Boooo!" Randy shouts when we pull away. "No tongue!"

My heart is pounding when I sit down. I can feel the vibrations working their way into my head. The heat in my cheeks spreads down into my core.

Heather sneaks up behind the table as Luke and I sit there awkwardly, neither of us wanting to talk about what just happened.

"Great job, guys," she says as she ducks down between us. "You two seem like you're actually in love!"

Luke and I shoot each other an awkward look.

"Aya's maid of honor speech is coming up," Heather continues, "and then Walter is going to make his big announcement. The President is still expected to come sometime after dinner! Exciting stuff!" She claps her hands and then disappears, heading straight for the DJ booth.

"I still can't believe my father is going to be running for President," Luke says, looking nauseous.

"Imagine your mother as the First Lady," I say with a shudder. "She'd start wars for fun. She'd probably tell some world leader that their flag was ugly and the name of their country was stupid."

Luke chuckles. "I bet her first order would be to have all the dogs in the United States killed."

We're giggling like kids when a warning bell starts ringing in the back of my head. Did Heather just say that Aya is making a speech? This can't be good.

I turn to her and she's casually eating her salad like it's a normal dinner at home in front of *Jeopardy!* and not like she's about to deliver a huge speech to seven hundred plus people.

Her lack of nerves is making me even more nervous.

"What are you planning to say in the speech?" I ask her. There's a slight tremor in my voice.

"Planning is not really my style," she says with a shrug. "I'm just going to wing it."

The alarm bells are now deafening.

"What does that mean? You don't know what you're going to say?"

She shoves a mammoth piece of lettuce into her mouth, but that doesn't stop her from talking. "I don't know now, but when I get up there…" She fires a finger gun at me.

"What does *this* mean?" I shoot her back.

"Magic."

"Oh god. Please don't mention I'm your boss. And make sure to call me Taliah."

"I can't talk about working together?"

"No! Absolutely not! We're supposed to be friends, not coworkers."

"Aww, that was half my speech. I was going to tell everyone about the time that guest spit on you because you yelled at him."

He wiped his mouth on a brand new tablecloth! I mean hello?!

Aya is lost in thought. I can only imagine the insane horrors that lie in her mind.

"Then what do I say?" she asks, not quite looking nervous, but not looking as confident anymore.

"I'm sorry to interrupt your meal," DJ Brain Damage says through the speakers, "but it's time for the maid of honor speech. Please put your hands together for Aya Wang."

Everyone claps as they turn to the head table. Aya and I both duck down, hiding behind the large flower arrangement.

"Just make up something," I quickly whisper.

The spotlight finds her and I start to get really nervous. Why did I tell her to make something up? Why did I pick her? She's crazy. She's unhinged. I went to her house to pick her up for work once and a raccoon answered the door. Not literally, but it was hanging out behind her legs.

Aya is all smiles as she stands up and takes the microphone from the DJ.

I feel twitchy all over.

"Hey, party people," she says to a smattering of laughs. "Taliah is my BFF and always will be."

At least she didn't call me Zoe…

"I've known her since we were little kids throwing nails on the street so we didn't have to chase down the ice cream truck."

Oh no. Does she know Taliah is from Turkey? Do they even have ice cream trucks in Turkey?

"She was my neighbor growing up and we played every day after school."

She's going to blow it. I have to do something before she blurts out that we lived in Connecticut or somewhere else that doesn't sound like it would be in Turkey.

I pick up my wine glass and hold it in front of my lips. "Turkey," I hiss. "Taliah lived in Turkey!"

Aya smiles at the crowd and then picks up her wine glass too. She takes a small sip and then holds it in front of her mouth. "Taliah lived with a Turkey? Cool."

"No!" I hiss as she lowers the glass and turns back to the crowd. *"Aya!"*

Shit. She's talking again.

"And of course, Taliah lived with that turkey she loved so much. What was his name again? Gobbles?"

"Yup!" I say, nodding my head with an unhinged smile on my face. "It was Gobbles."

Luke chuckles. I kick his leg under the table.

"We loved Gobbles so much," Aya continues. "We always laughed at how the skin hanging off his chin looked like testicles."

Oh. My. God. Did she just say testicles?

I glance down the table at Kathleen who is leaning over, glaring at me. "What the fuck?" she mouths.

"And then poor Gobbles died," Aya continues. "It was Christmas."

I'm staring straight ahead, holding my breath as I tense up all over. The only thing moving is my right eye that keeps twitching.

This is like watching someone driving toward a cliff in slow motion and not being able to stop it.

"Grandpa Taliah chopped his poor head off and we cried and cried and cried."

I swallow hard as I raise my wine glass over my mouth again. "Turkey the *country*. What are you doing?! *Stop* talking about turkeys!"

"Oh," Aya says with her forehead scrunched up.

"And that was in Turkey the country," she says into the mic. "Obviously. Probably why Taliah loved turkeys so much."

She looks down at me and winks like she just pulled off something clever.

"And now she's marrying a turkey. Carter." She pauses for a laugh that doesn't come.

"Wrap it up," I say through clenched teeth.

"So, congratulations to Taliah, Carter, and don't eat turkey. Meat is murder."

She flicks the microphone off and quickly sits down. There's silence until a few people start clapping politely.

The DJ exhales hard as he takes the microphone away. "That... was a speech."

"Thank you," Aya says, the non-compliment going right over her head.

"Did you have to say testicles?" I ask her once everyone's attention is back on their tables.

She shrugs as she eats her salad. "That's what they look like. Should I have said balls instead? Is that more polite?"

I take a deep breath, fighting off the migraine that's been lurking around in my skull all day. "It doesn't matter," I whisper to myself. "It's Taliah's life. Not mine."

It's not long before Walter takes the microphone and stands up for his big announcement. He gets a much bigger round of applause than Aya did.

"I'd like to thank everyone for coming to my son Carter and his beautiful bride's wedding." He looks directly at me and I feel the pit in my stomach getting deeper as he raises his glass. "Taliah, welcome to the family."

I'm smiling with clenched teeth as that fucking guy with the fucking spotlight finds me. Again. I *hate* that guy.

All eyes are watching me visibly sweat as I try really hard not to give what Aya calls my 'demented smile.'

Walter thanks some of the more prestigious guests by name as Luke breathes heavier and louder beside me. I put my hand on his and he squeezes my fingers in gratitude.

Walter goes on and on until he sucks in a breath and puffs his chest out. It's coming…

"Which brings me to a big announcement for Carter, Taliah, and the entire Whitfield family. I will be running for President in the upcoming election."

The crowd roars their approval as Walter closes his eyes and holds his arms out like a modern-day Jesus, only instead of helping the poor, he helps corporations get tax cuts.

I clap, but Luke can't seem to bring himself to. His arms are folded across his chest.

"Clap, *Carter*," I say as I elbow his bicep.

He unfolds his arms and gives three lazy claps.

Once Walter has had his fill of adoration for the moment, he continues. "I haven't selected my running mate, but my number one mate is here. My stunning wife, Kathleen."

She takes his hand and stands up as the crowd cheers. Maybe he does have a shot at winning…

"Ladies and gentleman," the DJ roars through the speakers, "the future President of the United States of America and the future First Lady, who is a lovely, *lovely* woman!"

Kathleen shoots him a venomous look.

"Keep that clapping going," DJ Brain Damage says as Walter takes her hand and brings her to the dance floor. "Their wedding song…"

There's a collective awwww from the crowd, which turns into a cheer as the big blue curtain hanging on the far wall gets yanked back, revealing a band.

"…performed by Mr. Marvin Hill and The Rolling Hills!"

Luke drops his head with a groan, but even I get caught up in the excitement, clapping my hands as I perk up in my seat. I *love* Marvin Hill. My parents used to listen to him during happier times and I still remember them slow dancing around the kitchen to his first record.

My pulse starts racing when I hear the familiar twang of the guitar.

It's *Kindred Soul*. I *love* this song.

Marvin must be in his early eighties, but he can still work the room as he struts around in his famous lavender suit, his big smile on display as he sings.

"Nothing gives me shivers like your voice
I'll stand on a mountain and rejoice
Girl, if it brings me back to you
I don't know what else to do."

Walter spins Kathleen on the dance floor and I'm caught up in the moment, watching with a big goofy grin on my face. They may be terrible, toxic people, but at least they're perfect for one another. At least they belong together.

I want a love like that. Not the toxic part, the perfect for one another part. I want someone to look at me like that after decades of marriage. I want to have a song with someone. I want to be happy.

Marvin gets to the chorus and everyone sings along, including me.

"My piece, my part, my whole
My love, my sweet kindred soul."

He continues with the chorus and I feel heated eyes on me. I turn and Luke is staring at me with a blank face.

"What?"

"You can't be buying this."

I shrug. "I like this song. It's a classic. And come on, your parents are literally the worst, but they're also kind of cute."

His mouth falls open. "Cute?"

He turns and watches his parents on the dance floor. His father dips his mother and people cheer.

"Not cute." His jaw clenches as he watches them. "No. They are bad people. This is a show. It's theater. It's bullshit."

I look at him and see no love in his eyes as he watches them.

"You want to know their true colors?" he says while they dance. "When I was a kid, about sixteen, I used to play hockey in a few towns over. My father called it a 'lower income' area. Mom called it 'beneath our stature.' I liked it because the kids weren't so preppy and entitled like they were around our house. I had a best friend, Pratham. He couldn't skate very fast, but everyone dove out of the way when he let his slap shot loose."

He smiles, the warm nostalgic kind of smile that's tainted with sadness.

"I practically lived at his house in the summer. His family was always so welcoming to me. They owned a laundromat and dry cleaning business and lived on top of it. Pratham was their only child, so they didn't mind having me around to keep him occupied."

Walter takes the microphone from Marvin Hill and sings a verse to Kathleen who's pretending to swoon. He's not nearly as good as Marvin, but the crowd doesn't seem to mind.

"One day we were playing hockey. It was in February. A Sunday. One of the kids showed off their own slap shot and the puck struck Pratham in the forehead."

"Oh god," I gasp, my hand flying to my mouth.

"He dropped immediately. Completely unresponsive. It was bad. I called his parents as someone called an ambulance. I rode with him in the ambulance to the hospital and Mr. and Mrs. Khatri met us there. He still hadn't woken up. They were devastated and taking it really hard. He was their only kid."

I get choked up as I watch Luke get choked up.

"His brain was swelling up. The hospital wasn't equipped to deal with it. He had to be airlifted to a hospital in Baltimore, but the goddamn helicopter company wanted cash since Pratham had no insurance. Mr. and Mrs. Khatri didn't have anything close to that and didn't know what to do. I borrowed their car and raced home. I caught my father just as he was leaving to play squash. I still remember he had a red jacket on and was loading his racket into his Bentley. I asked him for the eighty thousand dollars and he blew me off."

I look at Walter smiling as he hands the microphone back to Marvin and spins his wife.

"I tried to explain the situation and he kept brushing me off, saying he was late for his game. I begged him. I cried. I asked him to take it out of my college fund. My inheritance. I told him Pratham could die. He said that his parents should have gotten insurance, that it was the responsible thing to do. He spouted some bullshit, saying he wouldn't be doing them any favors in the long run if he helped their bad planning."

Luke shakes his head and glares at them as he takes a sip of water.

"I stood in the driveway and watched as the man who always claimed to be 'doing good for the people' backed away and drove off, leaving my best friend and his family in the lurch. I had to go back to the hospital and break Pratham's parents' hearts. Pratham died that night. The doctors tried to save him, but his brain swelled up and his heart stopped. All because *that* man refused to spend a small, tiny, insignificant fraction of his net worth to save his life."

I sigh as Luke squeezes the napkin on his lap.

"He showed up at the funeral, even though I told him he wasn't welcome. When I saw him sign an autograph, I snapped. I clocked him right in the mouth. Chipped his tooth. So no, Zoe, these people aren't cute. They're evil. This is all a show for the cameras, for the voters, for those idiot news-casters who fall for this bullshit every time instead of doing their jobs and finding out what kind of a man my father really is."

He crosses his flexed arms and looks at me. I can feel the frustration and hurt emanating off him.

"I hate this fucking song," Luke growls. "Two sociopaths claiming to be kindred souls when they don't have one between the two of them."

I swallow hard as I watch them dancing with dazzling smiles on their faces as they perform for the crowd.

I have to agree with him on that one.

These people are soulless.

CHAPTER Sixteen

Walter gives Kathleen one more dip as Marvin Hill finishes *Kindred Soul*. The band jumps right into *Candy Apple Baby* and half the wedding guests rush to the dance floor for the upbeat song as Marvin Hill spins around with a holler.

Aya leaps up and runs onto the dance floor with Ryan following close behind.

The spirited playful energy is contagious for everyone except for Luke. He's sitting there staring at it all like an old man watching skateboarders getting perilously close to his driveway.

"Want to get out of here?" I ask him.

His face softens when he turns to me. "More than anything."

"Give me a minute."

I dart out of my seat and head over to Frank. For some reason, he's putting Ryan's leftover steak into a plastic sandwich bag. He quickly shoves it into his jacket pocket when he sees me approaching.

"Frank," I say, letting my desperation show. "If I was your

real daughter, would you do me a huge favor on my wedding day?"

"You bet your butt I would. What do you need?"

Minutes later, Luke, Frank, and I are sneaking into the parking garage under the inn. There is an abundance of black limos down here, but Frank knows exactly where his is parked.

"Where are we headed?" he asks as he opens the back door for us.

"I heard something about a dive bar down the street?" I lost my first two guests to it. If I see Mario and Luigi in there eating soggy nachos instead of my crispy fig and olive crackers, I might have to give them a piece of my mind.

"I know the place," Frank says. "Let your daddy take care of it for you."

Ew. That turned from thoughtful to cringe real fast, like when your phone company texts you happy birthday and then charges you for it.

Luke snickers as he gets into the limo.

"Shut up," I mutter as I follow him in and sit across from him.

Relief hits me as we drive out of the inn and pull onto the street. I roll down the window and let the cool breeze wash over my face, happier than I've been in a while.

I catch Luke watching me, but this time, he doesn't look away. He doesn't hide it. He smiles warmly as he lets his head rest on the seat and his eyes rest on me.

I wish I could take a picture of him like this—tie loose, jacket open, relaxed grateful look on his gorgeous face. If this was our real wedding, it would be my favorite photo of the night.

"That's where you're taking me?" Luke says as Frank pulls into the parking lot of the dive bar.

I chuckle when I look outside.

It's certainly a dive bar. It's just called The Bar, but the r of the neon sign is burnt, so it reads The Ba. The owners seem to have put as much effort into the appearance as they did in choosing the name. It's a rundown dilapidated structure with a porch that's leaning to the left and missing two stairs.

"I didn't think it would be this bad," I say as I spot a few guys hanging by their motorcycles outside.

"If my parents aren't here, it's perfect."

Luke's eyes are full of gratitude. This is exactly what we both need: a break from this horrible day.

Heads turn as we walk in, but even a woman in a wedding dress can't keep the men from turning back to the baseball game on the TV. Johnny Cash is playing on the jukebox and there are a smattering of professional drinkers lounging in the duct-taped scarred booths. There's a dart board in the corner with no darts. They've probably been missing since the nineties, which is a good thing since the beer is only $2 according to the sign over the bar.

Frank heads over to the poker machines and starts talking to the grizzled old man hunched at the machine next to him.

Luke and I head to the bar. The floor is as sticky as you'd expect in a place like this, but I don't even care that the train of my wedding dress is dragging on it, probably picking up cigarette butts, bottle caps, and the odd tooth from last night's bar fight.

Ever the gentleman, Luke takes the wobbly bar stool and gives me the one with the gash down the middle of the pleather cushion.

"What can I get you two lovebirds?" the bartender grunts as he approaches. On paper, he has the look of a hipster—long beard, curled moustache, arms full of tattoos—but with him, it's not ironic. Or stylish. The bird's nest of a beard hanging off his chin looks like it's based in laziness, not style, and the tattoos on his arms look like they were drawn by a toddler who scribbled on his grandad while he was napping on the couch.

"Can I see a menu?" I ask, looking around for drink ideas. Everyone is drinking draft beer.

"We don't have a menu." He waves an unenthusiastic arm at the basic bottles on the shelf. "What you see is what you get."

"Two Jaegermeisters," Luke orders. I look at him. "What? You said you loved Jaegermeister."

"I thought it was a board game."

He laughs. So do I.

"It's not?"

"It's a drink."

"Oh. Well, I'm sure I'll like it."

He shakes his head and chuckles. "I'm sure you won't."

The bartender puts two shots in front of us and my nose crinkles up from reflex. This looks like something I should be putting into the engine of my car. I smell it and my eyes start to water.

"Is this demon blood?" I ask while examining the red liquid.

"Just try it."

We clink glasses and then I down the fiery liquid. It burns and unleashes a coughing fit that has heads turning.

Luke smiles at me. He took his like a champ.

"Ugh," I say with another cough. "I'll never forgive you for that. That tasted like poison."

"You said you liked it," he says with a shrug of his big shoulders. "I'll let you pick the next drink."

I wave the bartender over and he takes our empty shots. "If

you lovebirds are looking for a honeymoon spot, we got a room out back for rent. Twelve bucks a night."

Twelve bucks? Wow, I bet it even comes with free bedbugs.

"We're good, thanks," Luke says as he shoots me a look out of the corner of his eye. "Just a couple more drinks."

"Can we get something fruity?" I ask. "A cocktail with a pineapple on it or something?"

"Fruity?" the bartender repeats with a blank stare. "We have maraschino cherries and dried-up orange slices."

I sigh. "Two beers, please. And one for the guy on the poker machine."

I'm very aware of my heartbeat as the bartender leaves to get our beers. It's just me and Luke. There's no one next to either of us. No buffers. No guests or unwanted family members interrupting every thirty seconds. It's just us.

It almost feels like a date.

"What do you think Heather is going to do when she realizes we're gone?" he asks with a grin.

"I'm glad we won't be around to find out," I say with a laugh. "Did you see her flirting with the DJ?"

"DJ Brain Damage?"

I nod.

"Wow," Luke says with a grin. "Imagine the very organized, very brain-damaged children they'll have."

The bartender slides our beers in front of us and I sit back with a moan as I take a delicious sip.

Luke is smiling as he watches me.

"What?" I ask, sitting up and suddenly feeling self-conscious.

"Nothing, it's just… I like seeing you like this."

"Like what?"

"Smiling. Happy. Having fun…"

"I'm *a ton* of fun," I remind him.

He smiles as he takes a sip of his beer. "I can see that now."

It's nice to see him like this too. Away from all his family and all the aggravations they cause. I wonder what he would be like on a real date. Maybe it wouldn't be so bad…

"I think we collided into each other's lives at a stressful time for both of us," I say.

"Yeah," he says with a sigh. "I would have done things differently if I knew the kind of girl you were."

I lean forward, playfully narrowing my eyes at him. "And what kind of girl is that?"

"The keeping kind."

I'm not sure if it's from the shot or the way he's looking at me, but my whole body fills with a warm glow. I'm tingling all over.

I want to tease more compliments out of him. I want him to bare his soul to me. I want this to be a night that changes everything.

But I'm a chicken, so I change the subject.

"I'm sorry to hear about your friend. If you liked him, I'm sure he was a really nice kid."

"He was," Luke says with a sad smile. "I know I'd still be friends with him if he was alive today."

"For sure."

He takes a deep breath and exhales slowly. "You asked me what I was getting out of this."

"You don't have to tell me," I quickly say. "That's between you and your father."

"No, I want you to know. The reason why I didn't go to college was because I gave it away."

"Your college tuition?"

He nods. "Mr. and Mrs. Khatri were so excited for Pratham to go to college. He was going to be the first one in the family to go. Pratham was working so hard to get an academic scholarship and he was going to get one too. At the funeral, I had promised his parents that I'd set up an annual scholarship in his name. I told them Pratham couldn't go to college, but because of him, every year someone who wouldn't be able to afford tuition would be able to go. They were so happy. So touched. They both cried. I cried. But it was all bullshit. I didn't know it at the time, but I was lying to them. Lying to grieving parents who had just buried their son."

"Luke..."

He pushes on. "I tried to get my father to help me set it up and help fund it, but he said no. My mom's side said no. My grandma offered to pay for one kid. I've been ashamed of this for a decade. I couldn't do it on my own."

"But you gave your college fund away," I tell him. "That's nothing to be ashamed of. Someone got to go to college because of you, because of Pratham."

"Yeah and he dropped out senior year," he says with a laugh. "I can really pick a winner, can't I?"

We both look down at the carvings on the bar. Someone named Doug carved his name into it three times. I hope he doesn't show up tonight because I'm clearly in his seat.

"If I act as the groom tonight, my father agreed to fund the foundation for ten years. That's only ten kids who get to go to college."

"That's great, Luke. I'm sure Mr. and Mrs. Khatri will be thrilled. You're going to change the lives of those ten kids."

"It's not even close to what I promised them."

"Don't be so hard on yourself," I say as I place my hand on his. The feel of his warm skin sends heat coursing through me. "You're doing what you can."

"No, I'm not," he says with a sigh. "You said it yourself, right? I was born into a family who can get things done and I ran away to a small town and hid from the responsibility."

"I said that before I knew the story. Before I knew you."

"Doesn't make it any less true."

"It does a bit."

We sit in a comfortable silence for a few seconds, glancing up at the baseball game playing over the bar. I never understood why it takes the pitcher so long to throw the dang ball. Do they get paid by the hour or something?

"You know I can help you set the charity up," I say.

He looks at me without a word.

"I would have loved to have had the opportunity to go to college when I was younger," I say, starting to get into it. I can feel my heart thumping and adrenaline coursing through my veins like it always does when I get excited about a new idea. "It would be nice to help others have the opportunities that I didn't."

"That would require you seeing me again," he says with a raised chin and narrow eyes. "You sure you're ready for that?"

"I mean…" I'm trying to act cool and calm, but my hot blushing cheeks are betraying me. "It wouldn't be the worst thing in the world."

"That's not what you said this morning."

"A lot has happened since then. We got married for one."

He grins as he takes a sip of his beer. A part of me wants to watch his lips on the cold glass and another part wants to watch his strong hand wrapped around the handle. I glance at his Adam's apple bobbing while the two parts battle it out.

"So," he says as he puts the mug down with a thump. "You want to see me again?"

"Maybe for the divorce settlements…"

"How about for a date?"

I choke out a cough. *Smooth, Zoe…*

"A date?"

He grins. "This is all out of order, but after we get divorced, I'd love to take you out."

"Me?"

He laughs. "Yes, you, Zoe. I like you."

I'm not sure if I believe him. If he's setting me up for some kind of trick. Luke likes *me?*

"Where do you live exactly?"

"Horrendland Pond. It's a small town about two hours away."

"Never heard of it."

"That's probably a good thing."

I laugh. "Two hours… That's far."

"Before you answer, I'm seriously thinking of moving back to DC."

I perk up in my seat. "Really?"

He nods. "I have an employee, but there's not enough business for both of us. He has a baby girl at home, so I don't want to lay him off. I was thinking of leaving him to it and starting a larger shop in DC."

"That's… interesting." *Very* interesting.

"Living in DC would allow me to work on the charity on the side. I've been thinking about all of this for a while, but I've just needed a push. I think I finally found one."

He's staring right at me as he says it. The air charges with heat between us. He leans in, my body follows.

"Will you go out with me, Zoe?"

I turn away and take a deep breath. Did someone crank the thermostat up?

The empty pool table in the corner catches my eye.

"Beat me in pool and I'll go out with you."

He glances over at it. "If I beat you, I get a date?"

"Yeah."

"And a kiss?"

I grin. There's no way he's going to beat me. "Sure."

He hops off his stool and heads over with his beer. I follow him with mine.

My eyes are glued to him as he takes off his jacket and hangs it on a hook. I swallow hard as I watch him roll his sleeves up his thick forearms like it's my own private show. He catches me checking him out, but is a gentleman and doesn't say a word about it.

Luke pulls two cues off the rack and hands one to me. I walk right up to him and take it. "I'm breaking."

I'm all business as I chalk up my cue while he puts some quarters in and racks the balls. My game face is on. I wouldn't mind going on a date with Luke, but there's no way I'm going to let him win.

I grab the cue ball and toss it up and down a few times as he removes the rack.

"You look good with a ball in your hand," he says with a mischievous grin. His eyes roam over my body before slowly making their way back to my face.

I line up and break it *hard*. The balls crack. He winces.

Three solids drop in.

The look on his face… omg, priceless.

"Are you hustling me, Fitzpatrick?"

I lean down low and line up my shot. I can feel his heated eyes on me and for the first time today, I'm not bothered by the amount of cleavage I'm showing.

"That's Captain Fitzpatrick to you."

The seven is an easy shot, but I'm in the mood to show off a little. I bounce it off the long rail and sink the three in with a backspin. Luke whistles low.

"How do you know how to do that?" he asks as I slowly get up and look for my next shot.

"I know how to do everything," I answer with a smirk.

I strut around the table and spot myself in a mirror hanging on the wall. I'm in a wedding dress in a dive bar, playing pool. This day has certainly gone off the rails.

I nail a spot shot—very tricky shot—which sets me up to easily tap in the two.

"Seriously," Luke says with his jaw hanging open. "How do you know how to play like this?"

"My dad had a table," I say as I drop the one in the side pocket. "I never had many friends growing up and it was a game I could play by myself. I got really good."

He laughs. "I can see that."

"There's a table in my building," I say as I lean down and line up my shot. "It's like meditation for me. I go up there a few times a week and my mind quiets down."

I methodically sink my remaining balls like a pro and then put the eight ball away. Luke is staring at me in shock as I toss the cue on the table and walk over to my beer.

"I don't get a turn?"

I laugh at the look on his face. It's like he doesn't quite know what hit him.

"Sorry, biker boy." I take a long swig of my beer. "The game's over. You lost."

"I guess that means no date and no kiss…"

I won the game but lost out on the prize. There's nothing more I want right now than to wrap my arms around Luke's neck and feel his soft lips on mine.

I grin.

I have moxie.

Moxie girls don't ask for permission or wait to be kissed. They go for anything and everything they want with grace, grit, and guts.

I start clinking my beer mug with the wedding ring on my pinkie. Luke laughs. I don't stop until the whole bar is turned and clinking their mugs with forks and lighters, cheering us on to kiss.

Luke stands there, eying me shamelessly with a hungry look.

The pool table is between us. I lower my beer onto the edge of it, my skin prickling with desire as I drink the stunning sight of him in.

Our eyes never leave each other as I climb on the table and crawl to him. The clinking gets louder when we're face to face, our lips almost touching… so close… I can taste his breath and it gets five delicious stars.

His strong hands grab me and I gasp as he pulls me against his hard body.

My arms slide around his neck as his heated eyes drop to my lips.

I'm shivering from anticipation… I'm melting with need…

He lowers his lips and our mouths connect. It's like lightning. It's like magic. It's like heaven.

His lips are so soft. His tongue is so fucking incredible.

More… I want *more…*

I grab a fistful of his shirt and yank him against me.

He kisses me deeper, devouring my mouth as I devour his.

His hands on my hips… the grip tightens… he pulls me into him…

Yes…

The desperation… the intensity… I've never been kissed like this before…

Everyone hollers and cheers like they did back at the wedding, only this time, it's better.

This time, it's on our terms.

This time, it's our choice.

This time, it's real.

CHAPTER
Seventeen

I could stay in this bar forever, but there's only so long a bride can disappear during her wedding before people start to ask questions.

We get Frank—who was very happy to win nine dollars on the poker machine—and head outside.

"Stupid tin can piece of shit," one of the bikers hisses as he kicks the tire of his motorcycle.

"It won't start?" Luke asks as we're heading to the limo.

"Nope," the man says as he yanks the handkerchief off his head and assaults his motorcycle with it. "Useless fucking bike!"

Luke looks at me, the moonlight shining in his blue eyes, and my breath lodges in my throat. "Would you mind if I take a quick look?"

"I'm in no hurry to get back," I say with a grin.

He takes off his jacket and I can feel my eyes widening as they roam over his chest, spotting the enticing patches of skin visible between the stretched-out buttons.

"Would you?" he asks as he holds out his jacket.

I struggle to hide my enthusiasm as I casually, cooly,

nonchalantly take it and hang it over my arm. The second he turns and walks away, I bring it to my nose and inhale his intoxicating scent. The warm sexy smell fills my lungs and sends shivers tingling through me. *Mmmm, that's good.*

"I'm a mechanic," Luke says as he rolls up his sleeves and takes over.

"Thank you," the biker says, looking relieved. He looks at me and his face scrunches up. "Are you guys headed to some kind of costume party?"

"Something like that," Luke answers as he crouches down and starts examining the bike.

Frank walks over with his shoulders back and his chest puffed out. "I can help too," he says in a voice that's deeper than it has been all night. "I don't like the look of that gear head. Must be over torked."

I can tell by the way Luke looks up at him that those are not real words and that Frank has no idea what he's talking about.

With the rugged scent of Luke's cologne swirling in my head, I watch him as he inspects the motor. I'm not usually into a man who's good with his hands, but it's really doing something for me now. I take a deep breath as my eyes wander over his large muscular back. His shirt is strained tight against it, lit up with the warm saturated glow of the moon.

My mind heads to some lewd places. I'm picturing all sorts of dirty things. Things that would leave Luke's oil-stained fingerprints all over my body.

I suck in a long breath of the cool night air as I watch him do what he does best. I have to be careful here.

I have a tendency to go all-in with things. I get too intense. Too attached. Too quickly.

Guys don't like that.

It seems like every time I'm interested in someone, they cut and run. Maybe I'm too passionate, too all-consuming, too eager, or all of the above, but it's the only way I know how to operate.

I have two modes of being: off or all-in. There's no in-between.

That works great when you're running a business, not so great when you're trying to fall in love.

I can feel myself starting to fall hard for this man. I have to try and reign in my eagerness a bit, temper my intensity, or he's going to run like the rest of them did.

Luke cranks the engine and nothing happens. "It's your spark plug," he says as he looks up at the owner.

"That's what I was going to say," Frank adds, practically hanging over Luke's shoulder. "Definitely the spark plug."

The guy thanks Luke as I take one last quick delicious whiff of his jacket before I have to surrender it back.

It's like my own private show as I watch him take it and slide it up his big hard arms. His collar is folded in on itself and I rush in before he can fix it.

"Hello," he whispers as I reach around his neck and flip the collar up. Our mouths are so close. Closer than necessary, but still way too far apart for my liking.

I want to stand on my toes and tease another magical kiss out of him, but I have to play it cool if I want to advance to the next level with this man. My instincts always lead to a short ending. Thank you, play again. Next.

I don't want it to end like that this time. So quick. So sudden. I want to try for something real with Luke.

He groans as I pull away with a smirk on my lips.

"You're cruel," he whispers as I spin away.

I give him a wink over my shoulder. "Welcome to married life, my love."

The drive back is way too short and before we know it, the

limo is parked and we're in the elevator heading back up to the hall.

Our chaperone Frank is eating from another sandwich bag and the unsexy crunching of his trail mix is the only thing keeping Luke and I from jumping each other's bones. I can see it in the ravenous way he's watching me from across the elevator.

"Thanks for the break, Frank," I say when the doors open with a ding. The sight and sounds of guests everywhere makes me want to cringe.

"My pleasure," he says as he stuffs the bag into his pocket and walks out. "Consider it a wedding present."

Luke steps beside me and offers his arm. God, that smile… it kills me every time. I'm powerless against it. It's magically delicious.

I wrap my arm around his and our eyes linger on each other before we walk out. Heads turn. People smile and whisper. The photographers find us and start snapping away like Paparazzi harassing a world-famous power couple.

I feel like a bombshell on this man's arm. Like an Oscar-winning actress. I feel like I can do anything.

I imagine us like this at our real wedding and then remind myself to tone it down. I go all-in. It's a problem. I'm quite aware.

But still, I can't control my thoughts and I definitely can't control the way my body reacts to his. It's like we're operating on the same electrical current. The same bodily wavelength. The same emotional frequency.

I step a little closer to him, letting the side of my breast graze his arm as we walk. He notices. Of course he does. Guys have finely tuned boob radar and Luke is no different.

We jump apart like two kids caught with their hands in an Oreo box when we see Kathleen enter the room. There's no chance of blending in while wearing a wedding dress, so she spots me immediately.

She charges over with her hands balled into fists and her eyes practically feral. "Where the hell have you two been?" she hisses like a cat being forced to take a cold bath. "People are starting to notice. The Ambassador of France asked me if you two went back to your hotel room to make love!"

"What did you tell him?" I should just keep my mouth shut, but I'm curious.

"Her," she snaps. "And I told *her* you did."

"Mom," Luke says with a sigh. "That's a foreign diplomat."

She waves a dismissive hand. "Oh, it's just France. I don't understand all the hype. These people are known for style, but have you ever seen their flag? *Ugh*. Blue, white, and red. Three rectangles in a row. It's a flag for heaven's sake, take longer than ten seconds to design it."

"Well, we're back now," Luke says, starting to move past her and taking me with him.

"Don't you walk away from me!" she snaps as she jumps back in front of him. "Don't forget who's going to sign your check."

Her vicious eyes dart from her son to me.

"Don't think I was bluffing," she warns in a low voice. "I always follow through on my threats."

"What threats?" Luke asks. He looks at my face and I must look as pale as I feel because he steps forward while pulling me back protectively.

"This is between us," Kathleen says dismissively.

Luke doesn't back down. "What threats?" His voice is louder, more forceful. Kathleen looks around with a nervous smile on her face. Luke's eyes are locked on her like he doesn't care who hears.

"It's nothing," Kathleen whispers. "Just part of the deal, that's all."

"You don't threaten her," he growls. "You understand? I'll grab the microphone and tell every single person in here what's going on."

She backs up with fear in her eyes. "What are you getting so worked up for?"

That's when she spots our hands clasped together. He's squeezing me tight enough not to hurt, but tight enough to let me know he's got my back.

I'm really digging this growly protective version of Luke. No one has ever stood up for me like this before. I don't even know how to react, so I just let him take care of the situation. Letting someone else take over is a novel concept for me, but so far it feels nice not to have to be the one leading the charge for once.

"She's done everything you've asked," he says, not backing down. "You leave her alone."

"I see," Kathleen says with a sneer. "You've fallen for the help. I guess we're not the first great family in history to have one of their own fall for a pretty-faced servant. Probably the first one in history to fall for the one in the parking lot though."

"You stay away from her," Luke warns in a tone I wouldn't mess with. "I'm going to dance with my bride."

Kathleen stares open-jawed as he pulls me away. I want to ask her about the status of the seamstress, but I don't think it's very often that the queen of mean is put in her place and I don't want to ruin the moment.

Her eyes narrow ominously on me as I get swallowed into the crowd. I'm going to pay for that later.

Luke is barreling through the crowd and dragging me along with him. He looks tense. His back is all tight and he's moving fast enough that I have to hurry to keep up. These damn Barbie doll shoes are making that difficult.

People turn to talk to him, but he ignores them all as he pulls me into the ballroom. He heads straight for the DJ.

"Say You Won't Let Go," he says to DJ Brain Damage. "James Arthur. You got it?"

"Internet, baby!" DJ Brain Damage says with a nod. "I got everything."

"Put it on. I want to dance with my girl."

My girl.

"Coming up!" The DJ gets to work and slows down the song, an oldie that has everyone dancing, and puts on the tune that Luke requested.

The tension seems to ease out of him as he guides me onto the dance floor while the ethereal sound of a soft guitar strumming ripples through the speakers.

Bodies part as we approach. He leads me to the middle of the dance floor, under the huge chandelier.

The soft lights are hitting the crystals, painting us in tiny reflections and making it feel like an enchanting surreal dream.

Couples old and new pair up around us as Luke turns with a tender smile. We come together, my palms sliding up his chest as his hands fall on my arms and then slide down to my hips. We fit so perfectly.

He's looking down at me like I'm the most beautiful thing he's ever seen.

My heart flutters. My cheeks glow. Our hips sway to the beautiful song as we gaze at each other, completely absorbed in one another's eyes.

This man makes me feel so special. So seen. So wanted.

Those are all new sensations for me and I don't know how to deal with any of them. I'm learning on the fly here. This is all uncharted territory.

I take his hand in mine and look at the ring I put on his finger.

Luke must not like my eyes off him because he gently takes my jaw and tilts my mouth up. My lips part as I taste his hot minty breath.

Our mouths are so close…

I swallow a moan as the yearning intensifies.

I want him something fierce. It's unlike anything I've ever felt before. It's unexpected. It's unnerving. It's unreal.

His big hands slide onto my lower back and he lifts me and spins me around slowly. I'm fixated on his heated blue eyes as my dress twirls at my feet.

Luke lowers me back to the floor, but doesn't loosen his grip. Our foreheads come together as we watch each other with silly enthralled grins on our faces. I'm falling hard…

I can feel it in every cell in my body from my curled toes to my tingling fingertips. I'm getting lost in this man. He's addictive. He's intoxicating. I want him to be all mine.

He smiles warmly as I slide my hands up to the back of his head, threading my fingers through his soft short hair.

My mouth tilts up. Our lips hover within kissing distance.

I feel so hyper-aware in every spot his body touches. I have goosebumps on my arms. The hair on the back of my neck is standing straight up.

We're surrounded by people, but it feels like we're the only ones in the room. The couples all around us fade away. We're Belle and the Beast in the empty ballroom. It's just us left on the planet.

I close my eyes and curl into his body, resting my cheek on his chest as he holds me like he's never going to let go. He kisses my hair as we softly sway to the music as one. With a moan, he rests his chin on top of my head.

Everything feels different now. It feels amplified. Exciting. Magical.

I hope I'm not the only one feeling it, but I don't think I am. The way he looks at me… the way it makes me feel… that can't be one-sided.

The universe isn't that cruel.

I sigh as the song ends and our romantic moment is over.

He cups my cheeks as I look up at him.

"You're beautiful," he whispers as he gazes into my eyes. "Breathtaking in every way."

Another love song comes on, but this one is a bit more upbeat—*Lover* by Taylor Swift. Instead of holding their partners tight, the couples around us begin to move a bit more and do the occasional spin.

"You're not too bad yourself," I tell him with a flirtatious look. "You're kind of hot when you're yelling at your mother."

He throws his head back and laughs. I feel a warmth clenching my core at the sexy rumbling sound.

"Yelling at my mother, huh? Any other weird kinks I should know about?"

"You'll find out on the honeymoon."

He smiles as he holds me a little tighter. "I can't wait."

We dance a little more as the intoxicating scent of his cologne swirls in my lungs and makes me lightheaded in the best possible way.

Our eyes are never off each other for long. They connect once again and I get that familiar fluttering in my stomach. The night is moving way too fast. I don't want it to end.

"Yes, Luke," I whisper to him.

"Yes, what?"

"Yes, I would love to go on a date with you."

His eyes light up as he smiles. "I'm thrilled to hear that."

We stare at each other with big goofy smiles on our faces.

We're kids experiencing puppy love for the first time. We're seniors still holding hands after fifty years of love. We're full of hope and excitement with only a touch of fear mixed in to keep things interesting.

The song finishes and *Hey Ya!* by Outkast comes blaring on. That's my cue to leave.

I push away from Luke about to hurry off the dance floor and head for the safety of the carpet, but Victoria pops up in front of me, refusing to let me pass.

"We're dancing!" she says as she shakes her hips and pushes me back to Luke.

"I have to—"

"Nope!" she says with a grin.

Luke catches me and smiles as he turns me around. His hips are moving so seductively as he dances in front of me. I know I wouldn't be able to leave now if I tried. My eyes are fixated on him.

Aya and Ryan pop out of the crowd and start dancing with us. "Wooooo!" Aya shouts as she shakes her shoulders like a Polaroid picture. Ryan watches her with his tongue practically hanging out.

Victoria takes my hand and shows me some moves. I follow along and add some fun new moves of my own. We're all in a circle, laughing and singing and dancing and having a blast.

The tension and self-consciousness melts out of me and happiness takes over. This is fun. *Really* fun.

I swallow hard when I see the heated intensity brimming in Luke's eyes as he watches me move. Maybe I was all wrong about dancing. It has its uses.

Aya whispers something in Ryan's ear and his eyes bulge out as his cheeks turn red.

"Hey," I say as I dance over to Aya. "How is it going in the tent?"

"No way!" she snaps. "This is your wedding, Z. No work talk. Let's fucking party!"

Her enthusiasm is contagious and I can't help but laugh as she jumps up with a holler.

I let it all go. The stress, the worries, the ambition, the discipline. I release it all on the dance floor and let myself have some much-needed fun.

And it feels incredible.

CHAPTER
Eighteen

We're all sweaty, but still going strong. The energetic crowd is alive all around us, dancing like it's our last night on earth. Dancing like there's no tomorrow.

Victoria's excitement is contagious and I'm having fun as I try to keep up with her.

"You're cool," she yells in my face over the music.

"Really?" I shout back, not quite believing her.

"Yeah! You should totally come to my show next Friday with Luke."

"Okay!" I say, maybe a little too quickly. A little too eagerly. "If it's okay with Luke."

She grins knowingly as she looks at her brother. "I think it will be okay with him," she says with a chuckle.

I can't stop smiling as she dances away.

With a burst of energy, I turn and narrow my eyes playfully on Luke. He smiles as I dance up to him, biting my bottom lip.

"I think I have an idea for our first date," I say as I lean in, keeping my swaying body out of his reach. He's not having any of that. I grin as he steps in and puts his arms around me.

"Oh yeah?"

"Your sister invited me to her show," I tell him. "Can I go with you?"

"I'm not waiting a week for our first date," he says as he stares down at me. "How many days is that away? Six? That can be our sixth date."

I laugh as my heart quickens.

"My family likes you," he says.

"Half your family maybe. The other half hates me."

"Yeah, but they hate everyone."

I chuckle. "That's true."

"I like you too. A lot."

I shake my head, not quite believing it. It feels too good to be true. "Why?" I blurt out. "Why do you want to go out with me?"

His eyebrow raises. "Seriously?"

I nod. "Yeah. Seriously."

He takes a deep breath, giving himself a few moments to collect his thoughts. "I wish you could see yourself how I see you. I've never met anyone like you, Zoe. You look at the world and think you can conquer it all. If you were born a thousand years ago, you'd be commanding armies through Europe. I don't know anyone who would've put on that dress and did what you're doing."

"Because I'm so nefarious?"

"No," he says with a fierceness in his tone. "Because you're so brave. You don't let anything stop you."

My breath catches in my throat with the intense way he's looking at me.

"You're compelling to me. I feel myself drawn to you in a way I've never experienced before. I'm captivated in your presence. I have a hard time looking away."

My hand slides down to his and he grips my fingers.

"I'm crushing hard on you, Captain."

I stand on my toes, about to kiss the bottom of his adorable chin when Heather taps my shoulder, killing the moment.

"It's time for the bouquet toss."

"Shit," I mutter. I was having so much fun that I forgot I still had some bridal duties left to perform.

"Where is it?" Heather asks.

"On the table," I say as I look over at my seat. "I'll go get it."

I need a second to process. To think. To sear the image of Luke saying he's crushing hard on me into my brain forever.

With a deep breath, I head over to my seat, smiling at everyone I pass. It's easier to look happy now.

Luke has taken over my brain and I can't believe that I haven't been obsessing over work the entire night. This is so not like me. My crew is working outside, catering my biggest event to date, and I couldn't care less how it's going. They're fine. I trained them well.

I wind around the tables and spot Cindy and yellow dress girl deep in conversation at one of them. Cindy is crying. Again. Yellow dress girl looks fed up.

"Will you grow up?" she snaps. "It was *six* years ago!"

"I love him!" Cindy wails.

They both spot me and I hurry along as Cindy drops her head into her arms with a sob and yellow dress girl gives me an awkward smile and a pathetic wave.

Poor girl. I hope Carter wasn't a jerk to her.

I'm back to thinking about Luke as I arrive at the head table to grab my bouquet.

"What did you do with Taliah?" a voice hisses at me from behind.

I spin around with my heart pounding and jerk my head

back in surprise when I see Lily the flower girl glaring at me with her arms crossed.

"I met Taliah this morning," she says with an evil stare. "You're an imposer."

"An imposter?"

"Don't correct me when I'm confronting you!"

I gulp as she steps forward. This pretty little lady definitely takes after her aunt Kathleen. She's terrifying.

Normally, I wouldn't be so intimidated, but I can't get caught arguing with a seven-year-old in the middle of a crowded place. That would be a lose-lose situation.

"Where's Taliah?" she snaps. "Are you a witch? Did you put a hex on her?"

"Okay, you know those Disney movies are fake, right?"

She leaps forward and grabs a fistful of my dress. "Tell me where Taliah is or I'll rip your dress off!"

I gasp as she gives it a tug and I hear a tear. "Okay! Okay!" I shout in a panic. "I'll tell you everything!"

Her little eyes narrow on me.

"Taliah is the witch," I tell her in a low conspiratorial voice. "I'm a secret princess."

Her eyes widen. "You are?"

"Totally."

She's still not letting go. "Princess of where?"

"Vermontland."

What did Luke tell me? Specific details?

"I don't have much time," I whisper to her. "When the clock strikes twelve…"

She leans in. "Yeah?"

"If I don't find true love…"

"What? Tell me!"

"I'll be turned into a mermaid."

She lets go of my dress as she stares up at me in awe. "How can I help?"

I smile warmly at her. She's so damn cute. Terrifying but cute. "You can give your mom a big hug and tell her you adore her. Can you do that for me?"

She nods her head, lifts my dress to look at my feet, and then darts off to find her mother Tammy.

That was close. I almost had the wrong Whitfield tearing my dress off. That's Luke's job.

I actually pulled that off. I'm getting better at lying. Thanks, Luke! You're corrupting me in all sorts of wonderful new ways.

I'm about to grab the bouquet for the second time when another voice interrupts me.

"You two looked beautiful dancing out there." It's Luke's grandmother Eleanor.

I smile shyly as my eyes drop away from her. "Thank you."

"It's so nice to see my grandson in love," she says, looking thrilled. "Can you bring him around at Christmas? He never comes and I don't know how many of them I have left."

"Oh, Mrs. Whitfield," I say, feeling my shoulders drop and my stomach sink. I can't lie about this anymore. Not to her.

"Eleanor," she corrects.

"Eleanor," I say before taking a deep breath. "I wish I didn't have to say this, but… Luke and I aren't dating."

She tilts her head. "What do you mean?"

"I'm just the caterer. I was working in the parking lot when Taliah left. Kathleen and Walter asked me to step in. I'm not his girlfriend." Ugh. Why do those words come with a stabbing pain in my heart? "I'm nothing."

"You may be a lot of things, dear. But nothing is not one of them."

My eyes dart up to hers.

"And you may have been the caterer when you walked in this morning, but you're not just a caterer anymore. My grandson is quite taken with you."

I open my mouth, but nothing comes out.

"We never know what the day has in store for us," she continues. "There are still a few hours left to go. Anything can happen."

She smiles at me as she plays with the tip of my hair. "Don't count yourself out yet."

"I'm sorry I lied," I eventually say.

"Lying is a sport in this family," she says with a laugh. "You'll get better."

I laugh too. This family is crazy, but it's not all bad.

"Go to him," she says as she nods in his direction. "Embrace the moxie flowing through your veins. Don't hold back."

I look over at Luke and he's watching me from the dance floor. My heart jumps in my chest when our eyes meet.

"Zoe!" Heather snaps, nearly making me leap out of Taliah's shoes. "Deion is waiting for you!"

"Who's Deion?"

"The DJ."

"DJ Brain Damage?"

Heather rolls her eyes. "Just come already."

I grab my bouquet off the table and smile at Eleanor. "Thank you."

"You can thank me by aiming for my daughter," Eleanor says with a sigh. "Try to knock that phone out of her hands. She needs to get laid."

I laugh as I follow Heather back onto the dance floor. The music stops and Heather begins to frantically clear people off.

"Where those single ladies at?" Deion (who will always be DJ Brain Damage to me) hollers into his microphone. "Dance floor time. Catch a bouquet and be the next in line to get married!"

He hits a button on his mixer and Beyonce comes on, screeching about all the single ladies as a bunch of girls rush forward, dancing, hollering, and throwing their hands in the air.

I spot Janet in the crowd, which is easy because the blue light from her cell phone is lighting up her face. Her son Owen is beside her, absorbed in his phone too. He doesn't look up as Eleanor grabs Janet's arm and pulls her onto the dance floor.

"Her," Eleanor mouths as she pushes her into the front row of excited women.

I start dancing too as I turn around and grip the bouquet.

Luke is leaning on the wall in the distance, watching me with a smile on his gorgeous face. I smile shyly as I look down at my flowers. Would it be cheating if I toss it to myself and catch it? I wouldn't mind being the next one to get married.

"The rules!" the DJ shouts as the excitement amps up. "No biting. No kicking. No pulling hair. Keep it clean, ladies. Here we go!"

My heart pounds as all eyes focus on me, only this time, I'm excited too.

"Three… Two… One…"

I throw the bouquet over my head, aiming right for Janet. She doesn't even look up from her phone. It's sailing right for her head, but Victoria leaps in front of her and snatches the flowers out of the air at the last second. She comes down hard on the ground, taking two girls with her. The crowd cheers and bursts out laughing. Victoria thrusts the bouquet into the air triumphantly.

I'm glad she caught it. She deserves some love coming her way.

"Nice catch!" I say when she comes dancing over with it.

"You should try out for the NFL. I didn't know you could tackle."

She laughs as she holds the mangled bouquet of flowers to her nose and smells them. "Thanks. I really need a boyfriend."

We both laugh. "You and me both."

She glances at her brother and smiles. "Maybe, but you're much closer than I am."

I swallow hard. "You think?"

She waves her hand around. "This may all be fake. But you and Luke… That's not fake. I saw the way you were dancing, and where were you after dinner? Forget it! I don't want to know."

My cheeks burn as I look at him looking at me. Someone comes up to him and starts talking, but he never takes his eyes off me.

"I think you should go for it," Victoria says with a confident nod. "I'd love to see you around more."

"Really?"

"Yeah and maybe if it doesn't work out with you and Luke… I don't know, maybe we could still hang out?"

"I don't understand. For work?"

She shrugs shyly. "I was thinking as friends…"

"Oh!"

"We don't have to," she quickly adds.

"No. Yes." I take a quick breath. "I'd love to be friends with you."

"Okay," she says.

We're both blushing shyly as we smile at one another.

"Boys' turn!" DJ Brain Damage says, interrupting our little moment. "Taliah get ready to lose that garter belt!"

The freaking spotlight guy finds me again and I can feel my face going pale as everyone thinks about the garter belt wrapped around my upper thigh.

"Calling all single men to the dance floor!" the DJ shouts. "If you ain't got a ring on your finger, get your ass on the dance floor."

Heather comes over and grabs my wrist. My heart is hammering in my chest as she pulls me to an empty chair set up under the large chandelier.

"Just sit down and let Luke do the rest," she says as she practically pushes me into the seat.

I gulp as dozens of eligible bachelors crowd all around me. My mouth goes dry and I feel a faintness until Luke comes strutting over, looking hot as ever.

I'm Too Sexy by Right Said Fred begins to play and I can't help but laugh as Luke grinds playfully to the beat. He's giving me a real show as he pops his collar, dips his knees, and gyrates his hips while giving me a hilarious look.

I burst out laughing. I'm dying…

He straightens back up and struts down the line of guys, giving high fives as he goes. I can't breathe as he circles back and twerks his ass at me.

This man is not shy at all. He's willing to do anything to tease a smile out of me and I'm here for it.

I holler and clap my hands as he comes strutting forward like a headliner on the Magic Mike tour. He drops to his knees and I gasp as he picks up the bottom of my dress.

He gives me a devastatingly sexy grin before tossing my dress over his head and dipping between my legs.

Heat blooms within when I feel his strong hands on my thigh, peeling the garter belt down. My core clenches. My heart pounds.

Can he see my underwear? What exactly is visible down there?

He takes his time, sliding the garter belt down my trembling thigh and over my scraped knee. I'm practically panting by the time he pulls it off my foot and comes back out with a sly grin on that frustratingly sexy face.

His hair is a mess. I grin at him as I lean forward and fix it.

"He made it!" DJ Brain Damage hollers into the mic. "The groom entered uncharted territory and has lived to tell about it."

I shoot him a look and he moves on. "Gather around bachelors and loosen up those hands! One rule. If it comes to you, you must catch it."

Luke takes the garter belt and stuffs it into his pocket. "Not going to happen," he says in a possessive tone. "It's all mine."

He's breaking all the rules tonight.

The DJ is about to argue, but he takes one look at Luke and decides to put a song on instead. The dance floor fills back up and Heather comes to take the chair away.

"You're doing great," she says. "Just cutting the cake in a bit and the President should be here soon, and then we're pretty much done."

Pretty much done?

It's almost over?

My heart drops as I look at Luke.

I can't believe the night is moving this fast.

And I really can't believe that I'm this upset about it.

CHAPTER
Nineteen

"Hopefully, that's the last time," I say as Victoria helps me out of the bathroom stall.

"It's only ten o'clock," she says with a grin as she holds my dress off the tiles. "And we have lots more drinking to do. I don't mind at all."

"Good, because I lied. I'll never make it to the end of the night without another trip."

She laughs as we head to the sink. My flower girl is waiting there holding a big glass of water. She's looking right at me as I wash my hands.

"What are you doing, Lily?" Victoria asks.

"Are you okay?" I smile as I bend down in front of her.

She nods and leans into my ear. "It's to throw on you. If you turn back into a mermaid."

Awww. She's so cute. I can't even.

"That's not for another two hours," I tell her. "You can have a glass ready at midnight."

"Good," she says, looking relieved as she pours the water into the sink. "It was getting heavy."

"What are you guys talking about?" Victoria asks with a raised eyebrow, just like Luke does.

"Important flower girl bride stuff," I tell her as I wink at Lily. "Top secret."

Janet walks in and plows right past us to plug her phone into the wall. She's grinding her teeth as she gets absorbed back into the screen.

Victoria rolls her eyes as she shoots me a look. "Hi, Aunt Janet."

Janet barely looks up, getting only halfway to her niece's face before her eyes drop back down. "Hi girls. Having fun?"

"Yup."

"Great. Hey, let me know when the bouquet toss is. I haven't had a date in ages."

Victoria looks at me with a scrunched-up face.

"We just had it, aunt Janet. Remember? I fell in front of you?"

"Oh right!" she says as she grabs her forehead. "Sorry, I'm just a little distracted tonight. Are you freaking kidding me?"

Something pulls her back into her phone and she says another curse word under her breath. This lady is consumed by her job. It's ten o'clock on a Saturday, at a family wedding, and I haven't seen her eyes yet.

"Why don't you take the rest of the night off work and have fun with the family?" Victoria asks as she hops onto the counter.

"You're always on your phone," Lily says scathingly. "It's pathetic." Gotta love the brutal honesty of young kids. You can always count on them to bluntly say what adults won't.

Janet looks up with a stressed-out impatient sigh. "If I don't hit my quarterly quotas next week, my entire division loses their bonuses. They need me. You ladies are young and free. You don't understand what it's like to have people relying on you."

I know what it's like. I have workers relying on me right now.

I also know what it's like to be consumed by your job.

I've spent the last several years like this poor lady, not realizing there's a whole rich world around me to experience. My eyes are fully open now.

I'm not going back.

"Ugh," Janet snorts with a roll of her eyes. "The reception in here is horrible."

She unplugs her phone and the four of us leave the bathroom together.

Owen runs up to us. Janet barely looks at her son.

"Let's go, Lily!" he whispers, waving her over.

"Is it time?" she asks.

"Yes!" he says before turning to Janet. "Mom, are you going to watch?"

My heart breaks when I see the hopeful yet weary look in his eyes. Something tells me he doesn't get a lot of his mother's attention.

"Yes," she says, finally looking up. "Yes, of course."

"Watch what?" I ask as the two kids run away.

Victoria watches them go. "It doesn't matter."

They're up to something and my bridesmaid is in on it.

I'm about to pry deeper when Cindy comes over, looking like a broken-hearted raccoon with her mascara running.

"Taliah," she says with a tremor in her voice. "Can I talk to you for a second?"

I look at Victoria and she shrugs.

"Sure," I say as we step to the side. Victoria stays nearby, but out of earshot. "What's up?"

She takes a deep breath, her hands shaking. "I just..."

I jerk back as she lunges forward and wraps her arms around me in a bear hug. "Take care of him," she whispers into my ear.

"Okaaaay," I say stiffly as she pulls away, looks at me with a sad smile, and then runs off holding a sob in.

Victoria is back at my side. "That girl took my flip-flops when we were on vacation," she says as we watch her rush out of the hall.

"She also took your brother."

She gasps. "What? Luke?"

I shake my head. "Carter."

She thinks about it for a second and then nods. "I can see that. It was a pretty boring vacation. It rained the whole week and there was no internet."

The music stops and Victoria grabs my hand with a gasp. "Come!"

I don't have time to protest before she's pulling me through the crowd and up to the stage.

"What's going on?" I ask with my heart pounding. "Do I have to dance again? Or sing? Please don't make me sing."

"Just stand here," she says with a big smile as she places me in front. Ringside seats.

My pulse is still racing and now there's a fluttering in my stomach as she bounds onto the stage and disappears behind the blue curtain.

Luke pops up beside me and gives me a breathtaking smile. The nerves melt away as I look at him. I feel like I can do anything with him by my side.

"What's going on?" I ask. "What are they up to?"

He shrugs. "I have no idea."

Heather arrives on my other side as the blue curtain gets pulled open. The crowd cheers.

It's not Marvin Hill and The Rolling Hills. It's better.

They're all up there. All of Luke's cousins.

Owen is in the back with two wooden spoons on his thigh, Ryan is on the guitar, Lily is holding a tambourine, and Victoria is at the microphone looking like a star with a guitar hanging off her shoulder.

The stage is lit up with soft white lights, giving it an ethereal, dream-like look. It's gorgeous.

"I thought they weren't doing this," I whisper to Heather.

She shrugs. "They changed their minds."

Victoria looks directly at me with a smile on her face. "This is for the newest member of our family. Welcome to our crazy little world. We're not all bad."

I take a deep breath, feeling a thickness in my throat as I get choked up.

"This song is called Family Is Family written by Kacey Musgraves," Victoria says to the gathering crowd. "We hope you like it."

I do.

They're so good.

Victoria commands the stage as she sings the fun upbeat quirky song, strumming her guitar while smiling at me.

No one has ever sung to me before. Even as a kid, it wasn't something my parents ever did.

I get emotional as I watch, my eyes filling with tears. They didn't have to do this. They weren't going to do this. What changed?

Luke puts his big comforting arm around me as a warmth expands in my chest. A rush of emotions swirls through me as they play—joy, gratitude, surprise, sadness. I don't know what's wrong with me. I'm feeling it all.

They're all so talented. Lily is on the tambourine and dancing around. How is she so good at such a young age?

The boys are making it look easy. Owen is smacking the

spoons on his thigh to the beat. Ryan has all eyes on Aya as he plays the guitar with a grin.

And Victoria? She's a star in the making. She could be selling out stadiums one day.

The song comes to an end with a flourish and stops abruptly.

"Family is family," Victoria says, "and welcome to ours."

Luke's arm leaves my shoulders as we clap and cheer as loudly as we can. I rush onto the stage and hug each of them, feeling tears of gratitude sliding down my cheeks.

They actually made me feel like I'm part of the family. I'll never forget it.

"That was incredible," I say to Luke as I step back down. I'm still shaking. I don't know why this is hitting me so hard.

He wipes a tear off my cheek. "It was."

"It's your turn," I say as a joke.

His face turns serious. "Okay."

"Wait, what?"

Before I can grab him, he hops onto the stage and approaches Victoria.

"Is he going to sing?" Heather asks me. "This isn't on the schedule."

I never thought I'd ever say this, but fuck the schedule.

I'm laser-focused on him as he whispers something to his sister. She smiles, puts a hand on his shoulder, and then hands him her guitar.

Her eyes dart to mine and she grins while hopping off the stage.

Is he actually going to sing to me?

Adrenaline rips through my body as he straps Victoria's guitar over his big round shoulder and steps up to the microphone.

I feel like my insides are vibrating as all seven hundred plus people in the room watch him. He's only watching me.

The crowd hushes into silence as his fingers loosen up on the strings, soft notes filling the vast room and making it feel like an intimate little open mic night in a coffee shop rather than a huge hall with hundreds of people.

His eyes are fixated on me. Once again, it's just us in the room. Everyone else melts away.

"This is a song for my girl," he says in a smooth voice that gives me warm shivers all over. "Our future starts today."

His fingers begin dancing on the strings, the soft lights casting him in a warm glow. He's so beautiful. How can this gorgeous man be singing to me? How can I be the one he picked?

A weightlessness hits me as he begins to sing in a low sexy voice. I recognize the words. Perfect by Ed Sheeran, but coming out of Luke's mouth, the song is beyond perfect. It's magical.

People begin turning their heads to look at me, realizing they're witnessing something special. I don't take my tear-filled eyes off him. I can't. I'm mesmerized by him.

I'm breathless as he sings about being kids and falling in love. I'm no kid, but this is my first real love. And in this surreal moment, it feels like it's going to be my last.

I'm actually falling in—

Nope! No, no, no, no, no, no, no. No!

I can't do this again. It can't be like the other times.

But it was never like this *the other times.*

Look at me. Making excuses.

I take a few deep breaths and focus on Luke's sweet tear-jerking performance, letting the romantic lyrics coat the inside of my ears like warm sugar.

My mental breakdown is over. I'm fine now. Good as new.

I glance over at the ice sculpture of the angel. She's watching me with clear eyes and a soft smile. "Please let it work out," I whisper to my icy guardian angel. "Just this one time."

I shove my hope, worries, and anxieties away and enjoy the rest of the song, letting Luke's soft singing fill me with pride and joy.

He really is good. Shockingly good.

He's so calm, so confident. I stare at his lips as he sings with such emotion, realizing that I kissed those lips and they kissed me.

When the song finishes everyone claps and cheers.

I can't. I just stand there stunned, staring up at him in awe as he takes the guitar off his shoulder and lowers it onto the stand.

His eyes never leave mine.

He smiles at me as he heads for the stairs. My heart starts going as my head gets all light and airy. I feel like I could float to the ceiling without his big arms anchoring me.

"Wow, Luke," I say when he arrives, the crowd still clapping around us. "I don't even know what to say. That was beautiful. No one has ever done anything like that for me before."

He takes both of my hands in his, leans down, and kisses me softly on the lips. The crowd roars.

DJ Brain Damage puts on Billie Jean and the crowd starts dancing all around us. I can't dance right now. I'm still too shaky after that enchanted performance.

I lead him outside where it's nice and dark with a cool breeze. It feels electric on my skin.

"So, does your family always sing to each other?" I ask.

First Walter, then his cousins, then Luke. I wouldn't be

surprised if Kathleen sings me a tune the next time I run into her. Even the villains sing in a Disney movie.

"Yeah," he says as he leans in closer to me, the wind rippling through his hair. "I'm guessing yours didn't?"

"No. My parents put headphones on me and played music while they yelled at each other. Does that count?"

He gives me a sad look and I immediately want to take the words back. I want him to go back to looking at me the way he was before.

"Seriously, though. Thank you for that. It was really special to me."

He steps in with those hungry eyes brimming with need and want. I shiver as his hands slide onto my tingling hips and he kisses me long and deep. It's the best kiss yet.

My head is swimming when he pulls away.

"I'm really excited for our date, Zoe," he whispers. My chin tilts up to him.

"You are?"

He nods.

"I'm really excited too," I whisper back.

His hands slide into mine and we just stare at each other, smiling excitedly.

I can't believe I have to wait until Friday. This is going to be the longest week of my life.

"Carter!" one of Carter's frat-boy buddies shouts as a group of them come storming over.

"Not now," Luke mutters.

"Hollywood Stinger time, baby!" the one with the pink tie shouts as he slaps a big palm on Luke's shoulder. "Bar. Now."

Luke's hand shoots out and he grabs my wrist as the boys pull him back inside. I'm getting dragged along, but I don't mind. I could use a drink.

"Hollywood Stingers!" the most dude-bro of all the dude-bros hollers at the bartender. "Twelve of them!"

The one with the thick neck and earrings in each ear rubs his hands together. "We're doing two each!"

Luke looks like he's going to be sick. "Not again…"

"Yes, again!" king dude-bro shouts way too loud.

"What's a Hollywood Stinger?" the confused bartender asks.

"What's a Hollywood Stinger?" king dude-bro shouts, looking offended. "Jack Black Sambuca, Captain Morgan Freeman, Grey Goose and Maverick, and Crown Royal Tenenbaums. Mix it all up."

"What's the stinger part?" I ask.

"I almost forgot," king dude-bro says as he reaches into his jacket pocket and pulls out a little red bottle. "Christopher Walken's Watch In My Ass Hot Sauce."

All the bros start banging on the bar like a troop of chimps. "I only got one case of these babies left in my garage," he says as he holds it up.

"In Walken we trust!" they all shout at the same time.

Luke gives me a look out of the corner of his eye and I laugh.

The bartender has all of the bottles out, but he's looking at them like he can't bring himself to pour them. "You want me to mix all this together?"

"Hell yeah!" king dude-bro shouts.

"That's disgusting."

"I know," king dude-bro says as he rubs his hands together in excitement. "That's why it's so awesome!"

King dude-bro's wife, Queen dude-bro, rolls her eyes as she walks away. "I guess I'm driving home," she mutters to no one in particular.

"Pour it! Pour it!" they all chant like gorillas until the

bartender gives up all his professional standards and starts mixing them up.

"These are your brother's friends?" I whisper to Luke with a grin.

Luke shakes his head as he looks at me. "My brother is an idiot."

I laugh. "No kidding."

The bartender looks like he's ready for a vacation by the time the shots are ready.

"*Very* nice!" king dude-bro says in a horrible Borat impression as he starts sliding the shots over to everyone.

Luke is already looking queasy before king dude-bro thrusts one into his hand. He reluctantly takes it with a sour look on his face.

I feel so bad for him. I can't let him take it. He already had more than his fair share earlier.

"Bottoms up, boys," king dude-bro hollers as they all clink their shots together, spilling most of them.

Luke grimaces as he looks at the shot. "I can't take any more of these," he whispers to me.

I grab it out of his hand with a grin. "Pussy."

His eyes widen as I quickly down it along with the guys.

Oh, gross! Ugh! That's vile.

Disgusting. And it burns… fucking hell, it burns! My eyes are watering. My hands are shaking.

Another one appears out of nowhere.

Oh, crappers. I just called him a pussy. I have to take it now.

I grab the shot out of king dude-bro's hand and down that one too.

It's even worse the second time around.

With the cocktails, the wine at dinner, and the beers at the bar, these shots hit me hard and fast. I'm not much of a drinker and I've barely eaten anything all day.

The room spins as I stare at Luke's worried face.

And just like that…

…I'm a drunk bride.

Just what I need.

CHAPTER *Twenty*

"Are you drunk?" Luke asks as I try to sit, but slip on the stool. Why is his forehead all scrunched up like an old man? I'd like to see him as an old man. He'd be soooo hot.

"You're a sexy old man..."

"What?" He grabs my arm. This whole place is woozy. Why is the floor moving like this? "Shit, you're drunk."

I hit his arm with a limp hand. "Noooooooooo. You are the drunk one."

He grabs me as I fall into him and start giggling.

"Oh shit," he whispers to himself.

The room is all spinny, but Luke is in perfect focus. How can he be so perfect? Perfect, purr-fect... That's a funny word...

That face... *Mmmmmmm*... I just want to eat it like a baked potato. I want to claw his shoulders and bite his cheek. He's *soooo* hot...

I lean on his big sexy chest and step on my toes. I'm a vampire. Luke is my prey.

"Ow!" he says as he looks down at me funny. "Did you just

bite my cheek?"

"Noooooo… how dare you… you're being ridicu-lush…"

Look at that tux… that ass…

"Not here, my dear. People are watching."

He grabs my wrist and pulls my hand away. No fun…

I just want to climb him like a fire pole…

"My feet hurt," I whine. "These shoes suck."

"Easy," Luke says as he grabs my arm. I take off my shoes and slam them onto the bar.

"You keep 'em," I tell the bartender.

"Sorry about that," Luke says as he grabs them.

"Noooooo," I whine. "They're Satan's shoes. I hate them."

He tucks them under his big stupid hot arm and holds me up.

This room keeps teetering… What is happening…

"More shots!" I yell out. The dude bros holler. They know…

"None for you," Luke says as he tries to pull me away. I want more…

"Hey! It's you guys!" I shout when I see Victoria and Aya and that other guy with the hair.

"What's going on over here?" Aya says. She's so smiley… I like her…

"She snuck a few shots," Luke says. "Now she's feeling them."

"Shots sound like a great idea!" Victoria orders some more.

I'm so thirsty… When are they going to stop driving this room?

They're all talking. Why are they talking so much?? Why can't I concentrate on what they're saying?

I grin when I see Luke's face. He's holding me so tight. *Mmmmmm…*

"You have a sexy chin."

He laughs and then smiles at me.

"You so pretty. I wanna have allyour babies."

"Okay." *Mmmmmm,* his arms feel good on me. I just want to put my cheek on him and sleep forever.

"Is she okay?" It's a voice. I don't know who. Who cares...

"She needs more alcohol." That one is Aya.

"No, she doesn't." That one is my boyfriend. Luke is my boyfriend. I love him...

There's so much talking. Why is everybody talking so much?

"Why are her eyes glazed over like that?"

I moan as I push away from Luke. The guy with the hair catches me.

It's Heather. She looks mad.

"She had a few shots." Luke.

"They were gross. Two thumbs down."

Her mouth opens like a ping pong ball when I point my thumbs at the ground and blow a loud raspberry.

"I'm digging this Zoe!" Aya.

I high-five her, but hit her ear. Oopsies.

"You let her get drunk?" Why does Heather keep talking to Luke about me?

"I'm standing ray here!"

"Standing?" Heather. "Honey, you're leaning on the bar."

Oh, look at that. I am. Oops!

"We're supposed to be doing the cake cutting now!" Heather looks stressed out. She should chill. Oh, we should get some shots for her! "We can't do it with her like this. Shit. We'll have to wait. This throws everything off schedule. Why did you let her have shots, Luke?"

I lean back onto him and grin as I look at his sexy chin. "Yeah, Luke. Why did you letter have shots?"

"She downed them so fast," his sexy chin says.

"I'll get her some coffee." Heather rushes away. My hair hurts.

Luke holds me and hugs me and smiles at me. I love him.

"You're causing all kinds of trouble, aren't you?"

He kisses my forehead. He's perfect…

I'm giddy as I lean on his chest.

That grin… *Mmmmmm*. I just want to bite it off his face…

"What the hell is going on here?!" It's the witch. What's her name? Cathy? Kitty? Catwoman?

Victoria puts down her shot. Awww, her face… She looks so upset. What's wrong?

Kathleen. That's her stupid name. *She's* what's wrong.

"The President of the United Fucking States will be here in less than ten minutes!" she hisses. "Put those shots away! This is not a keg party! *You* are not even twenty-one!"

It's the guy with the hair. Aya's guy. Kathead is pointing at him.

"You said you were twenty-six." Aya.

Awww, they're holding hands. Oops, not anymore.

"And you!" the witch. "Diving for that bouquet like a desperate forty-year-old! You're a Whitfield, act like it!"

My friend looks sad. That makes me sad.

That witch is doing it.

"I taught you to act like a lady, not like a—"

"NOPE!" I yell way too loud. Everyone looks at me, but I don't care. The alcohol is driving now.

The witch… she's glaring at me…

"She's drunk!"

"Go away." I say it loud. I don't even fucking care…

"You can't just—"

"BEEP!"

"What is she—?"

"BOOP!"

People are looking. She smiles nervously.

"Go somewhere else," I tell her. "Or else."

She leans in. She's maaaad.

"I'm not going anywhere else! I paid for this—"

I start pounding my chest and hooting like a gorilla. That does it.

She practically runs away.

Everyone looks at me in shock. Then, they start laughing. Hard.

"That was awesome!" Victoria gives me a high-five. This one connects. "I've never seen anyone successfully stand up to her before!"

"You're amazing," hair guy says.

Aya orders more shots. I take one when Luke isn't looking, but it spills all over my hand. Probably a good thing.

I'm all buzzing and woozy on the stool. Luke holds me. He smells like man sex. I love him.

"Drink this."

"Huh?"

Coffee. It's cold. Yuck.

"Drink it all." Heather again. When did she get back? "The President is on his way. We can't wait any longer."

"We're going to have to." Luke.

"You're just going to have to hold her up with one hand and cut the cake with the other. We'll keep it short."

Luke's face is in mine. He's soooo hot. Look at that nose. I didn't know noses could be sexy. Is it weird that I want to make out with it?

"Are you okay to do this?"

"Do what?"

"Oh, Christ." Heather again. Why is she still here?

"The cake cutting. Can you do it?"

"I can do anything."

He smiles. "I know you can."

Suddenly, I'm on my feet, Luke's arm wrapped around me.

"Wait, my shoes! That bartender stole them."

"I have them right here."

Oh. He does. He thinks of everything.

Walking is hard. I hate walking.

I hit someone's chair. "Sorry, Mr. bald man."

Luke laughs. Such a pretty sound… I love him.

"You're doing great."

"I'm not. I suck."

"You don't suck."

"I'm the worst bride ever. I fell down the stairs now I'm drunk."

"You do put on quite a show. But I wouldn't want anyone else to be my bride."

"Hurry up." Heather. What's her problem? Geez…

"That's a big cake."

"Just try to stand still. I'll cut it."

"Okay."

I keep swaying. Is this wedding on a cruise ship? What the hell? What's wrong with the floor? Someone should fix it.

Why is everyone looking at us?

Why does Luke have a knife?

Oh, right. The cake.

People clap as he cuts it. Why are they—oh shit, not that guy again!

It's that Turkey guy. The ambassator.

Why is he staring at me like that?

I stick my tongue out at him.

Oh no. That doesn't work. He's coming here.

"Luke…"

Luke is cutting the cake. I tug his jacket.

Uh oh. He's right in front of me.

"Bütün gece benden kaçtın."

My mouth falls open. I stare up at his bushy eyebrows.

"Beni hiç dinliyor musun? Davranışlarından rahatsızım."

Why is he so loud? Everyone is looking. He keeps waving his big arms, making a scene.

Luke is back. Awww, I love him.

"We'll talk to you after the cake cutting," Luke says to the loud man.

The ambassador doesn't stop glaring at me. His eyebrows are so scary.

"Onunla neden ülkesini aşağıladığı hakkında konuşmak istiyorum."

He's so loud. Like a big frog.

More people are looking. Even I can tell this isn't good and I'm hammered.

"Luke..." He'll know what to do. He always knows... "Do something."

"I'm sorry," Luke says. Why is he smiling?

My shoulders droop as he takes a handful of cake and smooshes it into my face. It goes all over my mouth and on my nose. Vanilla. Tasty.

People laugh at me. That's okay. It's funny. I'm laughing too.

"Let's get you cleaned off." Luke says it loud. He grabs my arm and brings me to the bathroom. The big family one with the lock on the door.

I stare at his sexy blue eyes as he lifts me onto the counter.

So strong... *Mmmmmm...*

"Are you mad?"

"Why?"

"I put frosting all over your face."

Oh yeah. I turn and burst out laughing when I see the mirror. I look like a frosting Santa Claus.

Luke laughs too.

My hair is coming undone. Everything is coming undone.

"Kiss me."

He grabs paper towels instead. "You have frosting all over your mouth."

I grab his tie and pull him closer. "I'll be tastier."

"You're already deliciously tasty."

"Then kiss me."

My mouth tilts up. I need him so badly.

He kisses me on the lips and has a frosting moustache when he pulls away. I grin as I scoop it off with my finger. *Mmmmmmm*. I lick it off.

His eyes get that hungry look as he watches my mouth.

I'll do anything for him. I'm a wild woman for this man. I'd wear a leopard-skin skirt and top if he wanted me to.

"Do you get horny for leopard skin?"

He laughs. "What?"

"Never mind."

I'm hunched over, gazing into his blue eyes as he dabs my face, taking the frosting away.

"I love your face. I just want to *grrrrrrrr* all over it."

"You can do anything you'd like to my face," he says as he dabs the side of my nose.

I grin as I start to touch it. His cheeks are so prickly. The line of his jaw so hard.

"That's all of it," he says as he tosses the crumpled-up paper towel into the garbage.

"Don't go." I hook my legs around him and hold him there. He's my prisoner. He'll have to do whatever I say from now on.

"I'm here." He tucks a strand of loose hair behind my ear. "I'm not going anywhere."

"Good." I drag my hand down his arm. "I want you to be

my boyfriend."

He grins. Those sexy lips…

"I want to talk to you in the mornings and text you all day and watch TV and go to restaurants and open presents with you on Christmas. I think that would be pretty cool."

His lips come in nice and close. His breath is so warm and minty.

"I think that would be pretty cool too."

"Really?"

He nods.

And then he kisses me. I grab onto his collar and pull him closer, moaning as his tongue slides against mine.

Our hands start moving everywhere.

I hook my ankles behind him, trapping him here. His hands tighten on my hips. He kisses me harder, deeper. It's rough and urgent, the pent-up desire we've been feeling all day combusts into a frenzy of desperate hands and pounding hearts.

My fingers slide into his hair as he yanks my hips closer to his hard body.

I need this. I want this.

I want him. So. Fucking. Badly.

He groans as I grab a fistful of his lapel, pulling him into me.

Three loud slamming knocks on the door causes us to explode apart. It's jarring and unexpected and such bad freaking timing.

"What?!" I shout at the stupid door.

"The President is here!" The voice is muffled, but I'd recognize that witch voice anywhere. "Get your asses out here! *Now!*"

"The President?" I say with a gasp when I look at Luke and his messed-up hair. "But I'm drunk!"

CHAPTER
Twenty-One

"Is that makeup waterproof?" Luke asks as I splash handfuls of cold water onto my face.

"I don't know," I answer as I splash more and more of it in a desperate attempt to sober up. Luke's lips and hands did the majority of the sobering-up work, but I still have a little bit of the Hollywood Stingers clouding my brain.

"That's better," I whisper as I turn the water off and let the water drip off my face into the sink. Luke hands me a paper towel.

I wipe my face with it as I stand up.

"No!" I gasp when I see my face. It's a horror show. A sloppy mess of smeared, smudged makeup. I look like a drug-addicted clown waking up from a weekend bender.

Even Luke winces when he sees me. This shouldn't be happening now! This is all out of order. He should only see my smudged makeup the morning after sex when I already have him trapped. Not now. Not like this!

"Look away!" I cry as I turn my head and put my hand up. "I'm ghastly."

He chuckles softly as he gently pulls my arm down. "Stop. You're beautiful."

"I'm a mess," I say as a sob bubbles out. "I'm a hot mess."

He takes my hand and dips down so our faces are level. I can't even look at him. Look at those freaking blue eyes and that adorable dimple in his cheek. I'm a monster compared to him. I didn't realize it dancing out there, but *I'm* the beast and *he's* the beauty. I want to die.

"I can't meet the President like this!" Oh no. Even my dress is wet from all the splashing. "I look like I was in a wet t-shirt contest!"

He laughs. "No, you don't."

"You laughed!" I say, pointing at his frustratingly flawless face. "That means it's true!"

"You look like you were having a ton of fun at your wedding," he says calmly. "There's nothing wrong with that. You're allowed to have fun. You didn't do anything wrong."

"I didn't?"

"No. It's okay. I can guarantee the President has seen a drunk person before."

"Not in a wedding dress."

He smiles. "Probably not, no."

"I have to put on my shoes," I say when I spot my bare feet. "Where are my shoes?!"

"Here they are," he says in a calming voice as he grabs them off the back of the toilet. "But are you sure that's a good idea? You can barely walk in them sober."

"I'm not meeting the President with bare feet. I'm not Fred Flintstone!"

Luke bends down and gently takes my foot. His hand caresses my sole before he tries to slip Taliah's shoe on. He's graceful and gentle at first but then has to shove them on with a grunt like a dad shoving one last sleeping bag into the trunk of a packed car. "Wow, those are tight."

"I know that!"

He manages to get them both on with a lot of grunting and a couple of curse words.

"Oh shit, your dress is all ripped here," he says when he spots my seam on the way back up.

"Like I said. I'm a hot mess."

I grab his hand and open the door. Heather and Kathleen recoil when they see me.

"What happened to her?" Walter asks, looking horrified.

"I'll fix it!" Heather says as she opens her purse and storms into the bathroom. "You can wait outside, Luke."

She closes the door, pushes me against the sink, and attacks my face with a slew of makeup products.

"Ow!"

"Stop moving!"

I close my eyes and hold my head still while she does her thing. After a few minutes of feeling like an octopus was giving me a makeover, I'm back to looking decent again. Maybe even a little bit hot.

"Much better," Heather says as she looks me over. "We're going to meet President Brody now. Smile, shake his hand, let him lead the conversation, okay? Keep it simple."

"Simple," I repeat, feeling my head swaying again. I'm still a little bit tipsy. Why did I have those damn shots?

We head outside and Luke exhales long and hard when he sees me. I'm happy to be back on his arm as we hurry to a secure room on the first floor where a team of secret service agents are waiting outside in the hall.

The big one by the door looks so scary. He's got a big scar on his bald head and thick rolls on the back of his neck. He looks like he's half pit bull.

A woman in a dark navy blue pantsuit who was certainly the Valedictorian at every school she graduated from struts up to us with a clipboard neatly tucked under her arm. "Hello. I'm Rebecca Porter, the Chief of Staff to President Brody. We'll meet him briefly in here and then he'll be making an appearance in the ballroom. He has a hard out in thirty-seven minutes."

I feel so tired as I lean on Luke. I just want to close my eyes and sleep forever.

Rebecca taps the earpiece in her ear and stares into space. "Copy that. We're coming in now."

I must be giving off more drunk vibes because Rebecca stops at the door when she sees me. She points to my face with her pencil. "Is she okay?"

"She'll be fine," Luke says.

I burp.

"I'll hold her up."

There's an uneasy look in Rebecca's eyes as she looks me over one last time before turning to the door and opening it.

The secret service agents are the first ones in, followed by Rebecca, then Walter.

There he is… The President. I gulp as I step into the room, sobering right up. He's standing in the middle of the suite next to a white table with a big vase of fresh orchids on it. It hits me. Hard.

I'm meeting the *President*. Eight years ago I was selling homemade peanut butter and jelly sandwiches at construction sites. All this work. All this hustle. All of this drive and ambition. It's all paid off.

I'm in the same room as the most powerful person on the planet. I step forward with my chin up and my shoulders back, feeling a rush of energy surging through my veins. I feel like I can do anything. For some reason, I really wish the kids from high school could see this.

He's looking sharp in a black suit, black tie, gray hair, sprightly smile—attributes that got him elected over the other guy who was way more qualified and much smarter. I didn't vote for the guy, but he's still a big freaking deal. He's the President of The United States!

"Nice to see you again, Mr. President!" Walter bellows as he walks in and gives him a hug.

"Easy," the scary secret service agent warns as he steps in close.

"Relax, Merrick," President Brody says to the agent. "You're going to be working for him after me!"

"If all goes to plan!" Walter says with a jolly laugh.

"Well, you're going to like having Merrick around," President Brody says as he slaps the big grump on the shoulder. "I once had a terrorist pull a pin off a grenade and run up to me. Merrick shoved it into his mouth and didn't so much as burp when it went off. He's a killer."

Merrick doesn't crack a smile as he glares at us.

"Charles," Kathleen says as she walks up to him with a warm smile and wide-open arms, transforming into a different person before my very eyes.

"Kathleen," President Brody says as he hugs her. "It's been too long."

"Too long indeed," she says as they break apart. "Give Marla my best wishes."

"She's busy redecorating the East Wing for you!"

I picture a building decorated for Kathleen and wince. Are they even allowed to put satanic imagery in the White House?

"She's too kind," Kathleen says as Walter beams at them. "Tell her I hate pink."

They both laugh. "I will."

His eyes turn to me. Uh oh.

"This must be the bride," he says with his arms out. "Congratulations on joining the wonderful Whitfield family!"

This is surreal. The President of The United States is kissing my cheeks. It suddenly hits me how powerful Luke's family is. They're on a first-name basis with the President and the First Lady. They may be moving into the White House next year. It's crazy.

And it's really starting to freak me out.

"Thank you," I say as my pulse starts to race. I look back at Luke and feel a little bit better. He seems to have a calming effect on me, even in a stressful situation like this.

"And you must be Carter," President Brody says, flashing his molars. "I've heard so much about you. Walter is always gushing about your performance on Wall Street and your swim meets at Yale. You're quite the young man."

"And what about his other son, Luke?" Luke asks. Uh oh.

"I'm sorry?"

"Does he ever mention my twin brother Luke?"

President Brody's forehead scrunches up. "I didn't know you had twins, Walter."

"Well, yes," Walter stammers nervously. "My son Luke is another cherished member of the family of course."

Luke looks pissed. Kathleen and Walter are getting increasingly agitated. Merrick is still glaring. President Brody looks confused.

I have to do something to diffuse the tension. I'll change the subject.

"I'm going to be working with you soon, President Brody," I spit out.

"Oh really?" he asks as he turns to me. "In what capacity?"

Walter and Kathleen are behind him, fiercely shaking their heads.

"As a caterer," I say proudly. "Catering By Zoe will soon be the official caterer of the White House."

His head tilts to the side. He looks confused. "Who's Zoe?"

"I'm Zoe," I say, suddenly feeling like there's a brick in my stomach. "Professionally, of course. My real name is Taliah Osodogru, but when I'm working I go by Zoe Fitzpatrick."

My eyebrows raise as I hold in my breath, hoping he's going to buy it. He looks even more confused.

"It's like a catering pen name," I continue, rambling on nervously. "Why are musicians, actors, and writers the only ones able to change their names? It's not fair. Right?"

"Okaaaay," he says, looking at me funny. "But the White House has its own permanent staff. They've all been vetted and have gone through the rigorous security clearance process. Have you?"

I open my mouth but nothing comes out. I can feel the blood draining from my face as I slowly realize…

"We can fast track you through the security clearance process," he says as he nods to Rebecca to make a note. "Then, you'll be free to apply to any department you like. Rebecca, maybe we can put in a good word to get her in as a waitress?"

Rebecca nods as she scribbles something on her clipboard.

"A waitress?" I whisper.

I look past the President at Walter and Kathleen. They look terrified as I glare at them.

"We should be getting back to the wedding," Kathleen quickly says, hurrying to the door. "Lots of important guests outside."

My shock turns to fury as everything becomes crystal fucking clear. There is no Golden Contract. There is no Craig Watson head of the event planning committee for the White House and Capitol Hill. There is nothing but lies.

I got swindled. I got bamboozled. I got played.

And I am fucking pissed.

My back straightens as I clench my fists, my fingernails digging into my palms. There's a tightness in my chest as I stand firm in the middle of the room while Kathleen and Walter quickly flee toward the door.

"Get back in here," I hiss as a primal urge to break something comes in hot.

Kathleen gulps as she turns around with a tight smile. "Come now, dear. You've had too much to drink." She laughs nervously as she glances at the President. "You know kids and their weddings."

"There is no Golden Contract?" I say with my voice rising.

Merrick perks up, looking ready for anything. With the rage surging through my veins, I could take him down easily even though he's got a hundred and fifty pounds on me and a body full of hidden weapons.

"Let's talk about this *outside*," Kathleen warns.

"*No*," I snap. "I did all of this for nothing?!"

Luke winces at my words.

"You knew all along that it was a lie," I say, rearing on Walter with my finger pointing menacingly at him. "You thought I wouldn't find out until after!"

"What's going on?" President Brody asks, looking from me to them.

"They're big fat liars!" I shout at the President.

The pit bull doesn't like that and steps between us with his big meaty palm in the air. "Stay back, ma'am."

"Or what?" I shout, not caring who's in the room. My dream just got shattered and I don't give a fuck about anything anymore. "You going to arrest me because I do *this*?"

I feign a lunge at the President and Merrick gives me a warning look. "That's close enough!"

"What about *this*?" I go for another feint, but I trip on these stupid shoes and stumble right into the President.

He catches me as Kathleen screams and we both go down. Merrick rushes over. He grabs a hold of my dress as we're falling and tries to pull me back.

One hard tug and the dress explodes off me.

"No!" I scream as I land on the President's body, his arms wrapped around me, my tattered dress hanging from Merrick's big sausage fingers. I'm only in my underwear.

Holy shit, I'm only in my underwear.

Chaos erupts all around us.

Merrick grabs my leg. Two other secret service agents try to jump on me but Luke slams into them both and they fall to the ground.

"Everybody relax!" Walter hollers.

Luke rushes over and starts wrestling Merrick over my leg as Kathleen and Rebecca scream.

And the whole time, poor President Brody is lying helplessly under me while my boobs attack his face.

There goes my chance at a security clearance.

CHAPTER
Twenty-Two

"Is this some kind of prank camera show?" President Brody asks while I have him pinned to the floor.

I sigh. "Unfortunately, this is real life."

I'm just about to push myself up when cold hard metal wraps around my wrist and clicks closed, tight and sharp. I cry out as my arm gets yanked behind my back, nearly popping out my shoulder as some asshole handcuffs my other wrist.

It's Merrick. He grabs my arm and President Brody's arm and hoists us both up at the same time.

Luke charges over and pulls me protectively behind him. "She tripped," he says in a tight voice, getting right into Merrick's face. "Back off."

"Her shoes are too small!" Kathleen practically screeches. "What are you doing?! Charles!"

The President catches himself and shakes his head. "Get the cuffs off her, Merrick. This has all been a terrible misunderstanding."

Merrick slowly, reluctantly, takes the cuffs off as Luke and him stare each other down.

Luke yanks his jacket off and covers me with it. With his

huge body blocking the view, I quickly put it on and sink into the safe comforting smell of him.

I'm swimming in the jacket. It covers my top half, but it stops a little short—a couple of inches below my ass.

Great, now the guests can see an inappropriate amount of leg. You can't say I don't put on a show.

"Twenty-three minutes until wheels up, Mr. President," Rebecca adds.

"Well, then," President Brody says as he smooths out his suit. "Let's head out there and shake some hands."

He walks over to the door and stops at Luke. "That's quite a woman you got there," he says in a low voice. "You're a lucky man."

Luke looks like he doesn't know what to say as the President pats his shoulder and keeps moving. Walter and him walk out chatting about election catchphrases as if none of this even happened.

Merrick sucks his teeth as his heated eyes look Luke up and down. He's still holding my tattered dress. He dumps it into Kathleen's hands on the way out.

Kathleen looks at me as I rub my wrists. "Brides are supposed to get handcuffed on the honeymoon, dear. Not at the wedding."

I'm about to let her have it when Heather pops her head into the room. "The seamstress is here! What are you wearing?!? Where is your dress?!"

She gasps in horror when she sees it in Kathleen's hands. "Oh my God!" She takes off her glasses and rubs her eyes as she stumbles out, probably contemplating a career change.

Luke, Kathleen, and I shuffle out and follow Heather to the elevator. All the guests are at the wedding, so the hallway is empty.

"The seamstress is waiting in your room," Heather says to

me as she puts her glasses back on with a sigh. "I hope the dress can be saved."

"We don't need it anymore," I say in a low voice.

Kathleen whips her head around. Her eyes bore into me. I glare back at her.

"You still have a few hours," she says, not knowing when to quit. "And the brunch tomorrow."

My blood is boiling. I'm twitching all over as I try to hold in my anger. This lady doesn't know who she's messing with.

Heather is looking at us with concern as she repeatedly hits the button for the elevator, woodpecker style. "Why are they fighting?" she whispers to Luke. "What did I miss?"

"There's no Golden Contract," he whispers back.

Heather goes still. "Oh."

Luke sighs. "Yup."

The elevator doors open with a ding and the four of us head inside. Heather hits the button for the fifth floor as heated adrenaline explodes out of my core and sears through my veins like lava, filling every inch of my tense body with hot, pulsating anger. I'm steaming. I'm livid. I want to Hulk smash her into oblivion.

She made me dance in front of all those people! I fell down the stairs, I faked a nose bleed, I gave the President Of The United States a lap dance!

And she knew… All along she knew…

When the doors slide closed, it all comes bursting out.

"You knew there was no contract!" I shout at Kathleen. "This whole time!" My heart is pounding as I rear on her. "You are a deceiver! A con artist! A lying bitch!"

The corner of her lip curls up.

"Are you… *laughing?!?*"

My anger turns to disbelief as she bursts out laughing. Deep, breathless, belly laughs. I look at Luke in shock as she doubles over, cackling uncontrollably as tears pour out of her eyes. He shrugs knowingly.

"A Golden Contract..." Kathleen wheezes out between heaves of laughter. "Who came up with such an asinine concept?"

All I can do is stare in disbelief as she holds her ribs while choking out breaths, saying she's going to pee herself.

"That's the most secure building in the world and you thought that..."

She's crying laughing while me, Heather, and Luke watch with blank faces.

"...you thought that they'd hire you and..."

She can't even talk. She's dying of laughter.

"...they'd hire you and those drug dealers out there for the... for the... for the White House?!"

She claps her hands as her whole body shakes with laughter.

Luke hits the button for floor three. The elevator stops and the doors open.

Kathleen is laughing too hard to notice that Luke is pushing her out into the hallway.

"What is this place?" she asks when she sees where she is, her laughter quickly drying up. "Is this a lower floor? I don't feel safe here!"

I take a deep breath of relief as the doors close in her face and the elevator continues up.

"Thank you," I whisper to Luke.

He's shaking his head as he stares forward. "Anytime."

We get off on the fifth floor and Heather grabs the dress from Luke. She bounds out and races down the hallway as we slowly follow. The anger is gone. I don't even know what to think or feel anymore. I'm dead inside.

At least I have Luke's jacket. I wrap his coat around me

tightly, loving the feeling of being surrounded by his essence, his smell, his spirit.

"Sorry about them," Luke says softly.

I exhale long and hard. "You did try to warn me."

"Yup."

We walk the rest of the way in silence. Heather is speaking to the seamstress in Taliah's room—an old British woman who doesn't seem impressed with Kathleen's sewing skills.

"Awful, awful work," she says as she inspects the torn seams. "Amateur garbage."

"How long will it take?" Heather asks, looking at her watch.

"Forget it," Luke says as he leans on the dresser and crosses his arms. "We're not going back out there."

"We're not?" I ask, looking at him in shock.

"There's no Golden Contract. What's the point?"

"There's still your part of the deal," I tell him. And I could still use that fat check…

"How long will it take?" Heather asks, ignoring both of us.

"Three days," she says as she runs her finger over a tear.

Heather isn't having any of that. "We'll pay you triple if it's done in forty-five minutes."

"Forty-five minutes?" she says with a bit more enthusiasm. "Where's the sewing machine?"

"Oh shit!" Heather says, slapping her forehead as the seamstress looks around the room. "It's in Kathleen's suite! We have to find her, I don't have the key!"

"This doesn't come out of my time," the seamstress says as they hurry out of the room with the tattered dress.

The door slams closed and the sound echoes through the silent room.

It's just me and Luke again.

Only this time, there's no one around.

And there's a lock on the door.

And there's a bed.

The possibilities are endless.

I sit on the huge comfy bed with Luke's jacket wrapped around me, my back resting on the pillows. He's leaning on the dresser with his arms crossed over his big muscular chest, watching me with a brimming intensity in his hungry blue eyes. His tight shirt is clinging to his round biceps, his tie loose around his thick neck. He's so hot. It doesn't even seem real.

I get tingly all over as we hold each other's eyes, grins on both of our faces.

He rubs his jaw. I nibble my bottom lip seductively.

"Forty-five minutes to kill…" I say with a flirty look.

His ravenous eyes slowly glide down my body, leaving blooms of heat in their wake. "Whatever shall we do?"

My heart pounds in my chest as the air charges with desire and possibility. I want him. Badly.

I want to feel his hands on me, his breath on me, his *weight* on me. I want all of him and I want it now.

It's all I can think about. All kinds of dirty erotic thoughts are swirling in my mind. I'll save you the details, but it's definitely 18+ up there.

This is our wedding night. Pretend or not, it feels like we've been through something special. Something important. Something that makes us more than strangers, more than friends, more than whatever we've been so far. I want *more*.

I want *him*.

"Want your jacket back?" I ask as I open his coat with a seductive look, revealing what little I'm wearing underneath.

He sucks in a breath as he slowly, shamelessly, hungrily looks me up and down. "Yeah. I do."

I sit up with a grin on my lips and take it off. His eyes never leave me as I hold it to my stomach. "Come and get it."

I gasp as he lunges forward, crawling on the bed like a tiger about to devour its prey. I melt into the bed when I feel his hands pressing down beside me, the weight causing the mattress to dip. His mouth swoops in and those soft sexy lips press against mine in a delicious devastating kiss that has me moaning into his mouth.

I slide my hands up his hard, perfect arms and continue over his round shoulders onto his stubbly cheeks. He pulls away and stares at me like he's never seen anything so beautiful.

"Are you still drunk?" he whispers, his hot breath washing over my tingling lips.

I shake my head as I glance at his mouth. "No. Surprisingly, standing in front of the President wearing only your underwear sobers you up real quick."

He grins. "Stop. You're making me jealous."

"Don't be. He's got nothing on you."

He kisses me again and my back arches when I feel his hardness pressing down on my inner thigh. I'm so ready for him. I'm *dying* for it.

"Lock the door," I whisper as he kisses my neck, his strong hand sliding down my bare ribs and dipping into the elastic of my underwear.

"Wait here," he whispers as he kisses the top of my chest. Like I would go anywhere.

He drags his stubbly chin through my cleavage and gets up with a sexy look that annihilates me. I'm *throbbing* down there. I *need* him back on me or I'm going to die.

I try to catch my breath as I watch him lock the door. He slides the chain into the brass track and then turns around with a look that tells me I'm in for a hell of a ride in the next forty-five minutes.

I swallow hard as he pops his collar and slowly unravels his tie, staring at me with those sexy cobalt blue eyes. He tosses it onto the chair and then gets to work on his cufflinks.

I'm aching as I watch him undo one at a time, those big thick forearms looking damn near lickable. He slides his cufflinks into his pocket and then starts with the buttons.

He's enjoying torturing me as I watch him slowly strip, his gorgeous muscular chest and abs coming into view with each flick of his fingers. After the last button, he peels off his shirt and I'm treated to a delicious sight of tight, taut, sinfully hot muscles. His abs clench and tighten as he pulls the shirt off his arms and then drops it onto the chair.

My whole body shudders with anticipation as those strong hands wrap around his belt buckle. His abs flex as he pulls his belt off and unbuttons his pants.

I suck in a breath and hold it when his pants drop and I see the long hard outline of his erection jutting out against his black boxer briefs.

"Forty-two minutes," I say as I glance at the clock. "We're running out of time. You better get over here."

He grins as he runs his hand through his hair and comes to me.

"We'll just have to make every second count..."

"Open up!" Heather shouts as she pounds on the door. I sit up in bed when I hear the lock click and the door swing open. The brass lock stops the door from opening more than an inch.

"Zoe!" Heather says, shoving her face into the crack The Shining style. "Luke! I have the dress! Open up!"

Luke looks at me and sighs. He's laying on his stomach

beside me in the bed, the sheets up to his waist. His hair is all messy as he lays on the pillow, groaning like his five o'clock alarm just went off.

"Hurry up!" Heather begs.

I slide out of the bed and quickly put my bra and underwear back on as my pretend groom sneaks a peek.

"Pervert," I whisper with a grin as I grab his jacket and slide it on.

I quickly fix my hair as I rush over to the door in bare feet. Heather has one eye poking through the slit.

"Thanks, Heather. I'll take it."

"Open the door and I'll help you put it on."

"That's okay," I say as I reach through the crack and take it from her.

"But the… You'll need help with the…"

"I'll be fine. I'll meet you downstairs."

I yank the dress through the slit in the door and then close it with a deep breath.

Three more hard knocks. "Zoe! *Zoe!* Open the door! Now!"

"I'll meet you downstairs!" I shout before taking the dress and walking back to the bed.

Awwww. Luke is putting his shirt back on. *And* his pants are on too? What the hell?! I missed the entire show!

At least I get to see him putting his cuff links and tie back on.

I have one eye on him and one on myself as I slip the dress back on.

"Oh, that is much more comfortable," I say as I move around. "I can actually breathe. Cleavage still very much present though."

"I slipped her a twenty to leave that part alone," Luke says with a grin.

Heather starts banging hard on the door. "Zoe! Open up, Zoe! *Now!* This isn't about the dress!"

"She is persistent," Luke says as he slides his jacket on and fixes his collar.

"One second!" I shout to her. "We're almost ready."

"Now!" she shouts back. "There's an emergency out here! *Zoe!*"

More fierce banging.

It suddenly stops. A part of me wants to push the dresser in front of the door and have a sex marathon with Luke all over this suite. We wouldn't come out until hotel security swings down from the roof and kicks the windows in.

"Luke," I say shyly. I don't know what I want to say, but I need to say something before we go back out there and become Taliah and Carter once again. I might not get another chance.

His stunning blue eyes fill with adoration as he watches me. It takes my breath away. I need a second to recover.

"Luke, that was really…"

"Incredible?"

I nod as we both smile. "Yeah. Incredible."

My body is craving him again. I can still feel him on me, under me, in me. I don't want that to be the last time we do that. It can't be.

He steps closer and takes my hand. A whiff of his cologne hits my nose and I nearly blurt out that I love him.

"Zoe," he says before I embarrass myself. "You are so—"

Banging on the door interrupts him at the best part and I nearly scream in frustration. *I'm so what? What?!?*

"Open this door immediately!" A new voice shouts out. It sounds kind of familiar…

No!

My eyes widen as my blood turns to ice.

"Who is it?" I ask as I hurry to the door, terrified that I might already know. I peer into the peephole just as she answers.

"Taliah Özüdoğru."

CHAPTER Twenty-Three

"What do we do?" I ask Luke as he rushes up behind me.

"I can hear you in there," Taliah shouts as Luke looks through the peephole.

"Heather and Carter are there too," he whispers. "We have to open it."

"No, don't!" I lunge on the handle, but he's too strong. He unlocks the brass latch and opens the door.

"Hello," Luke says calmly. "Heather, would you mind bringing my parents up here? Immediately."

Heather runs to the stairs, muttering 'Oh shit, oh shit, oh shit, oh shit, oh shit,' and disappears into the stairwell, click-clacking away as she runs down the stairs in her high heels.

"What the hell is going on here, Luke?" Carter asks as he pushes into the room with his chest puffed out. The door swings open and Taliah sees me for the first time.

She gasps with a horrified look on her face. "My dress! What did you do to it?"

Carter gets right into Luke's face. "You're pretending to be me at *my* wedding? Why would you do that?"

Luke backs against the wall, looking more flustered than I've ever seen him.

Meanwhile, I have Taliah limping toward me on crutches, her foot in some kind of boot, with a betrayed look on her face.

"How could you?" she asks with a gasp. "My dress. My wedding. You stole all of it!"

"I can explain everything," I say as I back away from her with my hands up.

She stops and stares at me. "Go ahead."

I swallow hard. I got nothing. "Luke?"

"Dad wasn't willing to give the wedding up," Luke explains. "He wanted to announce his run for the presidency, so he asked us to step in."

"And you said *yes?*" Carter roars. "You stole my identity, bro! Not cool!"

"Was this your plan all along?" Taliah asks with a pained look on her face.

I feel horrible. What the heck was I thinking?

"This was why you convinced me to leave? This is why you practically brainwashed me into eloping?"

"Again, I never said elope."

Her body stiffens as she looks me up and down. "Look at all that cleavage," she says with a shudder. "I can't believe people think you're me. That's so creepy!"

"Hey!" Luke snaps as he steps past his brother. "You were *lucky* to have her as a replacement! She handled the night with elegance, grace, and class."

Well, I did show the President my underwear and I fell down the stairs during the reception, but I'm not about to bring *that* up.

"Why aren't you in Anguilla anyway?" Luke asks. "I thought you were getting married on the beach?"

"Taliah slipped down the steps at the airport and broke her ankle. We've been at the hospital getting it fixed up."

"And guess what I saw at the hospital when I was suffering in agony?" she says with her hand on her hip.

"What did you see?" I ask with a gulp.

"My fiancé's friends dancing all over my Instagram at *my* wedding!" She starts limping toward me with a furious look in her eyes. I step back with every step she takes. "Eating filet mignon while I'm eating a stale tuna fish sandwich from a fucking vending machine! Dancing at the luxurious Royal Inn on the Bay while I'm lying on a cot in the hallway like a freaking animal! And networking with elites while I'm stuck beside a homeless man with rabies telling me all about his new shed!"

My back hits the wall. "How did he have a shed if he was homeless?"

"I don't know, but he was definitely homeless," she snaps. "He was wearing flannel."

"Maybe he just likes—"

"How could you steal my wedding?!" she shouts in my face.

I cringe away from her. "I didn't steal it. I just… *slipped* in."

"You *stole* it!"

I didn't think I'd ever be happy to see Kathleen, but I could kiss her as she charges into the room with Walther and Heather following behind her.

"What are you two doing here?" she snaps.

"This is our wedding," Taliah says, staring at her in disbelief.

"It's not your wedding anymore," Kathleen says in a firm voice. "You vacated the position. We refilled it."

"Vacated the position?" Taliah says, looking like she has a bad taste in her mouth. "Are you insane?"

"Mom!" Carter says with his hands out. "What did you do?"

"What did you expect?" Kathleen hisses as she angrily paces around the room. "You left us in the lurch. We couldn't cancel. You knew that! We're allowed to do what we can to survive. Your father is a US politician. Soon to be the President of the United States. The *best* President of the United States. Books will be written about him, statues will be erected all over the country, he will be the greatest man this world has ever seen! When I married him, I promised I would get him there, and I tend to deliver on that promise. And not a selfish son, a self-entitled daughter-in-law, a bitter absentee motorcycle mechanic, or a parking lot caterer who thinks she can con and manipulate her way into the most prestigious family in the country, will stop me."

Eyes drop as she glares at everyone.

"This was not just *your* night," she says.

"That was the problem," Carter says in a low voice.

She charges right up to him. "What was that?"

"Oh, come on!" he says as he looks at his father in disbelief. "You make everything about you! It was *my* wedding and all you've talked about for the past three months is how you were going to take it over with your stupid announcement!"

"*Stupid* announcement?" Walter says with an incredulous laugh. "The presidency? Stupid?"

"I should be going," I say as I slip toward the door. "This seems to be a family matter."

Taliah crutch-sprints across the room to block my path. "You're not leaving with that dress on. Take it off. Now."

"No!"

"This is ridiculous!" Walter shouts in a booming voice that gets everyone's attention. "You put us in this desperate situation, Carter. I would expect this from Luke, but not from you."

"How dare you!" I shout, surprising everyone, even myself. They all look at me, but it's no time to back down now. "Luke is a good man who's done everything you asked of him and more. You're lucky to be able to call him a son. It seems the problem in this family is *you*." I turn and point to Kathleen next. "And *you*."

She scoffs. "You're drunk."

"Not anymore, I'm not!"

"Why is the parking lot attendant talking?" Walter asks in an impatient tone.

"Don't call her that," Luke practically growls.

"What? Why not?"

"They're in love," Kathleen says with a roll of her eyes.

"Oh, that's just flipping great!" Walter says as he throws his hands in the air and turns around.

"I can't believe you, Luke," Carter says, looking betrayed. "I would never do anything like this to you."

"Yeah, right," Luke mutters under his breath.

"What did I ever do to you that's even half as bad as this?" Carter asks with a huff.

"Pratham!"

"What about him?"

"You didn't care. You didn't give a shit!"

"I cried at the funeral!"

"Fuck your tears, Carter!"

"Boys," Kathleen warns.

Luke doesn't even hear her. He's fully focused on his brother. "After the funeral, we were both furious at Dad for what he did. He tried to buy us off with new snowmobiles and it worked on you. You thanked him, hugged him, and forgot all about our dead friend before you zipped past the stop sign on the corner of the street. You're turning into him. You're as selfish and self-centered as he is."

Carter scoffs.

"Did you even bother telling Victoria you were eloping?"

"Shit," Carter mutters under his breath.

"Don't give me that bro code bullshit." Luke walks away, shaking his head.

"What about you?" Carter shouts as he steps forward, about to get his verbal hits in. "You think you're such a great guy? You ditch all of us. For what? An accident that happened *fifteen* years ago? A hockey puck killed your friend, not us. Get over it."

Luke drops his head. Carter doesn't know when to quit.

"You think you're so perfect, but all you do is fill yourself with bitterness and resentment. That's not noble. It's pathetic. You're not a good brother. You're not even a good person."

"That's not true," I say, but the damage has already been done. Luke's face twists up as he turns away. He looks crushed.

"This is not Dr. Phil!" Walter bellows. "We're in the middle of a wedding here. This is the biggest event yet for our family! Carter, you put the tuxedo on and be yourself for the rest of the night. Zoe will stay as Taliah."

"You can't be serious," Taliah says in disbelief.

"It will be a PR disaster if we switch brides now," Walter warns. "You had your chance, Taliah, and you gave it up. Zoe will remain as the bride for the rest of the weekend."

"And why would I do that when you lied about everything?" I ask.

He pulls the check out of his pocket and shows it to me. "You keep with the plan and I'll give you another one after the brunch tomorrow."

Eleanor's words from earlier ring in my head. *You could have gotten two hundred and fifty thousand.*

I stare the big man down. "Make it for one-fifty and you have a deal."

"Fine," he grunts.

"Seriously?" Taliah says with a gasp.

"Luke, we don't need you anymore," Walter says coldly. "You can go home."

"Go home?" he says with a drop of his shoulders. "It's still a family wedding…"

"And we all know how much you care about the family," Walter says sarcastically. He's not even looking at him. He's fixing his tie in the mirror.

"Alright, places people," Kathleen says, clapping her hands. "We've had enough incidents for one night. Let's land this plane smoothly. Luke, give Carter his tux."

Luke sighs in disbelief as he yanks the tie through his collar and tosses it onto the bed. I turn away while the two of them get undressed.

Taliah is shaking her head as she looks at the mangled dress on my body.

This is so bad. She's Luke's sister-in-law and a part of the family. I really wanted her to like me. I feel like we could have gotten along so well. I guess that's never going to happen now.

"Taliah, I—"

She puts her hand up and turns away from me.

Walter and Kathleen leave without saying goodbye or thank you to their son who just did them a massive favor. My jaw clenches as I watch them leave.

"I'm just supposed to stay here?" Taliah says with a huff. "And do what? Watch as she steals my life?"

"I'm going to wait in the hallway."

I glance at Luke as I head for the door, but he doesn't even turn around. He doesn't even acknowledge me. The amazing

Luke I've gotten to know looks like he's already gone. I didn't even get to say goodbye.

I lean against the wall in the hallway, waiting for him to come out. I can't believe the night is ending like this. I can't believe he's leaving.

He comes out in Carter's t-shirt and jeans.

"Luke," I say as he walks up to me. "Are you okay?"

He nods even though he doesn't look okay at all.

"So, I'll see you on Friday?" I ask with a tightness in my stomach. "For Victoria's performance?"

He sighs long and hard. Oh no.

"I can't drag you into this family," he says.

It feels like my heart is being squeezed into a tight little ball. "They're not all bad. I like Victoria and your cousins…"

"Maybe we should just… let this be."

"Are you… canceling our date?"

"You said it yourself, Zoe. You did all of this for nothing."

"Luke, that's not what I meant."

"And you're still going to get your money," he says with a shake of his head. "And an extra one hundred and fifty thousand too. Good for you."

"I don't care about the money anymore, Luke. Don't leave like this…"

"It was a fun day, but my family is right. I'm not any good, Zoe. It will be better for you if we leave this at one night."

"That's not true!" I say as he drops his eyes.

"Yes, it is. I'm going back home. I don't know what I was thinking… moving back here…"

He just walks away.

"Luke!" I shout to his back. He turns, sadness oozing off him. "But I was… starting to fall for you."

"Oh, Zoe," he says with a sad smile. "I'm so sorry."

And just like that, he leaves.

CHAPTER Twenty-Four

He left. He just… left.

I can't fucking breathe.

"Oh, shit!" Carter gasps when he sees that I'm about to lose it. "Oh, please don't cry. Please don't cry. I'm going to look like an asshole who made his bride cry at his wedding."

He bounces on his toes as he looks up at the descending numbers over the elevator.

A heaviness hits my stomach. A numbness wracks my core.

"I don't understand…"

He was feeling it. I know he was.

"Understand what?"

I was doing everything right. I wasn't being too passionate. Was I?

The elevator starts spinning. I feel like I'm going to be sick.

"Keep it together, Josie," Carter pleads. "Shit, we're almost there."

The spinning stops but the shaking starts.

I can't fucking breathe.

I'm breaking. I can feel the cracks tearing through me.

Ripping me into pieces. Cutting flesh, maiming muscle, slicing skin.

I grip onto the railing as my legs give out. My heart is racing. My head is racing. I can't fucking think. It feels like I'm losing my mind.

"Are you having a panic attack?"

My ass hits the ground.

"Shit, you are!"

I'm trembling. I'm sweaty. I don't want to be here.

Everything is all wrong. This is all wrong.

What is happening to me?

The elevator doors open with a ding.

"Get up, Josie! Get up! Please."

The lobby looks blurry through wet eyes. Fuzzy people are looking in.

Carter sees his swim team friends and lights up. "Chaz! Teets! Mikey! It's Hollywood Stinger time, baby!"

He looks excited to leave the elevator, but then turns around as he holds the doors open. "Are you okay? Do you need something?"

"I'll be fine," I say as I shake my head. "Just need some fresh air. Go on. I'm okay."

He looks at me with concern for a few seconds and then nods before bouncing out of the elevator.

The doors slide closed.

My mind comes back online.

I catch a breath. My heart slows.

The panic attack is over, but I feel even worse than before.

My head is pounding and I feel all shaky.

I crawl over to the buttons and hit the second floor.

The elevator moves. I sit on the ground, back against the wall, and focus on my breathing.

Focus on calming myself down.

The second floor comes too soon and the doors open abruptly.

"Come on, killer," I whisper to myself. "Get your ass up."

I grab the railing with a trembling hand and pull myself to my feet. With a deep breath, I head out and stumble down the hallway, feeling exhausted, defeated, heartbroken. I'm a human Adele song. I'm regret and sadness incarnate.

I start feeling a bit sturdier with each step and manage to head to the stairs and make my way down them. I exit the inn through a side door. The secret service agent stationed there nods to me and tells me congratulations.

"Are you okay, ma'am?" he asks when I stumble out the door.

"Yeah," I lie, barely turning to see him. "Just a little tipsy."

The cool night air helps. It's all tingly on my sweaty skin and fills my lungs and head with some clarity.

I haven't had a panic attack in years. They're always a good time.

I can't be here any longer.

Senator douchebag can keep his check. I don't even fucking care anymore.

I head to my tent in the parking lot with my shoulders dragging low as the last of the hope in my body leeches out.

I knew I shouldn't have taken a chance like that. I should have just kept it professional.

I have to remember this the next time I start having those unhelpful feelings. It's just going to end up with me having a panic attack on the floor of an elevator. It won't ever end well.

It's just going to derail me. It's going to take me away from my goals.

I step onto the concrete parking lot and walk around the dumpsters.

"Oh no," I whisper when I see the sad broken view of the

ice sculpture on the concrete. The angel is smashed into pieces, the banner of LOVE cracked down the middle.

I guess she was melting too much under the heat of all the sin floating around, so the staff threw her onto the concrete. The poor girl is demolished and mutilated in an angelic crime scene.

"Welcome to the club," I whisper as I step over her severed icy head.

It's not just my love life that is in a worse position than it was this morning. My business is screwed too. Kathleen will make sure that none of these people will ever hire my company again. I'll be blacklisted among the DC elite. Catering By Zoe will be a pariah. It will be untouchable.

Kathleen will have my business license revoked just for fun. I'll be put on a terrorist watchlist. She'll probably even bug my bedroom so she can laugh at the sound of me crying over her jerk-head son.

I shiver when I realize I might have to lay off all of my employees.

Jason was my first hire. I still vividly remember the addictive mix of excitement and fear when I shook his hand and told him he was hired. Sarah is a single mom with a kid. Carlos' mom is in a wheelchair and relies on his support.

I'm hard on them, but I do care. They rely on me for their livelihood and I don't take their trust lightly. It weighs on me even in the good times. But right now…

I don't know how I'm going to tell them. I don't know what they're going to do.

"Come on, Z," I whisper to myself. *Do you really think they're going to care?*

They'll find new jobs.

They all hate me anyway.

They'll probably be happy to no longer have me as their boss.

I stop under the maple tree, looking at the tent in the distance and watch them work. The tent is packed. It's actually full of people—secret service agents, drivers, assistants—and they're all hanging out and enjoying my food while Jason and Sarah serve them with smiles on their faces.

The place is spotless and the buffet is well-stocked.

I smile as I watch them, feeling pride that I trained them well. I'm proud of them too.

If I can salvage my business maybe I should trust them a little more. Take my hands off the wheel and let them drive for a change. They seem to be doing just fine.

Jason walks out with two bulging garbage bags and lights up when he sees me. "Hey, boss! I heard you were the bride? I can't believe it!"

He looks me up and down in the wedding dress with a huge smile on his face. "You look fantastic!"

"Really?"

He nods enthusiastically as he tosses the two heavy bags into the dumpster. "Oh yeah. Super hot. Are you coming to quarterback the closing up?"

I take a deep breath as I watch Sarah bringing a tray of soft drinks to some guys playing cards. "It looks like you guys are on top of things. Maybe I shouldn't be so hard on you all."

"Nah, you're a great boss."

"Really?"

He smiles as he walks over. "We like to bust your balls, but it's because we like you. That's why we all worked so hard for you tonight. We got three bookings! A baby shower and two engagement parties. It's not the wedding of the year, but they're—"

"Perfect," I say as I throw my arms around him in a hug. "They're perfect."

He stiffens as I wet his shoulder, but then loosens up and hugs me back.

"Can you tell everyone I'll pay them overtime since I'm not there to help clean up?" I ask as I pull away and wipe my eyes.

"A hug *and* overtime?" Jason says with a laugh. "What did you do with our Zoe?"

"I don't know."

He smiles and then hurries back into the tent to tell everyone the good news. I hurry away before anyone else sees me out here.

My pair of purple rubber boots catches my eye beside the dumpsters. I left them there after I hosed down the parking lot where our tent is. I got here early this morning to do it. I didn't want any cigarette butts or clumps of dirt at my guests' feet while they enjoyed my beet salad with goat cheese and balsamic vinaigrette dressing. How clueless I was…

"This wedding may not be done with me," I say as I yank Taliah's shoes off while walking over to my boots. "But I am done with these cursed shoes."

I smile as I throw them into the dumpster and then step into the purple rain boots.

"Much better." My dress drags on the ground all around me, so no one will even know, and if they do, well, I'm all out of fucks to give.

Kathleen would be horrified if she knew what was on my feet and that sends a giddy little thrill through me as I walk back to the wedding.

I'm walking through the grassy area toward the back of the inn when I hear some giggling and moaning coming from some nearby bushes. *What the—?*

A very familiar blue dress is peeking out from behind a bush.

"Aya?" I whisper. "Aya, what are you doing?"

"You mean *who* am I doing?" she says as she gets up with a giggle.

"Woot woot," a small voice emerges from behind the bush.

"Don't judge," Aya whispers as she rushes over. She's missing a shoe and there's a leaf in her messy hair.

"You and Ryan? Really?"

She shrugs as she glances back at the bush. "He's younger, but he's sweet and endearing. Endearing goes a long way with me. Sometimes you just have to follow your heart and ignore your brain."

"Smart."

She nods. "I ignore my brain all the time."

"Good luck with his family," I say as I picture Aya trying to fit in at Kathleen's house for Christmas dinner.

"They're going to love me," she says with a flick of her eyebrows. "They sing, I play ukulele. It's a match made in heaven, really."

"Yeah," I say as my shattered heart starts to ache again. "Aya, are you going to be okay if I don't have a ton of work for you?"

"I'm not worried. I can always sell a vintage ukulele if I get behind on rent. But you'll figure it out, Z. You always do."

"Yeah…"

"Where's Luke?" she asks with a relishing smile. "You two really made it look easy. I've never seen a bride and groom look so in love."

"He's gone," I say as tears burn my eyes, trying to get out. I refuse to let them. "He went home."

"Oh," she says, looking confused. "I thought it was starting to be more than just pretending…"

"Nope," I say as I take a deep breath and start walking. "Just pretending. I should get back."

"Okay," she says as she watches me walk away. "I should get back too."

She skips back to the bush and disappears behind it with a growl.

"Woot woot!" Ryan squeaks.

I hurry back to the party before I have to hear any more of that.

Guests smile at me as I walk past them and head into the reception hall. I force out smiles for everyone.

The first one I see when I walk in is Carter. My heart jolts in my chest at first, thinking Luke has returned, but then the dark cloud is back when I see the slimmer shoulders, the skinnier arms. His friends are gathered around him as he tells a story, his arms swinging around as he gets into it. They all suddenly laugh and I have to look away.

I can't believe I ever found him better looking than Luke. The little details make all the difference—The squareness of his shoulders. The thickness of his jaw. The way his blue eyes feel like they're peering into your soul.

Carter is all surface beauty. Luke's beauty runs deep.

He doesn't give his smiles as easily as Carter does either. Carter tosses them out like Oprah handing out cars during a season premiere. Luke is more guarded. More restrained. But once he does open up, he's the most incredible man you'll ever meet.

I'm already missing him. I'm already wishing he was still here by my side.

"It's almost midnight," a voice says from behind me. I turn around and see Lily holding a big glass of water.

I smile sadly. I shouldn't have lied to her. That was mean.

"I'm not really a magical princess," I tell her as she looks up at me, holding the huge glass with two hands. "It was all a fib. There's no curse. I'm not going to be turning into a mermaid tonight or ever."

She purses her lips as she looks at me skeptically. "That's what someone who is cursed would say. You *are* going to turn into a mermaid."

"No, Lily. I'm not."

She grabs the bottom of my dress and lifts it up to check my feet.

"I knew it!" she gasps. "Your feet are turning into a mermaid's tail!"

"What? No! Those are my rubber boo—"

Too late.

She tosses the (very cold) glass of water right into my face. An ice cube hits my forehead.

"I'll go put on my bathing suit!" she squeals before sprinting across the room and disappearing from view.

I stand up and hold in a scream as freezing cold water spills down my back.

Oh my god! Oh my god!

I'm gulping down air. That was so freaking cold!

Kathleen walks right up to me with a paper, pen, and a martini.

"Once again, dear. Brides are supposed to get wet on the honeymoon. Not at the wedding."

She dumps the paper and pen into my hands (keeping the martini for herself), not at all caring that my face is dripping with water.

"Sign this NDA," she commands.

I glare at her with crazy eyes as I grab the NDA and wipe my face with the crisp white pages.

She drops her mouth in horror as I dump the ruined contract back into her hands.

"No."

"Your shift is not over, lady," Kathleen warns in a low voice. "Watch yourself."

"Or what?" I say it loud enough for her to look around while smiling nervously. "I'm out of fucks to give. You have nothing you can threaten me with."

"You'd be surprised."

With my dead eyes locked on her, I drop two fingers into her martini and pluck out the olive. "So would you."

She recoils as I plop it into my mouth and chomp down on it.

"Get yourself together!" Kathleen whispers harshly as she leans in close. "We're paying you for a service. It's not my fault you fell in love with my idiot son. I have two of them, you know? You think you're the first girlfriend to cry at my feet? Usually, I'm the one making them cry, though. That's what I like about you, you give as good as you get. Finally some competition around here."

"You... *like* me?"

"You're tolerable," she begrudgingly says. "Barely."

Coming from her, that's as nice a compliment as I'm ever going to get.

"Now do the job we're paying you for."

I hate to admit it, but she's right.

I have a job to do. We agreed on the terms. It's not her fault that my heart has *Luke* carved into it.

"And sign the non-disclosure agreement."

I shake my head. Water drips off my chin. "Not a chance."

She spins around with a huff and click clacks away.

This whole family is *exhausting*.

I pick up my dress and waddle to the bar in my rain boots that are definitely *not* my feet growing into a mermaid tail.

I make eye contact with Eleanor and she waves me over. *Damn it.*

"I am leaving shortly," she tells me after I reluctantly walk over to her.

"So soon?"

She grabs my arms and gives me a warm smile. "You did wonderful tonight, dear. It was a joy watching you and my favorite grandson together. Where is he anyway? I'd like to say goodbye."

"He's over at the bar," I say, motioning to Carter with my head. I'm hoping her eyes aren't as sharp as her brain is.

She spots him and then frowns. "Not him. Luke."

I look down at my hands. "He left."

She holds onto my arms a little tighter. "You look upset."

I shrug as I fight back a fresh onslaught of tears. What is there to say?

"Stupidity among the Whitfield males," she mutters to herself. "It's an epidemic."

"It's not his fault," I tell her. "I was a bit too… much."

She shakes her head as she looks at me with those alert blue eyes. They're just like Luke's with their ability to peer into my soul.

"Don't ever dull your light so a man won't have to walk in your shadow," she says as she holds my arms and my gaze.

"Powerful women like us," she continues in a commanding voice. "Our passion is our virtue. It's our gift to the world. It's our gift to our lovers. Don't ever hold it back. Don't ever doubt it. Embrace it. Let it grow, let it flourish, and the world will be a better place for it."

She takes my hand, taps it lovingly, and then leaves.

I'm left standing here, not knowing what the hell to do.

CHAPTER
Twenty-Five

I'm slumped in a chair watching Luke's uncle Randy on the dance floor playing air guitar to some old classic rock song. He's the only one there. And he's really into it.

It's almost over.

The wedding, not the drunken performance.

It's one-thirty and the last of the guests are trickling out. The President is long gone. Happiness is long gone. Fun is a distant memory.

Scary Turkish ambassador guy has vacated the building so that's one less thing to worry about. Most of Carter's friends have left too. It's mostly just the Whitfield family left as the dining room staff cleans up and starts putting the chairs on the tables. The lights come on.

"Really good job today," Heather says as she steps in front of me with her clipboard. "The brunch starts at ten tomorrow morning. I'll come by your room around nine-thirty. You and Aya can have the bridal suite. Carter and Taliah will stay in the groom's suite. Do you have something to wear tomorrow?"

"No."

I just want to cry. I want this whole stupid night to be over.

"I'll get up early and bring you an outfit," she says without hesitation.

"Thanks, Heather. You're a really hard worker and an amazing wedding planner."

"Aww, thanks," she says, putting her hand on her upper chest. "That means a lot."

She gives the signal to DJ Brain Damage to wrap it up.

"Sorry, Randy," he says into the microphone. "I gotta turn it off."

Randy stops and opens his arms, staring at him in disbelief. "I'm in the middle of my solo!"

The song cuts out and Kathleen starts clapping. "Finally the DJ does something right."

Walter walks over as I stare ahead blankly.

"For the night," he says as he reaches into his pocket and hands me the check.

I unfold it and stare at all of the zeroes. They don't look as pretty as they did this morning. Just the sight of the check is making me nauseous.

This is the prize I wanted this morning, but now it's just feeling like a disappointment.

"Thank you," I mutter as I stuff it into my bra, not caring how unclassy it looks.

"You'll get another one for one fifty tomorrow after the brunch," he says. "Sorry about the silver contract. It's just business. You understand."

I glare up at him as he downs the rest of his scotch and slams the glass on the table beside me.

"Kathleen!" he hollers in his raspy voice that sounds similar to Luke's. "Let's go, my love."

The ice queen walks over and takes his arm. She shoots me a look over her shoulder as they leave.

As soon as she turns around, I give her the finger.

Carter sees and laughs as he comes over. "I can only imagine what my mother did to deserve that."

He plops down into the chair beside me and lets out a long breath.

"I'm sorry about your wedding, Carter," I say, feeling horrible. "I don't know what I was thinking. This was an awful idea and I can't believe I went along with it."

"I should have expected this from my parents," he says with a head shake. "Did Luke do a good job at least?"

I can't help but smile as I remember the way he was shaking his hips on the dance floor like Danny Zuko, the way he picked me up off the floor after I dove down seven stairs, the beautiful song he sang to me, a thousand other special moments—the looks, the kisses, the grins. I loved each one of them.

"He did a great job."

"You know," Carter says softly as he loosens his tie and stares straight ahead. "I hate to say it, but I think Luke was right. It was selfish of me to leave."

"You just wanted to give your bride a nice wedding."

He sighs. "Well, that didn't happen. And I pissed off my whole family."

"No offense, but I think your whole family would have been pissed off no matter what you did. It seems like every little thing sets your parents off."

"They are wound a little tight."

We're quiet as the waitress comes over and grabs the sugar, salt, and pepper.

"Do you think Taliah will ever forgive me?" I ask when the waitress leaves.

"If anyone would, it's her. That lovely woman has a heart of gold."

"I hope she does," I say with a lump in my throat. "I really do feel terrible."

"Don't sweat it," he says as he sits up. "It went well, my dad got to make his announcement, and now we'll be free to have the wedding we want. When Taliah's ankle heals, I'll bring her somewhere nice. Somewhere perfect."

"I hope it goes smoother next time."

"Oh, I forgot to ask! Did the President show up?"

I gulp. "Yup!"

"And how did it go?"

"I tackled him in my underwear."

He laughs as he gets up. "Good one."

I laugh nervously as he heads to the bar, chuckling along the way.

Heather and DJ Brain Damage slip out together, arm in arm. They're giggling and whispering to one another.

I'm done. It's over.

I could go check on the tent and make sure everything is completed to my standards, but I'm sure they're fine. Jason will take care of the closing. He'll make sure everything is done properly.

I guess there's nothing left to do but go to bed.

With a sigh, I get up.

Victoria comes over with a mischievous grin on her face. "Where are you going?"

"To bed."

"Nope," she says as she hooks her arm around mine and starts pulling me toward the exit. "It's your wedding! We're having an afterparty in the pool!"

"Isn't it closed?"

"Yup!"

I'm tired and sad. I just want to go to my room, wipe my

makeup off, slide under the gazillion thread Egyptian cotton sheets, and go to sleep.

But it is my wedding, as fake as it is. I should enjoy it. It could be my only one.

Oh god. That thought makes me want to join Carter at the bar and get another drink.

"But I don't have my bathing suit," I tell her.

Her grin deepens. "Follow me. You won't need one."

A few minutes later, we're sneaking under the fence to the pool with Aya, Ryan, and Owen. The whole area is definitely closed. All of the lights are off, including in the pool. The water is dark and perfect for sneaking around.

I've never done anything sneaky like this before. Normally, I'd be more likely to tell on people doing something like this rather than joining in.

I'm tingling with nervous excitement as I hold up the fence for Aya to go under. She slides through the dirt and then holds up the fence for me on the other side.

My dress gets snagged on the bottom of the fence and tears a bit as I pull myself through. What's one more tear? This dress has already been mangled and torn and Frankensteined together by a professional seamstress and a fake one. It won't be used again. It's cursed. It's garbage. It deserves its terrible fate.

"Are we skinny dipping?" Ryan asks excitedly as he looks at Aya and then at me once we've all slid under the fence.

"Gross!" Victoria says, looking disgusted. "We're family."

Ryan looks ready to argue his case, but Aya interrupts him. She runs past him and jumps into the pool with her dress on.

I laugh as Victoria jumps in next, quickly followed by Ryan and Owen. All in their fancy clothes. None of them caring that they're going to be ruined.

I'm smiling but hesitating at the edge of the pool.

"What are you waiting for?" Victoria asks with a grin as she smooths her wet hair back.

"It's not my dress," I say as I look around for security. There's no one around. "I shouldn't get it wet. It's going to ruin it."

Aya laughs as she looks me over. "That dress is already fucked. It looks like you played baseball in it."

I look down and gasp when I see the dirt stains smeared on my chest. I guess marine-crawling under a metal fence in a white dress was a horrible idea. I seem to be full of them today.

"Aw, fuck it," I mutter as I jump into the pool.

The warm water swallows me. I close my eyes and let myself sink to the bottom, blowing out bubbles until my lungs burn and my body's reflex forces me back up to the surface.

Victoria is grinning at me as I slick my hair back. "Can I be there when you give the dress back to Taliah?"

I'm suddenly filled with a cold dread despite the warm water. "You can give it back to her yourself if you want. Please."

"Not a chance," she says with a grin before diving under the water and swimming around.

This is cool. It's a nice ending to a shitty night.

Everyone is smiling and even Owen is looking like he's having a good time. He's so cute with his brown hair all spiky from the water. With his hair like that, he kind of looks like a younger version of Luke. A heaviness fills my body when the image of him leaving hits me again.

Maybe we should just… let this be.

I don't want to cry. Not here. Not now. This is the first time I've ever really hung out with friends and I don't want to ruin it by crying.

"It's nice to see you smiling, Owen," I say as I wade over to him. Ryan and Aya are busy in the corner and Victoria is swimming into the deep end. "I feel like I haven't seen your eyes all day. They're so blue like your cousins'."

He smiles shyly.

"Your mom works a lot, doesn't she?"

"Always," he says as he looks at his hand gliding through the water. "Some weeks she barely talks to me."

"I'm sorry to hear that," I say with a sad smile. "I know how it feels. I barely talk to my parents either."

"Really?"

"Yeah. I'm a single child too. Just like you."

We look at each other and just know. The loneliness, the isolation, the heartache. The feeling of being alone in the universe without a tribe. Of feeling like you're always on your own. It weighs on you. It eats away at you slowly. Until there's nothing left.

I feel like I got a piece of it back today. With Luke, with Victoria, with Aya, with Ryan, and now with Owen.

My heart aches as I feel it all slipping through my fingers again.

After the brunch tomorrow, I'll probably never see these people again. I might see them on TV if Walter wins the nomination and eventually wins the election, but it won't be the same.

It won't ever be the same.

Victoria is gracefully swimming on her back, her blue dress floating around her like a mermaid tail as she returns.

"This might be the last time I ever get to do something like this," she says as she puts her feet on the ground and stands up with a sad look on her face.

"Like what?" Owen asks.

"Like anything," she says with an ache in her voice. "I might be moving into the White House. I'll have the secret service following me wherever I go for the rest of my life. I don't want that."

"Have you told your father that?" I ask her.

She looks at me like I just said the most ridiculous statement ever uttered by a human. "He's making all these huge life decisions that effect all of us, but he doesn't care how we feel about it. He hasn't even asked what I think."

Ryan comes wading over with Aya clinging to his back like a baby koala.

"You should join the Taliban," Aya says. "America will never elect your father if his daughter is a member of the Taliban."

I'm expecting Victoria to roll her eyes, but she looks like she's considering it.

"Don't take advice from Aya," I warn her. "She lives with a raccoon."

"You do?" Ryan asks as he looks over his shoulder at her. "That's so cool."

"He doesn't live with me," she says like it's nothing. "He just comes to visit once in a while. I have an open-door policy with wild animals."

"See?" I say with a laugh. "Unless you're running a zoo, don't take Aya's advice."

"I would make a great zookeeper," Aya says with a nod. "I'd put the giraffes and sloths together so the sloths can cling to the giraffes' necks like furry scarves."

"Is that a flashlight?" Owen says with a gasp.

We all turn and then explode out of the pool as the flashlight starts bobbing.

"Hey!" the security guard shouts as he comes running over.

"Go under the fence," I tell them as I hold it up. "I'll take one for the team. They won't arrest the bride."

I hope.

"Thanks, Z!" Aya says as they all run over and crawl under it one by one.

They run off into the dark grounds as I let go of the fence and walk over to the gate. I suck in a breath as the security guard catches up to me. He points the flashlight into my face, blinding me.

"What are you doing in there?" he asks, surprised to see a drenched bride on the other side of the fence.

"I needed a break from my husband," I say with a shrug. "It's only been a few hours and he's already driving me crazy."

He laughs as he pulls out his key and unlocks the gate for me. "Don't worry, you only have about sixty years left. Fifty if you're lucky."

"Thank you," I say with a chuckle as he swings the door open and lets me out.

He has no idea that the rest of my late-night water crew are halfway across the resort by now. They escaped because of me.

I wish him a good night and leave with a smile on my face.

CHAPTER Twenty-Six

"There weren't many options in town," Heather says as she hands over the fancy bag. "But I think you'll like it."

I take a deep breath as I slowly take the bag and peek inside. White lace.

Heather sits on the bed with her large Starbucks coffee. She still has her big dark sunglasses on, which are probably hiding her bloodshot eyes. I wonder if DJ Brain Damage let her get any sleep last night.

"This looks like lingerie," I say as I grab the dress and pull it out. "Oh. This is really nice. Oh, wow! It's *beautiful*."

Heather looks pleased as I drape it against my body. It looks like it's going to fit perfectly. It's classy, respectable, and won't show any cleavage. It even covers my shoulders with short puffy sleeves.

"I told you," Heather says, clearly pleased with herself. "And don't forget the shoes."

I peek back into the bag and see an adorable pair of white open-toed sandals in my size. I could kiss her.

"How much was all of this?" I ask, afraid to get the bill.

She waves a dismissive hand. "I put it on the Whitfield's credit card. They won't even notice."

I thank her again as I turn to the mirror, excited to try the dress on.

"Where's Aya?" she asks. "I got a dress for her too."

"Check Ryan's room," I say with a laugh. "She never came back last night."

"Isn't Ryan staying with his parents and Lily?"

"Then you might want to check any raccoon lairs around the area."

"What?"

"Nothing," I say with a laugh. "You can leave it here. I'll text her to come pick it up."

"Hair and make-up?" she asks as she gets up and tosses her empty coffee cup into the garbage.

"Would you mind?"

"Not at all. Sit."

I sit down and pay careful attention to the way she does my hair, making it all wavy and loose, and then the products she uses for my face and how to apply them.

By the time she's done, I have a list of products to buy and am looking pretty good. I'm not sure if I can replicate this look on my own, but I'm going to try.

"You look amazing," she says as I walk out of the bathroom in the dress and shoes. "How are you still on the market?"

"I haven't been on the market," I say with a sad laugh. "I've been too busy working."

"I hear that," Heather says as she walks over and starts plucking at my hair. "The curse of the entrepreneur. We have to make a point of poking our heads out of the office once in a while or what's the point of it all?"

"I'm starting to see that now," I say as I smile at her. "I've been guilty of that for too long."

"Well, there's no better time to start than when you look like a knockout. I better go check on Carter. He was hitting the bar a little too hard last night and I'm worried he's still asleep. Are you okay getting to the brunch on your own?"

"I feel like I can run a marathon in these sandals," I say with a laugh. "I can make it downstairs."

She leaves and I'm about to kill some time with my phone when there's a knock at the door.

My heart races. I hurry to the peephole and sigh when I see Victoria there. I'm still excited to see her, but it's not the person I was hoping for.

"Wow! You look hot!" she says when I open the door.

"So, do you!" I say as I look her over in her adorable yellow summer dress. "Come on in."

"I'm glad to see you're not in the hotel jail," she says with a laugh as she strolls in and sits on the bed like she's already feeling right at home. "We were afraid you got arrested for grand theft pool or something."

"I played the bride card," I say with a laugh. "Worked like a charm."

We chat for a bit about the wedding and the brunch, laughing about the classified Presidential strip tease I was involved in.

A nagging thought won't leave me alone. I try to slip it in gracefully, subtly, nonchalantly…

"So, is Luke coming to the brunch?"

She gives me a sad knowing look and I feel my excitement draining. I already knew, but… I was still hoping.

"I haven't heard from him," she says with a sigh. "I went to his room, but there was no answer. I'm pretty sure he left. I can text him if you'd like."

"No, no," I quickly say. "That's okay. I was just wondering."

There's another knock on the door and I rush over to the peephole, letting myself get excited once again. Some people never learn. Apparently, I'm one of them.

It's Aya.

"Where have you been?" I ask as I open the door. She's still wearing the bridesmaids' dress and has an abundance of leaves in her hair. Maybe she did have a sleepover with a raccoon...

"Don't ask," she says as she walks into the room. She heads straight for the mini-fridge, grabs a bottle of water, and downs two-thirds of it in one long chug. "Woot woot."

"Oh my god," Victoria moans with a shake of her head.

Aya gets ready—looking fabulous as usual—and the three of us head out to the brunch. I feel better with my girls by my side. I've never had girls before and this is perfect timing—

The door in front of us swings open and Taliah limps out.

—because I'm going to need them.

"Carter," she calls into the room with a roll of her eyes. "Your *bride* is here."

"Give me a second," he calls back.

It's super awkward as we stand here in tense silence. Normally, Aya can be counted on to break the tension with a strange comment, but she's busy texting Ryan.

My cheeks burn as I look away from Taliah, suddenly wishing I wasn't wearing a white dress. It kind of feels like I'm rubbing it in.

"How's your ankle?" I ask with a thickness in my throat.

"Still broken," she answers in a tight voice. Her eyes drop to the wedding ring wedged around my pinkie. I casually, nonchalantly slide my hand behind my back.

My heart is pounding so hard as she gives me a stern glare with her arms crossed over her chest.

"I really am sorry," I squeak out. "I didn't mean to—"

She puts her hand up, cutting me off. "Just don't make a fool out of me at breakfast and then stay out of our lives for good."

"Hey," Victoria says, stepping in front of me protectively. "Don't talk to her like that. She was just helping the family out. Be mad at Mom and Dad, but not at her."

"What are you friends with her or something?" Taliah asks as she stares at us in disbelief.

Victoria hooks her arm around mine. "Yes, I am."

Carter is putting on his cufflinks as he arrives. It's not nearly as good a view as Luke putting on his.

"You girls look nice," he says as he steps into the hallway. "Babe, are you going to be okay with room service?"

She just looks at him.

He smiles awkwardly and then gets to work on his other cufflink. "Victoria, run over and tell Mom and Dad we're heading down." He's not even looking at her as he says it.

"No," she answers in a firm voice.

He looks up, making eye contact with her for the first time.

She looks at me and something unspoken passes between us.

You got this, girl.

With a deep breath, she turns back to him. "We need to talk."

"Okay?" Carter says, looking confused.

"It was really shitty what you guys did," she says.

Carter looks at me for help. My eyes narrow.

"You didn't even tell me you were leaving. After all the work I did in helping put this wedding together. The song list, picking the cake, the decorations, dress shopping, flower shopping, the invitations."

"We had Heather to do all that stuff," he says in a dismissive tone.

"*I* did it!" Victoria snaps. "And I would have appreciated a thank you *and* a goodbye."

He takes a deep breath as he looks at her. "I had to leave. Dad was making the day all about himself. You know how he is. He makes everything about him."

"And you make everything about you," she continues. "You don't even care that you broke Luke's heart and now you don't even care that you broke mine."

"Luke?" he says with a look of disbelief. "That was fifteen years ago. Why can't he just get over it already?"

"Have you ever apologized?" she asks with a firm look. "Maybe that would help! His best friend died and you just blew it off. Like you blew me off. I had to find out from Mom and Dad that you had left. Don't you realize how you guys made me feel? How excited I was for the wedding? You guys didn't even care."

Carter thinks about it for a moment then drops his eyes with a heavy breath.

"I'm sorry," he says in a low voice. "I should have told you."

"I guess we got caught up in the whirlwind of it all," Taliah says with a sad look. "I'm sorry we didn't consider your feelings."

"Thank you," Victoria says as she holds back tears.

"You'll be there for sure when we get married for real," Carter promises as he puts his arm around Taliah's shoulders.

"Put me down for two," Victoria says. "I'm bringing a plus one."

Taliah smiles salaciously. "Oooh, did you meet someone last night? Who are you bringing?"

"My friend Zoe," she says with her chin in the air. "She's a blast to have at weddings."

She hooks her arm around mine again and pulls me away. I

look at Carter and Taliah over my shoulder with an apologetic look. They both look stunned as they stare back at me.

We turn the corner and Victoria bounces up and down to the elevator. "God, that felt good!"

"You did great," I say as Aya and I follow her over. Aya is still absorbed into her screen, giggling as she texts Ryan.

"Thanks, Zoe," she says with a big warm smile. "You were right."

I laugh as the elevator arrives with a ding. "It's not so often that I'm—*oh crap!*"

The breath gets sucked out of my lungs when I see the Turkish Ambassador staring at me.

He's standing right there in the elevator. Close enough that I can see the gray hairs in his big black bushy moustache.

"Günaydın Taliah," he says in a deep booming voice. "Konuşabilir miyim."

Victoria steps in front of me. "We'll take the next one," she tells him.

"No." I stare him down as I pull her behind me. I'm going to end this once and for all. "I'll meet you girls downstairs."

Aya and Victoria reluctantly watch me walk into the elevator.

I give them a slight nod as the doors slide closed.

It's just the two of us now.

The elevator starts moving down.

Specific details… You can do this, Killer.

His arms are crossed over his big barrel of a chest and he's looking down at me with disapproval, like he's about to chastise me once again in words I don't understand.

He opens his mouth to start, but I slam the stop button with the side of my fist. The elevator lurches to a stop as I lunge in, stabbing my finger into his face while gritting my teeth.

"What are you doing?!?" I hiss at him. "Are you trying to blow my cover?"

He steps back with a shocked face. I got him on the ropes.

"I am a Turkish spy reporting directly to the President!"

Oh shit, does Turkey even have a President?

"I am on the cusp of infiltrating the immediate family of the next President of the United States and you are doing nothing but hindering my progress! Would you like me to report you? Is that it?"

"No!" he cries in panic as he waves his thick hands in front of him. "No!"

He doesn't know what hit him. His big mouth keeps flapping open, but no words are coming out. Time for the knockout blow.

"Your incompetence has put you on thin ice, Ambassador."

He drops his head in shame. I hit the button and the elevator starts moving again.

"Now, leave this hotel at once and never speak of my name to anyone ever again. Otherwise, I'll call the President on his personal cell phone—yes, I have the number—and report you immediately. Do I make myself clear, Ambassador?"

He frantically nods his head as he quickly backs away from me. "Evet hanımefendi," he grumbles, whatever that means.

I don't stop glaring at him until the elevator doors open to the lobby and he practically sprints out of the building.

A giggle bubbles up when I'm all alone. *I* did that. I actually lied. Successfully.

I wish I could tell Luke.

The giddiness gets pulverized out of me and is replaced with a deep heaviness that is becoming all too familiar.

With a heavy sigh, I step out of the elevator and walk through the lobby.

Janet is sitting on the couch by the fountain, sucked into

her phone as usual. Owen walks over to her and sits down. He says something to her and she barely answers. She doesn't even look up from the screen.

I'm already marching over to them as Owen pulls out his phone and slumps down beside her.

"Can I see these for a second?" I ask as I snatch the phone out of her hands and then grab the phone out of Owen's hands. They stare up at me in shock as I toss both phones into the large fountain behind me. They land in the middle with a splash.

"Wha—? What—?" Her brain is short-circuiting now that she has no screen to distract her. "Why did you do that?"

"Stop ignoring your family!" I snap at her. She stares up at me in shock. "You have an amazing son and you're not even realizing that he's growing up without you!"

She looks at Owen and then looks back at me.

"It can't just be about work," I tell her in a firm voice. "Life is deeper than that. We have to remember who we're doing it for otherwise what's the point?"

Her shock is starting to wear off and she's getting a slightly crazed look in her eyes as she stares up at me. It's probably time to move on.

"Enjoy your breakfast," I say with a gulp.

I quickly head outside to the brunch. The huge food table is set up on the patio by the water and there's a long beautiful row of tables under the giant tent. It's stunning. The flowers, the dishes, the decorative fruit platters, the covered chairs, another three-layered wedding cake. This place really is spectacular and the weather is perfect. Sunny with a nice refreshing breeze. All that's missing is Luke.

"Good morning, Zoe," someone says from behind me. I turn around with a gasp at hearing my real name. It's Father

Cliff. He's walking on the grass in black slacks and a black shirt with the little white square at his throat.

"It's a… Taliah. Remember?"

He gives me a fake smile as he arrives.

"Father Cliff, why were our real names on the papers?"

"You got married in the house of God," he says.

I can feel the blood draining out of my face as I stare at him in horror. "What are you saying? Those weren't *real* documents… right?"

He grins, clearly pleased with himself. "You can expect the marriage certificate in six to eight weeks. It was filed this morning."

My mouth drops open. *What?!*

"I was not about to sin under the eyes of the Lord," he says with a shrug. "Not for your family or for any price."

"But you still kept the ten grand, right?" I say through clenched teeth.

He sticks his chin in the air. "That's irrelevant."

A million thoughts are racing through my mind as he walks away like he didn't just drop a bomb onto my life and explode it all to pieces.

I'm married?! For real?

I have to tell Luke.

Luckily, I think I know exactly where he is.

CHAPTER Twenty-Seven

"Thanks, Frank!" I say as I run out of the limousine toward the dive bar from last night.

His elbow is hanging out of the window as he watches me. "It's only ten o'clock. Even the diviest of dive bars open at noon."

I run past the guy from last night who's sprawled out on his broken motorcycle and sleeping with his bandana over his face, and up to the bar. It's locked. Shit.

The bartender said the room to rent was around back. I run down the stairs and jump over the missing two. With my heart pounding, I race around the bar and take a breath of relief when I see Luke's motorcycle parked next to a tiny cabin.

Well, cabin is being a bit generous. At best, it looks like a converted shed or an oversized dog house.

I run over to it and knock on the door three times.

"Luke!" I call out. "It's me."

When there's no answer, I try the handle and it swings right open.

Wow. At twelve dollars a night, it appears that Luke overpaid. It's nothing but an old dresser with only one drawer, a stained yellow sink, a urinal, and a dingy cot.

Luke is sleeping on his stomach in only his underwear. I reach over to shake him awake, but I stop myself and take one last look.

He looks so peaceful laying there. A strong urge to gently brush the messy brown hair off his forehead wells up inside of me. I wrestle it away as I run my eyes along his muscular back as it slowly moves up and down with every tranquil breath.

His skin looks so warm and soft. I just want to crawl into the bed next to him, rest my cheek on his back, and drift off to sleep. I want to wake up with those big comforting arms wrapped snugly around me. I want to pretend like the evening didn't end so horribly and we're back in that magical place.

This is not helping.

A thickness grows in my throat as I straighten my back.

"Luke," I say in a firm voice. "Luke, wake up."

His head jerks up and he looks confused as he turns to me. "Zoe?"

The way he says it… it almost sounds hopeful…

"I'm sorry to barge in here like this—"

"No," he says as he sits up and pulls the blanket over his bottom half. "No, not at all. I'm glad you're here."

"You're not going to be glad when you hear what I have to say." I take a deep breath. "We're married for real. Father Cliff put our real names on the documents on purpose. He filed them this morning, which means we're officially married."

"Oh." He drops his eyes as it hits him that he's no longer a bachelor.

It's hard not to look at his arms and chest when they're so fully on display, so I look at the ceiling instead.

"I just wanted to tell you in case you wanted to get the divorce documents ready. I'll sign whatever you send over."

I turn and quickly exit through the door, letting it slam closed behind me with the super aggressive squeaky hinges.

I'm holding in tears as I rush back to the safety of the limousine.

The door opens. Luke stumbles out as he tries to pull on Carter's tight jeans.

"Zoe!" he calls out.

I stop, take a deep breath, and turn.

He opens his mouth, but doesn't say a thing. His face looks pained as he stares at me.

"I don't want it to end like this," he finally says.

I could say all of the things I have burning inside of me. I could tell him I don't want it to end like this either. I could tell him I want him. That I've never felt this way about anyone before. That I'm scared I never will again. That I need him. That I'm still falling in love with him even after he broke my heart.

I could say all of those things.

But I don't.

I don't say any of them.

"Goodbye, Luke."

I say that. And then I leave.

~

"Where did you run off to, dear?" Luke's grandmother Eleanor asks as she comes walking over in an elegant blue dress. She kisses my cheek and then holds my hand. "I wanted to tell you something."

"I just had a… phone call to make. Nothing important. What is it you wanted to tell me?"

"I heard that my son and his wife pulled a fast one on you," she says with an apologetic look. "Lying about the White

House catering contracts… They should be ashamed of themselves."

I let out a defeated breath as I look at her. I'm not even mad anymore. I'm too *blah* to be mad.

"Never agree to anything without a contract," she says with a firm nod. "If it's not in writing, it doesn't exist."

I'll try to remember that the next time I'm dealing with sociopaths.

"Anyways," she says in a lighter tone. "I'm always in charge of hiring the caterers for my bridge club tournaments. I'd be happy to hire Catering By Zoe for the next event."

"That's very nice of you, but you don't have to."

"I want to," she says as she squeezes my hand. "I'd feel like I was in good hands with you in charge."

I smile at her. She's so sweet.

"And it's not a small group," she continues. "Two hundred rich grandmothers who pay for their families' engagement parties, funerals, birthdays, baptisms, bar mitzvahs, weddings, baby showers, retirement parties, you name it. After one or two tournaments, you'll be swimming in bookings."

My heart starts to beat a little faster. "Really?"

"Oh yeah," she says with a sly grin. "These rich women throw money around like it's a sport."

"You don't mind?" I say with an excited tingling in my limbs.

"Not at all. I've been wanting to get rid of our caterer for a while now. I mean, how do you screw up a pig in a blanket?"

I shake my head. "Fucking amateurs."

She grins. "That's the spirit I like to see. I take it your food is good?"

"The best," I say with a proud nod.

"I have no doubt."

"Thank you so much, Eleanor. I won't let you down."

"I know you won't." She pats my hand. "I don't mean to pry, dear. But my grandson?"

I hold my breath as my eyes suddenly fill with water. I shake my head.

She sighs. "I don't know how he could let you pass him by. Just when you think the Whitfield males can't get any stupider…"

"I'm just glad I got to meet you all."

"I'll be seeing you again, Zoe. Sooner rather than later, I hope."

She pats my hand one last time and then leaves to talk with an older couple.

I let out a breath of relief as I turn to the sparkling bay. Two hundred rich matriarchs who throw around money? It's not the White House, but it sounds pretty damn amazing. I guess I won't have to lay off any staff after all. I might even have to hire a few more.

I'm already planning it out as I walk over to the shoreline and gaze at the lone sailboat in the distance. A young family is on the boat—a happy couple with an adorable toddler. The father is showing him how to hold a fishing rod while the mom watches with an encouraging smile on her face.

That's what I want. A family.

I can't go back. The genie is out of the bottle. Pandora's box has been opened. I can't pretend that all I care about is work anymore. I can't pretend like I don't long for more.

I smile as I watch the kid's excited face as he casts his lure into the water. He looks so proud as he turns to his mother who is clapping with glee. Meanwhile, the shiny lure is dangling a few inches above the water, but neither of the parents have the heart to tell him.

The sadness aches within, but I can feel an optimism brewing somewhere deep inside me as well. It didn't work out with Luke, but that doesn't mean it won't work out next time, or the time after that. I just have to stay hopeful. I just have to do whatever it takes.

"Taliah?" a shy voice says from behind me.

It takes me a second or two to realize the voice is talking to me. "Hi, Cindy," I say when I turn and see Carter's ex standing there sheepishly.

She looks at the grass between us as she fidgets with her hands. "I just wanted to apologize for my behavior yesterday. I had a bit too much wine and I made a fool of myself."

I put my hand on her shoulder and smile when her eyes meet mine. "*You* made a fool of yourself? Did you see me nose-dive down the stairs?"

She laughs in relief. "You almost stuck the landing."

"Yeah, I don't think so," I say with a laugh. "And you don't even want to know about what happened when I met the President!"

"What happened?" she asks, not looking nervous anymore.

"Top secret," I say with a wink. "Let's just say that I made an impression he'll never forget."

We both laugh and she smiles gratefully at me. "I'm glad Carter found someone cool like you to marry."

"You'll find someone too," I say and I mean it. "You'll find someone who gets your heart pumping like it's Christmas morning. Someone who makes every one of your dreams come true."

"I hope you're right," she says, looking like she wants to believe me, but she's not quite there yet. "I want to get married one day. I want a family, but sometimes it feels like I'll never get there."

"You'll get there when you're ready," I say softly. "Someone wise once told me that you can always make your own family.

All you need is love, respect, and a commitment to stay together."

We're both a little misty-eyed as we look at each other. "Congratulations again, Taliah," she says with a genuine smile this time.

I reach out and hug her.

"I guess, I'll see you around," she says as she pulls away to leave.

I nod, even though it's a lie. I won't be at any more family events. The next time she meets Taliah, she'll be pretty confused.

Victoria walks over when I'm alone once again. "Come," she says as she grabs my wrist. "We're going to hit the buffet. You're sitting beside *me*."

I start to feel better once I'm in line for the buffet and surrounded by my new friends. Victoria and Carter are in front of me, Aya and Ryan behind me.

"Where did you guys sleep last night?" I ask the giggling couple behind me.

"Sleep?" Ryan says with a goofy grin. "Who said we slept?"

"What are you guys doing this afternoon?" Victoria says as she hands me a hot empty plate. "Maybe we can catch a movie or take the boat out?"

"We're heading out for our honeymoon," Carter says as he grabs a spoonful of fruit salad and puts it on his plate.

"Oh, you're still going?" Victoria asks. "I didn't think you'd go since you didn't get married."

He shrugs. "I'm not about to pass up a free vacation to Anguilla. The beachfront villa is booked and Grandma already reserved the company jet for us."

We move up the line and Randy walks the other way with a whole lot of sausage piled high on his plate. He's wearing his bathing suit and a tank top, and doesn't seem to care one bit that he's wildly underdressed.

"What about you?" Victoria asks as we move down the buffet. I'm starving, so I load up on waffles, pancakes, bacon, sausage, and all kinds of other unhealthy delights. "Do you want to hang out?"

"I'd love to," I say, already knowing that my schedule is wide open.

We head over to the table when our plates have no more room to cram anything else on them.

I smile when I see Owen and Janet sitting beside each other. There are no screens in sight. Janet keeps chugging her coffee and Owen's hands are shaking, but it's a start.

"I didn't get to tell you last night that I loved your performance," Janet says to him in an awkward stiff tone.

Owen's face breaks out into a huge grateful smile. "You thought it was good?"

She puts her hand on his and smiles warmly at him. "I thought it was excellent."

Awww.

"Taliah," Carter calls out when I head for the middle of the table. "We're over here!"

Oh, right. I'm still the star of this show. I guess I have to sit at the head of the table with my new pretend groom.

I keep my eyes on Owen and Janet as I sit down with my overloaded plate. Frank makes his way over to the empty seat beside Janet. "Anyone sitting here?"

Janet looks stunned when she looks up and sees him. "No," she says, staring at him in awe. "It has your name on it. Where did you get those scrambled eggs?" she asks as she points at his plate. "I didn't see any up there."

He reaches into his suit jacket and pulls out a resealable

plastic bag full of them. "I got a few extra. You can have some."

She reaches into the mushy bag with her spoon and something passes between them when they touch hands. They can't seem to take their eyes off one another.

"I'm Frank."

"I'm Janet."

They're all goofy smiles and hearts in their eyes.

Owen sighs as he reaches over and takes Ryan's phone off the table. He slouches down and gets absorbed into the screen once again. Oh well. You can't win them all.

Just as I'm about to take a big, delicious, syrupy bite of my pancakes, Walter starts clinking his glass with his fork and stands up.

I roll my eyes. This guy will never pass up an opportunity to make a speech.

"I would like to thank everyone for coming to the Whitfield family brunch," he says in a booming voice. He holds up his mimosa and smiles at the fifty or so guests who made the cut. Kathleen is smiling in the seat beside him. "It was a wonderful wedding and a very special night for the Whitfield clan. Today we start two new chapters in our family's illustrious history. We welcome Taliah into the family and we start my bid to become the President of the United States."

He holds for applause and people clap politely. I notice that Victoria keeps her hands in her lap.

"I'll be on the *Mornings In New York Show* tomorrow morning, so be sure to tune in for that."

Yeah, definitely not watching that.

"Carter, Taliah…" he continues. "Grab your drink and please stand up."

I smile awkwardly at Carter as we stand up, clutching our mimosas.

"Taliah, now that you're a member of the great Whitfield…"

His voice trails off as the rumbling sound of a motorcycle fills the air.

"Now that you're a member of…"

The rumbling gets louder as a motorcycle comes roaring through the parking lot. It's heading right for us.

My heart starts thumping in my chest as I recognize it.

It's him.

What is he doing here?

Luke rides his bike right onto the grass and revs the engine as he comes flying toward us.

"What the hell?" Walter grunts as he watches the bike park next to the table.

I can't breathe as I stare at Luke's red helmet, knowing it's him underneath. I'm clutching my glass so hard I'm worried it's going to shatter in my hand.

He cuts the engine, steps off the bike, and takes his helmet off.

CHAPTER Twenty-Eight

It's Luke.

He's staring right at me—messy brown hair, wrinkled shirt, jeans. My heart aches for him. It *longs* for him. It wants to beat right out of my chest and flop across the grass to get to him.

He looks wrecked as he stares at me with desperation in his blue eyes.

"I don't want this to be over."

"I hope not," Randy says as he picks up a sausage with his fingers and bites into it. "Even my first marriage lasted longer than twenty-four hours."

"Wait," someone whispers. "Is that Luke or Carter?"

"I thought *that* was Carter."

Everyone looks so confused as Luke takes a step toward me.

I can't move. I can't breathe. All I can do is stand here trembling while holding my mimosa.

His beautiful blue eyes—so full of anguish—are *pulling* me toward them. They're *gripping* me. I'm *fixated* on them.

"I don't want to let this be," he says in a firm voice. "I don't want to keep it at just one night."

The weight on my chest begins to lift as I see the vulnerability, the honesty, the possibility.

"Yesterday should have been the hardest, most frustrating, roughest day of my life, but it wasn't. It was the best day I've ever had. I had the time of my life and it was because of you."

I swallow hard as I watch him. Everyone is staring at us, but he hasn't taken his eyes off me.

"I love seeing the fire in your eyes when you look at me. I love the passion burning inside you. I love your intensity. Your drive. Your fiery spirit. I love that you moved out on your own and started a new life. I love that you started your own business with nothing and grew it into a success. I love that you kicked my ass in pool. I love that you go for whatever you want and don't stop until you get it. No matter what."

He takes a deep breath as his eyes burn into mine.

"You inspire me, Zo-*Taliah*." He looks around nervously. "To do the same. I want you. I want to be the one you choose for your family. I want to be the one you choose to love."

I take a deep breath and am shocked to discover that I'm crying.

"What do you say, Captain? Can you please forgive me? Can I take you out after we get divorced?"

It's pure torment on his face as he waits for my answer.

Everyone is staring at me, waiting for me to say something. Anything.

I let my finger do the talking.

With a grin on my lips, I start clinking my glass with the wedding ring on my pinkie.

Everyone joins in, clinking their glasses with forks and knives as the tension rushes out of Luke and a slow loving smile takes its place.

"Kiss her already!" Carter shouts.

Luke rushes over, grabs my face with his warm smooth hands, and kisses me like there's no tomorrow.

Everyone cheers as he wraps his arms around me and holds me like he's never going to let me go.

He better not.

This is right where I belong.

CHAPTER Twenty-Nine

"Carter and Taliah, everybody!" Walter nervously shouts to the cheering crowd. "I guess my identical twins played a little trick on everybody. Good one, boys!"

Carter gets out of his seat and pats Luke on the back as he takes his plate to sit somewhere else. "Sit with your girl," he says with a smile.

"Thanks, Carter," Luke says as he sits beside me. He's clutching onto my hand and with the intense way he's gripping it, I'm not sure if I'll ever get it back.

Walter wraps it up and everyone gets back to their breakfast. I'm too amped up to eat, which is a shame since there's nothing worse than wasting perfectly good pancakes.

"I told the Turkish Ambassador off!" I whisper to him. "You should have seen me, you would have been so proud. I told him I was a spy!"

"I can't believe I missed that!" he says with a regretful smile on his face.

"I'm officially a successful liar now. Thanks to you."

His eyes fall to my mouth and he leans in and kisses me, just because he can.

The guests leave after breakfast until it's just Aya, me, and the Whitfield family left. Taliah shows up and picks over what's left of the buffet. My stomach twists into a knot as I watch her. At least, I won't have to pretend I'm her again. I hope.

Luke takes my hand and we head over to the water. It's a gorgeous sunny day and I feel so blessed to enjoy it with this wonderful man. We sit on the grass and watch Owen blowing bubbles while Lily runs around trying to catch them. Aya and Ryan are whispering and giggling under a maple tree.

"So, how many bedbug bites did you get on that gross cot?" I ask with a grin as we sit on the grass.

Luke starts subconsciously scratching his legs even though he's probably fine. "It was even more uncomfortable than it looked. It was like sleeping on a bag full of coat hangers."

"Serves you right for leaving me," I say, but there's no bite in it.

He takes my hand and squeezes it. "It won't happen again, Zoe. I promise."

God, those eyes… that face… I can't even…

We're leaning in for another kiss when Walter arrives, clearing his throat to get our attention. He has the fancy box of envelopes under his arm.

"Your payment for services rendered," he says as he reaches into his jacket and hands me another check. One hundred and fifty thousand dollars. I run my fingertip over all the zeroes. I can't wait to see the look on the bank teller's face when I deposit both of them.

"I'm glad I could be of service," I say with an overly polite smile. "Catering By Zoe. We do it all. Tell your friends."

"If any of my friends are looking for a last-minute bride, I'll tell them to call you."

He looks down at the box of envelopes and takes a deep breath.

"Luke, I owe you an apology."

I can feel Luke stiffening beside me.

"I'm sorry I was insensitive when your friend died," he says with a regretful look. "I was wrong. I should have done more to save Pratham. I should have done whatever I could to help. I was leaving in a rush and didn't grasp the severity of his injury because I wasn't listening to you. And after, when it was too late, I didn't acknowledge my role in the tragic event. I'm sorry, Luke. I let you down as a father. I have a lot of regrets in my life but how I handled that one is at the top."

He lets out a heavy sigh.

"I'll happily add on another five years to your charity," he says in a low voice, "in addition to the ten that we already negotiated. So, that's fifteen years, plus this."

He offers the box.

"Please put this toward your charity as well. Hopefully, it will make up for the years we missed."

"That belongs to Carter and Taliah," Luke says with his hands on the ground.

"They didn't get married," Walter says. "You did. Plus, we paid for the wedding, so we don't owe them squat."

Luke shakes his head. "I still don't feel right about taking it."

"Take it, Luke." Carter walks over and nods to his brother. "It would have made Pratham proud. His parents will be thrilled."

Luke looks up at his brother and then at his father. I can tell he's touched. His chin quivers.

He takes the box, opens the lid, and lets out a low breath

when he sees all of the fat envelopes inside. The guests must have really opened their wallets to curry favor with the next President of the United States. There's a fortune in there.

Luke puts down the box and stands up.

Walter offers his hand. Luke's eyes are watering as he wraps his arms around him, hugging him instead. "Thanks, Dad."

Aww, now I'm crying as Walter wraps his arms around his son.

Luke hugs Carter next. It looks like Eleanor will get her wish—Luke will be around at Christmas time.

I wander away to give the men some privacy.

Oh no.

Hopefully, the forgiveness in the air is contagious because Taliah is limping over on her crutches.

"I didn't know you and Luke had real feelings," she says softly.

"Surprise!" I say with a nervous smile.

"Did that happen last night?"

I nod my head. "It was just one of those magical nights that come around once in a lifetime."

She smiles as she reaches over and runs the tip of my hair through her fingers. "I wish I would have been there to see it."

"Maybe one day you'll be there for the real thing."

"I'd like that," she says with a warm smile. "I don't want to fight with you, Zoe. I want to be friends, and if things go as well with Luke as they did with me and Carter, we might even be sisters one day."

"I'd like that too," I say. "So, we're cool?"

She nods. "We're cool."

I probably should tell her that the Turkish Ambassador thinks she's a spy, but maybe that can wait for another time.

"I'm pretty amazed that you pulled this wedding off," she

says with a laugh. "That was so ballsy. I don't think I would have had the guts to do it."

I laugh, thankful it's finally over. "It was pretty wild."

"It reminds me of the time when I was getting started in real estate and I pretended to be a Moroccan princess to get a meeting with a rich investor. It did *not* go well."

We both laugh. "You did that?"

"Oh yeah," she says with a grin. "When you start with nothing like I did, you got to do whatever it takes."

I can't help but smile. "I think we're going to get along just fine."

Kathleen comes slithering over with a scowl on her face. "Why are you still here?" she asks coldly. "You got your check. Leave."

Taliah hooks her arm around mine and clutches it protectively. "She's with me. *I* asked her to stay."

Kathleen narrows her eyes on her. "You also asked my son to elope. You're playing a dangerous game, lady."

I got rid of her once, I can do it again.

"The next time you think you can ruin a—"

"BEEP!"

"You can't possibly think—"

"BOOP!"

"Are you finished, because I—"

She stops talking and glares at me when I start pounding my chest and hooting like a gorilla.

"If you think that's going to—"

Taliah joins in and starts beating her chest as well while we both make gorilla sounds.

Kathleen grits her teeth, huffs out a breath, and then leaves with her fists clenched, muttering something under her breath.

We both burst out laughing when she's gone.

"Dealing with her is going to be a lot more fun with you around," Taliah says as she looks at me with a big smile.

I can't wait.

"We have to go get ready," Carter says as he walks over. "The jet is scheduled to leave in three hours."

Taliah looks unsure. "I don't know, Carter… Our honeymoon? We didn't even get married."

His eyes widen in panic. "Are you kidding me, babe?! It's a free trip to Anguilla. Five bedroom villa on the beach, private jet, we're not missing this!"

Taliah suddenly turns to me. "Come with us!"

"What?!" I gasp.

"Yes!" she says as Luke comes walking over. "Come on the trip with us! We'll get to hang out and get to know each other. It will be so fun!"

Aya overhears and comes over with Ryan. "Can we come too?"

"Absolutely!" Taliah says. "And Victoria! You're coming too!"

Luke looks at Carter as if waiting for his approval.

"It's been too long since we've hung out," Carter says with a smile. "Come on, we'll have a blast."

Luke grins. "I'm in!"

Everyone is getting excited. Except me.

"I can't," I say. Everyone turns to me in disappointment. Once again, I'm the party pooper. "I have a booking on Thursday. A business conference."

"James can handle it," Aya says. "Put him in charge."

I suck in a breath as everyone waits for my answer. "Okay," I finally say. "I'll let James be in charge."

I'm expecting to feel fear and regret at handing my business over to an employee, but I don't. I'm okay with it. Life is for more than just work.

"You'll come?" Taliah asks, looking thrilled.

I smile as I look at all of the happy excited faces staring at me. "I'll come!"

They all cheer and then explode into action.

"The plane leaves in *three* hours!" Carter shouts as everyone rushes to get ready. "Get your shit and we'll meet at the airport. Private hangar number sixty-three!"

"I have to get home and feed my raccoon!" Aya says as she sprints to the parking lot.

"I'll help!" Ryan says as he follows her out.

"I have to go pack," I say as my heart begins to race. "I don't have anything here."

"Come on," Luke says as he hurries over to his motorcycle. He pats the seat. "I'll give you a ride. Captain."

I grin as I hurry over.

I've never been on a motorcycle before and I'm not sure if I'll like it.

Luke hands me his red helmet and kisses me before I put it on.

He gets on first and I climb on behind him. I wrap my arms around his large frame and grip my hands on his hard stomach. *This is not so bad…*

Lily comes running over before we leave. I lift up the visor and look down at her.

"You are a Disney princess," she says with a look of awe. "You got your happily ever after."

"She sure did," Luke says with a grin. "I'll make sure of it."

I blow her a kiss as Luke starts the engine and drives off, both of us eager to start the rest of our lives.

Together.

CHAPTER *Thirty*

Five weeks later…

"I wrote two new songs," Victoria says as she tunes her guitar at the table. "Will you let me know if they're horrible?"

"We will," Luke says with an encouraging smile. "I'm sure they're great, though."

Carter and Taliah nod in agreement.

Victoria looks right at me. "Zoe?"

I look her dead in the eyes. "I'll tell you."

She takes a breath of relief. "Thank you."

I smile as I watch her bound up from her seat when the manager waves her over to the stage. We're at the pub where she plays on Friday nights and I'm here watching with my friends.

"Luke, did you sign the place?" Carter asks from across the table.

Luke's jaw tightens as he gives him a look.

"What place?" I ask as my heart starts racing.

Luke sighs as he drops his eyes to his beer. "I was going to surprise you *later*," he says as he shoots Carter another look. "But I signed a lease for the shop."

"You did?!" I perk up in my seat and grip his big arm. "Where?"

He laughs. "Beside The Ba."

"Where?" Taliah asks, looking confused.

"It's a dive bar near the wedding venue," I quickly tell her. "We escaped there for a while during the reception."

"And Zoe trounced me at pool," Luke adds with a sly grin as he looks at me.

"So, it's happening?" I ask in disbelief. "It's really happening?"

Luke nods. "Signed, sealed, delivered. Hopefully, I can have the shop open by Christmas."

"Just in time for all of the motorcycles to be put into storage for the winter," Carter says with a laugh.

Taliah smacks his arm. "I think it's great, Luke. I can come by this week to help you with the zoning requirements and give you some ideas on the layout."

"That would be amazing," Luke says with an eager nod.

I can't stop staring at him. I'm in awe. This is really happening.

He moved down the street from me two weeks ago and now he's opening up a business to be near me. I can't even with this guy. He's too much.

"There they are," Taliah says as she looks at the door.

I turn and smile when I see Aya and Ryan rushing in. They grab a seat at our table as Victoria sets up.

"Did we miss it?" Aya asks as Ryan flags down the waitress.

"She's just starting now," Luke says as he shifts a little closer to me.

I lean over and kiss his shoulder, just because I can. He looks at me and chuckles.

The past few weeks have been indescribable. A pure dream.

I didn't know that life could be so fun.

We all had a blast in Anguilla.

Taliah is amazing and we connected immediately. She's unbelievable with all the things she's done. She moved here from Turkey when she was nineteen with nothing more than two thousand dollars and now she runs this amazing real estate empire. She's incredible and I have so much to learn from her.

Even Aya and Ryan fit in perfectly. We hung out by the pool or beach all day and had these long fun dinners, just talking and laughing all through the night. Sitting there with Luke by my side, laughing until my ribs ached and becoming closer with these wonderful people, I just had the most blissful and happy feeling vibrating through my body. I was wishing I could live in those moments forever or at least bottle them up to bring home. Whenever I felt lonely, I could open that bottle and be engulfed with all of that hope and love and friendship.

It was paradise until Kathleen and Walter showed up midway through the week and caused some chaos, but that's a story for another time.

Things are going so well with Luke. The days and evenings at the villa were fun, but the nights with this extraordinary man… unforgettable.

We got the marriage annulled when we returned home. It was pretty easy once we showed the judge the video of Father Cliff using Carter and Taliah's names throughout the ceremony instead of ours.

I was a bit disappointed to no longer call Luke my husband, but I'm pretty sure it's not going to be the last time he puts a ring on my finger. At least, that's what he keeps saying.

"What are you grinning about?" Luke whispers playfully when he catches me staring at him.

"I'm just happy," I say with what feels like a permanent smile on my face.

He smiles back at me, leans in, and kisses my forehead.

The DJ turns off the music as Victoria steps up to the microphone with her guitar slung over her shoulder. Aya cheers so loud that the whole bar looks at her.

"Thanks for that, Aya," Victoria says into the microphone with a laugh. "I'm going to play a few songs for you tonight. This one is called, *In The Deep End*."

I cling to Luke's arm as she begins to strum on the guitar and sing softly into the microphone. She's so talented. I love watching her perform. I've only missed one performance since we met and that was because I had a booking.

Eleanor's bridge club is keeping Catering By Zoe very busy. The phone is ringing off the hook with bookings and we're almost fully scheduled up until Christmas. I had to hire six more employees.

We've been busier than ever, but the days of me putting work before everything else are over. I promoted James to manager and he does a good job covering for me when I have more important things to do, like last week when we went to Capitol Hill with Walter for a family photo shoot.

You should have seen Kathleen's face when I showed up on Luke's arm. I wish I got a picture of that.

Victoria sings a few more songs, including the two new ones, which I'll be happy to tell her are amazing.

"Thank you," she says as our table cheers the loudest. "Now, if you wouldn't mind, my very talented older brother would like to come up here and sing a song."

Luke pushes his chair back and gets up.

"You're singing?" I ask as I stare up at him in shock. I had no idea.

"For you," he whispers as he looks down at me with that look I love so much. He's looking at me like I'm the most precious thing in the world.

"Go, Luke!" Aya shouts with a holler. She's clapping her hands as everyone in the bar looks at her again. Well, not everyone. Luke's beautiful blue eyes are burning into me as he leans down and whispers into my ear.

"I love you."

He leaves before I can answer. Before I can process those words I've been dying to hear. It's the first time he's said it—the first time either of us has said it—and I'm sitting here stunned as I watch him casually walk to the stage like he didn't just change everything.

I tear up as I watch him take the guitar from his sister, a comforting warmth radiating through my body.

Can life be this perfect? What did I do to deserve all this?

I lean back in my chair as Luke stands up to the mic, looking confident, at ease, and so fucking sexy.

His eyes land on mine and my heart does a little flip in my chest.

"This is for the girl I'm going to marry. Again."

My cheeks hurt from smiling as everyone around the table chuckles.

Luke sings *Wicked Games* to me and I'm ready to kick everyone out of the pub and jump his bones right there on the stage by the time he's finished the sexy erotic song.

I need to leave. I need to get this man alone. I need to do wicked things to him.

But first, I need to tell him something. Something important. Something I've been waiting to say to him since that first enchanting night together.

He sits back down beside me and I lean into his ear. With my whole body brimming with joy, happiness, and satisfaction, I say those magical words I thought I might never get to say.

"I love you more."

The End

Come visit Luke, Zoe, and the whole gang on their vacation in Anguilla with a FREE 20,000 word novella!

Join my newsletter to read Borrowed Honeymoon for FREE!

Sign up at www.NoahHardy.com/newsletter.html

Note From The Author

If you enjoyed the book and it made you laugh, please leave a review. I'm a new author so every review will help *tremendously*.

If you want more books like Borrowed Bride then let me know it in a review!

I read them all!

Thanks so much.

- Noah Hardy

Noah Hardy is a father of two and a husband of one. When he's not writing a novel (and laughing to himself) in a coffee shop, he's trying to be as good a father as Bandit from Bluey, but man, that cartoon dog sets a high bar.

He also writes Adventure Comedy books for kids ages 8-12 under his Middle Grade name, Marc Lewis.

Learn more here —

For you…
www.NoahHardy.com

For kids…
www.AuthorMarcLewis.com

Coming Soon...

The Proposer

By Noah Hardy

Coming May of 2024

Check out www.NoahHardy.com for news!

Also by Noah Hardy

Want more Borrowed Bride?

Get the Audiobook! Available now!

Also by Noah Hardy

Noah Hardy writes Adventure Comedy Middle Grade books under Marc Lewis.

Perfect for boys (and girls) ages 8-12, including reluctant readers!

How the heck do you escape space?

Wyatt can't stand his annoying new stepbrother, Duncan. First, he spills lemonade on his bed, then he messes up his video games, and now he's gotten them both abducted by aliens!

The bickering boys are taken to a distant planet where they become the star attraction in a strange alien zoo. Wyatt is not about to spend the rest of his life trapped in a cage with Duncan, so they come up with a plan to escape. Between them and the exit? Only a bunch of mysterious enclosures, each housing an alien species more frightening, weird, and freakish than the last.

Surviving smoldering Lava Snakes, hungry Sand Squids, terrified Leaferoos, and a snarling Grimhound is one thing. Surviving each other might be a little harder.

From Middle Grade author Marc Lewis comes a thrilling, hilarious, action-packed middle grade novel that even the most reluctant readers won't be able to put down.

Made in the USA
Las Vegas, NV
31 October 2023